STOLEN *hart*

HART'S BAY

E. DAVIES

Stolen Hart / E. Davies. – 1st ed.
ISBN: 978-1-912245-38-3

To every broken-hearted, starry-eyed dreamer.

1

AARON

In the week since the grand opening of his coffee shop, Howya Bean, Aaron had learned that serving coffee here had less to do with beans than people.

Hart's Bay was a small enough town that everyone knew their neighbors by name, face, and grudge. And, most importantly, relationship status.

Aaron already knew—in the Biblical sense or otherwise—most of the gay population in town. So when *single* gay guys walked in, he sure as hell paid attention.

Quinn had been here twice this week on dates with different guys. It looked like he'd lined up a third this drizzly Saturday morning. It was impossible not to notice the broad-shouldered man with the easy smile. Aaron had never been more grateful for his excuse to ask everyone's names.

Especially the ones who made him lean on the counter so he didn't swoon.

Quinn filled the doorway sideways, and most of the way vertically, making him a good six foot one. He moved with an easy grace that said he was confident in his skin. It drew Aaron to him like a moth to flame.

He'd shown up last Saturday wearing a disappointingly thick flannel shirt. Luckily, he'd rolled the sleeves up, revealing forearms that distracted Aaron completely and made him ring up the wrong coffee twice.

The second time he visited, Quinn had chosen a crisp collared shirt and tie under a frankly adorable patterned sweater. He'd looked every inch the perfect boy to introduce to your parents. If your parents weren't the kind to tell you that you were bad for their public image, of course.

This time, Aaron scanned Quinn as he unzipped his winter jacket. Another nice choice—a plain gray T-shirt under a blue damask collared shirt. More importantly, the T-shirt stretched over pecs that Aaron longed to nuzzle. If only Quinn took off his outer layer, Aaron could see more. Maybe he'd have to crank up the heating in here.

Aaron gulped as Quinn approached, all rational thought escaping out the front door before it closed with a faint jingle. *Here goes.* "Morning, Quinn," Aaron greeted him by name with a cheery smile. "Vanilla latte?"

He'd practiced the words in his head so he didn't get tongue-tied. Being within touching distance of Quinn made Aaron want to see what the view was like from his knees.

A pleasant shiver danced along Aaron's skin as Quinn gave him a slow smile back. Quinn's deep green eyes caught Aaron's interest like the key to his pants. His dirty-blond hair was a little longer on top and swept back.

"Oh, good morning." Quinn sounded faintly surprised. He probably had no idea Aaron had memorized the curve of his lips, let alone his name and coffee order. "Yeah, that'd be great, thanks."

Aaron's fingers danced over the tablet to enter the order, and then he pirouetted to the coffee machines while Quinn paid. Focusing on what he knew so well—the knobs and levers of the machines that produced liquid gold with just the right touch—gave him enough confidence to chat.

Quinn checked his watch. "Came a little early."

Oh, God. The temptation was real. In any other situation, Aaron would have leaped on that pun like he would a six-foot hunk smiling at him. *No*, Aaron told himself firmly and bit his lip, looking away to grab a mug.

"Did you? Any fun weekend plans?" Aaron asked, his gaze flickering to Quinn.

Quinn chuckled, tucking his wallet back in his pocket. "I hope so. We'll see how it goes today."

Aaron was dying to ask whether he had another date with one of the guys he'd already seen, or if it was someone else. Having some hot gossip might satiate the unreasonable jealousy monster in his belly.

But Quinn wasn't forthcoming with any more details, and Aaron knew better than to pry. He didn't want to scare the guy off.

Just because he'd daydreamed about that razor-sharp jawline under his lips and that round ass between his hands... didn't mean he should share that with his customers. Aaron had never been to business school, but even he knew that was Business Ownership 101.

"Hope you get lucky, then." Aaron winked, sliding the mug across the counter. The outfit he'd chosen for the coffee shop was a crisp white shirt, and his dark jeans hid the current tenting situation. Phew.

"Thanks." Quinn gave Aaron another of those easy grins

with perfect, white teeth and strode for a table while Aaron melted across the counter behind him.

Fuck, he was hot. But for Quinn, Aaron was just part of the scenery. He had to resign himself to that fact. After a few moments, Aaron recovered his wits and wiped down the machines.

What kind of guy would walk in to meet Quinn today? The last couple of guys had been pretty average. Quinn could definitely do better.

Aaron had slept with the first of Quinn's dates last summer. Thank God he hadn't seemed to remember Aaron, but Aaron sure remembered his amateur blowjob skills.

He didn't know the second guy, but he'd been just as boring in conversation as the first one was in bed. Aaron had fiddled with the music to drown out his monotone while Quinn fidgeted his way through the date.

Was he going to be young, slender, and showy? Or was he quiet and reserved? Was Quinn after a discreet, straight-acting dude who played football every weekend? God, Aaron wanted to know his type.

He hoped it was "five foot eight, spunky as in loves being covered in spunk, more inappropriate than Great-Aunt Mabel at Thanksgiving, and coffee shop owner."

Apparently, Quinn's type was also "late to everything." As Aaron tidied behind the counter, he kept an eye on the situation. Nobody who came in was remotely likely to be Quinn's date.

His customers included some of the guys from the Harts' construction firm, a few of his friends from the art gallery, and Victor, who owned the grocery store in Hart Square. Victor definitely wasn't Quinn's date, because he came in with Jesse's mom, Laura Stone. Aaron was pretty sure Victor and Laura were dating now. She was always a bit kooky, but Aaron loved it. She'd even brought a Christmas wreath for Aaron to hang on the shop door.

Time ticked past the hour. By fifteen minutes past, Quinn was tapping his phone on the table, his brow furrowed as he stared out the window. His mug was empty now.

Aaron slipped out from behind the counter with a fresh vanilla latte and set it in front of Quinn. The quiet click of the mug on the table made Quinn look over and then up.

"Stood up?" Aaron asked with a sympathetic smile. "Here. It's on the house."

Quinn's deliciously full lips parted in surprise for a second before he smiled. "Oh, that's awfully nice of you. Thank you." He looked at his phone, but no notifications beckoned. "Yeah, it looks like he chickened out."

"Men." Aaron clicked his tongue as he gathered Quinn's old cup and stir stick. "Coffee is more reliable."

"So true." Quinn sighed and raised his new cup to toast that, then sipped. "Your coffee is great. This is the perfect first date spot, you know."

"I've noticed." Aaron grinned. "Why the rush? Trying to find a date for the holidays?"

He hovered on the other side of the table, tempted to sink into the chair opposite Quinn and start talking. But he didn't want to cross that boundary. Customer service was one of two things Aaron did well—servicing a cute guy was the other. At his old job, he'd mixed up the two, but he had no room for inconvenient flings here in tiny little Hart's Bay. They were supposed to stay nice and separate.

"Not quite." Quinn propped his chin on his fist, elbow on the table as he looked up at Aaron. "I wanted to find a boyfriend this year."

"And you're running out of time," Aaron finished with a nod. "Gotcha."

"But the family pressure is real. It's crazy around the holidays, isn't it?" Quinn stuck his lip out in an adorable pout. "Like they're desperate to marry me off."

Aaron sighed and snapped his fingers. "Amen to that." He'd made a fresh start in life and just started a new business, yet his parents didn't care about any of that. They wanted him to meet a nice, clean-cut, quiet guy so he'd stop being a ticking time bomb of bad PR.

Quinn laughed. "If only it were that easy."

"Well, if you want any recommendations, let me know," Aaron said with a grin. "I know lots of men who want commitment. I ran away quickly when they brought it up." He leaned in and whispered, "And all of them are *much* more interesting than your last two choices."

"Thanks," Quinn said, his gaze flickering from the window to Aaron and back again. "And thanks for the coffee. Do I get to know your name?" The rain cloud over Quinn's face cleared as he smiled at Aaron.

"Aaron," he managed, his voice tight with excitement.

"Aaron. Thank you."

"Welcome," Aaron said lightly. He spun and headed for his little sanctuary behind the counter to contain his squealing. Hearing him say his name out loud did weird things to his heart.

Sure, he wanted to hear his name grunted, deep and loud, while Quinn was fucking him into the floor... but for now, he'd take this.

Am I an asshole to be glad his date's a no-show? Aaron bit his lip as he tidied another table in the corner. *Just so I could talk to him?* He tried to bring himself around to feel disappointment for Quinn's sake and couldn't manage it.

Damn it, of course Quinn was looking for romance. It seemed like everyone out there wanted a relationship. That made it harder and harder for Aaron to contain his jealousy.

He wasn't just jealous that they were finding love, but that they *wanted* to find it. Aaron wished he had it in him to trust people like that.

Ever since last New Year's, when his now-ex had thrown him out of the apartment they'd shared, Aaron had focused on keeping the strings off. It had been a lot more fun than tearily packing up his belongings and drinking away January.

But even though Aaron sampled the menu more than any of his friends, one by one they were pairing up happily. Meanwhile, Aaron just swiped his life away on Grindr.

Aaron refused to compromise on what mattered. His sex drive was the center of his life—fantastic sex made everything tick along well. Dating some guy who was perfect on paper yet sparked no chemistry? No, thanks. That was Aaron's version of hell.

None of Aaron's dirty parties, dim back rooms, or mid-afternoon quickie hookups had gone anywhere. Which was a good thing, he'd persuaded himself.

How the hell his friends had found men who fit them so perfectly, Aaron had no idea. Rusty was cool and responsible, taming Ezra's flighty emotional moments. Colt was fiery enough to rein in Rain—the two of them owned this very building, and had become Aaron's friends in the process. Justin, one of the strong and silent construction crew, had his own sweet, bubbly little Harry on his arm. And Finn was just as ambitious as Jesse was enthusiastic.

Maybe Aaron was too weird to have an "other half" out

there—someone willing to crush the walls he'd put up in this last year.

Lost in his thoughts, Aaron almost missed when Quinn took off. Luckily, the deep voice by the door grabbed his attention. "Thanks for the coffee. See you soon."

"Have a good day!" Aaron answered automatically, beaming at Quinn until the guy raised a hand and walked out. Then his smile faded as he folded his arms on the counter and sighed. There went his foolish daydream of getting laid today.

Aaron kept on sinking down until his forehead rested on the counter, overdramatic even when nobody else in the cafe was paying attention.

For a guy who needed to be ridden hard and put away wet as often as possible, Aaron's last few weeks had been dry as a desert. The chaos and stress of opening this place—painting, getting furniture, crying in the car after bank appointments— had overwhelmed him.

A good dicking-down would solve all his problems. Especially the stupid, lonely ache that was swelling in his chest as he straightened up and sidled to the end of the counter. From here, he could see out the glass extension of the building to the parking lot that lay between the edge of the boutiques and the art gallery. He watched Quinn get into his car and drive away.

It was impossible to feel lonely with a guy balls-deep inside him, right? But today, every time Aaron imagined someone's weight pressing him into the mattress, his fingers tight in Aaron's hair, it was Quinn.

Maybe he could make one exception to his "no fucking the locals" rule. In the quiet moments between customers, Aaron searched Grindr and the other half-a-dozen hookup apps on his phone. He checked them all, but he couldn't spot any profile that looked like Quinn's.

That left two possibilities: Quinn was one of the creepy blank profiles in the area, or he just wasn't online, like some hopeless romantic. Aaron had to wait for the guy to come back so he could make his move.

Hitting on customers was easy. Aaron had done it dozens of times. He'd found ways to invite guys to leave their phone numbers safe in his keeping—and later, their loads safe on his face. Rejection didn't faze him.

So why did the thought of hitting on Quinn next time he walked into the cafe make Aaron's palms sweat? Clearly, the dry spell was driving him to extremes. He didn't have a chance with Quinn anyway.

Aaron had decided a year ago that he'd never let a guy shatter his heart again, but Quinn was totally looking for marriage material. He couldn't be more opposite. The way his eyes had shone with hope when he talked about finding a boyfriend? Ew. No way. Love was nice to look at on other people, but condoms were, too. And they were a lot cheaper.

If only Aaron could show Quinn that—preferably before Quinn ended up dating a loser who couldn't show up on time to a date.

Okay, I'll do it, Aaron promised himself as he locked up the shop that evening, his feet and back aching. His roommates —all of whom worked in the art gallery within eyeshot of his cafe—had left for home, so he had to walk.

At least the town was small, so it only took ten minutes to get home on foot. It was a chance to cool down and shake off his workday before he got home to the usual chaos.

Aaron stretched, shivered in the crisp December air, and started the slow walk home. *Next time he comes in,* Aaron thought, *he's mine for the night.*

2

QUINN

As soon as Quinn's spoon touched the hot water, he groaned. "That's not coffee at all, you dumbass."

Instead of instant coffee granules, he'd dumped a spoonful of gravy granules into his mug. He half-heartedly stirred, watching it dissolve. It would sure as hell wake him up, but at what cost? Ew—the very thought made him shudder.

Setting aside his mug with a sigh, he yanked open the cupboard to grab another. He'd laugh about it later. At six o'clock on a winter morning, after spending hours last night wrestling with his pillow and wondering what sucked about him so much he'd been stood up... the humor was hard to find.

He shoved the offending jar in the top shelf of his cupboard and grabbed the coffee. Once it was mixed up, Quinn sipped and made a face. After a week of regular visits to the new coffee shop right by the harbor of Hart's Bay, he was getting spoiled.

Coffee was his one treat. As a personal trainer, he had to be an example of good health and nutrition to his clients. But coffee? He'd sooner give up breathing.

Quinn wrapped one hand around the mug, one hip against the counter as he poked at his phone on the countertop. He didn't have any clients today. Most of his current clients trained before or after work—early mornings or evenings. Things were especially quiet when most people had given up on healthy living for the rest of the year.

Originally, the plan had been to see Eric again if all went well. Since the asshole hadn't bothered showing up for the date yesterday, it looked like Quinn had some time to himself.

"Speak of the devil." As Quinn scrolled through notifications, a text from Eric popped up. It had been sent around two in the morning. *Sorry I couldn't make it. Family emergency. Rain check for Sunday?*

The first thing Quinn checked was Instagram. It was the only social media Quinn used, and technically it was for promoting his business. But he occasionally spied on his clients to keep them accountable. Especially the gay clients, who might have cute, single friends like Eric.

It only took a few moments for Quinn to find the lie: a photo of a group of smiling shirtless men at a bar last night, including Eric. Squinting at the photo, Quinn spotted Eric's hand on someone's ass.

He scoffed. "Family emergency, my ass." If he were a little more vindictive, he might have had a bruising reply for Eric. But Quinn didn't waste energy on assholes who weren't worth it, so he just ignored the text message.

It was a lot more fun just taking some time for himself. He'd really enjoyed his time sitting in the window of the cafe, watching people come and go from the boutiques.

In his year of seeking dates, when was the last time Quinn had taken *himself* for a date without trying to attract some potential future husband?

At least Quinn had gotten free coffee from that sweet barista, Aaron. Now, *he* was a cutie pie—and more interesting than either of his last dates. Quinn kind of wanted an excuse to talk to him again. Maybe he hadn't been joking when he'd offered to set up Quinn with people he knew. He'd seemingly known everyone who came or left, and most of their orders.

The only other place in town as juicy with gossip was Cher's End Table, the local bar. But Quinn didn't want to go there to find a hookup or a date—and more to the point, Aaron wasn't there. Sure, he was paid to make Quinn want to come in for coffee, but he'd done exactly that.

After breakfast, Quinn would stop by, get some real coffee into him, and get the gossip. If anyone knew of potential dates, it had to be Aaron. And with any luck at all, maybe Aaron himself was single. Quinn's luck in love might come back from wherever it had fucked off to for this entire year.

No luck.

Quinn felt bad that disappointment was his first reaction to a friendly young woman waving at him from behind the register.

"Hi," he said anyway and smiled, trying to cover up the disappointment so she didn't think she'd done anything wrong. "A vanilla latte, please."

Of course someone else had to work here. Quinn hadn't even thought of that, but it was obvious. Aaron couldn't work ten hours a day, seven days a week.

"Sure thing. Is that for here or to go?"

"For here," Quinn said, swallowing the guilt.

Part of him said he should hop on Instagram and offer a

discounted session, or call one of his gyms and ask if they had anything they needed covered today. But his realization earlier that he hadn't treated himself to a date like this in ages had startled him.

In unrelated thoughts, Aaron might come into the shop a little later.

After Quinn paid, he watched his barista make the coffee and tried to subtly drop the question in. "Is Aaron around?"

"Oh, sure. He'll be here soon. He's usually in a little bit later on Sundays." She offered him a smile. "Do you need to talk to a manager?"

"No, not at all." Quinn waved a hand. "I just wanted to continue a conversation."

She gave him a sly smile. "I see. Well, grab a table, and I'm sure he won't be long."

"Thanks." Quinn nodded to those sitting here he recognized, but he didn't feel like making small talk with them today. Instead, he took the mug over to the same window table for two where he'd sat last time.

The cafe was L-shaped and on the end of the unit. All windows, this section of seating extended from the building. From here, the other boutiques stretched out to the right, and beyond them, a few hundred feet of parking lot. He could see the side door to the art gallery, and just a peek of Hart Square between that building and the grocery store.

Quinn watched as his neighbors went about their day. A dark shape on the dock had to be the resident seal—everyone in town had practically adopted Lucy as their collective pet.

She slipped into the water as a boat slowly came into the harbor. After the guy in it had tied up and headed up the ramp to the parking lot, she popped her head out of the water, slowly rotated once, and heaved herself back up.

The man who'd been in the boat entered the side door of the art gallery, and then the door opened again for someone else to step out.

Not just anyone—it was Aaron.

Quinn smiled to himself and looked at his mug, as if Aaron would catch him spying from all the way over here. But his whole body had lit up like a Christmas tree.

That was half the reason he'd wanted to come back today —to figure out what the hell *that* was about.

Relax, act cool. Don't be weird, Quinn told himself, but he could feel Aaron walking across the parking lot toward the cafe. Acting desperate was not the way to win anyone over. His year of failed dating experiments had shown him that much.

A minute passed, and then the door rattled as it opened.

"Morning, Yolanda! How goes the battle?" Aaron's cheery tones floated through the coffee shop air, and Quinn had to resist the urge to greet Aaron in return.

Quinn peeked out of the corner of his eye as Yolanda waved. "Oh, it's great. I've got everything under control. The note you left—you meant for me to use the small bag first, right?"

"Sure did."

"Phew." Yolanda laughed. "Then I did."

Quinn smiled to himself. It was nice to feel the positive energy between them. Aaron obviously treated his staff well. And this interaction made it obvious that Aaron was the manager or owner.

That was kind of hot. He'd sure like to see Aaron get bossy. He was overflowing with personality already.

"And..." Yolanda cleared her throat. "You've got company."

Quinn glanced over, and Aaron grinned at him and held

up a finger in a *wait a moment* signal. He nodded and watched Aaron circling the room, saying hello to the regulars.

His heart pounded as Aaron finished and made a beeline for him. Now he had to start that conversation.

Hey, you're cute and funny, thanks for cheering me up yesterday, and I just wanted to say hi and ask if you know anyone single who is into dating, preferably if they're you.

Oh, man. After a year of taking chances and being shot down, Quinn should have grown thicker skin. But here he was, nervous as hell.

"You're back." Aaron smiled and pulled out the chair opposite Quinn. He plopped himself down in the chair. "Who's the lucky guy this time?" He crossed his knee and playfully grinned. "I hope I'm not about to make things awkward for you, but it feels like it should be my turn soon."

Oh, crap. There went Quinn's heart, melting again at that sassy little grin and Aaron's boldness. "It is," he countered. "You offered to help me out yesterday, and... well, I'm out of options."

Aaron gasped and clutched his chest. "I'm used to being the last resort at three in the morning. This makes a pleasant change."

Instantly, Quinn saw through the self-deprecating grin. He didn't have to know Aaron to see the mask he was wearing. He really thought of himself as the last option, and that was ridiculous.

Quinn leaned forward, a frown on his lips. "I bet you're not their last option. And if you are, well... screw that."

"I usually do. It's fun," Aaron said with a giggle that was genuine, and it made Quinn smile in return. "But my offer stands. You want to know the single gay guys around here?"

You would have been my first choice if I'd met you in January, Quinn thought. He kept it in and just nodded.

Aaron winked at him. "Top? Bottom? Power bottom? BJ king? Kink? XXL or boyfriend dick? What are the specs?"

A blush swept Quinn's cheeks. He could hardly look at Aaron. He was *so* not used to talking about his sex life in public, but the guy seemed to have no filter and no judgment when he said any of those words.

"Or are you ace? That's cool, too. My Cupid powers are primarily rooted in my little black book, though."

"Um... no, that's not it," Quinn said with a laugh, rubbing his face. "I'm just looking for a date I get along with before we figure out how the, uh, bedroom stuff works."

Aaron chuckled. "Way out of my area of expertise. So, what happens when you get along? After your nice innocent suppers and drive-in movies, or whatever the classy dudes do these days?"

Quinn squinted at him. "What do you mean what happens?"

"What happens when you suddenly find out that you're both bottoms and nobody brought the important, double-headed gear to solve the problem?" Aaron grinned. "I mean, granted... I'd take anything I could get after my last couple months. Opening this place has put a serious damper on fun."

Quinn laughed. "I haven't even thought about compatibility in ages," he admitted. With Aaron's tongue so free, it made him unwind a little bit and not feel so embarrassed. "I haven't had a boyfriend in a few years. And I hate the thought of going to a meat market on my phone to try to find someone. I'd rather click with someone offline first."

"Aha." Aaron stared at him. "The rare specimen who isn't on Grindr. That's why I haven't seen you before."

Quinn laughed. "Yeah. I really wanted to stay that way. But now that it feels like I've tried everything and everyone... maybe I'll have to."

"Find true love on Grindr?" Aaron gasped. When Quinn nodded, he clicked his tongue. "Oh, hon. That's not gonna happen. Nobody on there wants anything serious. Trust me."

Again, the edge crept into Aaron's voice. His peppy tone nearly hid the sadness, but Quinn picked it up.

"So what do I do?" Quinn ran a hand through his hair and sighed. "I've tried blind dates with friends of friends. I've met way too many guys at bars. And... yeah, I'm tired of not getting laid, too. But I don't want to give up on hope."

Quinn's throat felt tight as he looked out the window at the choppy waves in the harbor.

For years, he'd daydreamed of meeting someone who could fall into a nice, simple pattern with him. He didn't need to be wooed with flowers and ballads. All he wanted was someone whose eyes lit up when he saw Quinn walk in.

Aaron leaned in, about to say something. But he patted Quinn's hand, and a static shock flashed through both of their hands.

Aaron gasped. "Ow!"

"Hey!" Quinn laughed, yanking his hand back at the sting. "Well, that was electrifying."

Aaron shook his head. "Weird. I haven't even been rolling on the carpet like usual." He batted his lashes. "Maybe that's the problem."

Quinn laughed again. Aaron was the complete opposite of him, happy to see someone only once. "That must be nice, though. A lot easier to find men for a night than... you know, the future."

"It is," Aaron agreed with a thoughtful hum, folding his

arms. "But I've been waiting for someone to ask me out for ages." He didn't look away from Quinn, the invitation written all over his face.

Oh, shit. Aaron was definitely flirting with him, wasn't he? And he had been all along. "Are you propositioning me?" Quinn asked.

"I thought you'd never notice," Aaron sighed, raising his hands above his head for a moment as if thankful—or victorious.

A smile crept across Quinn's face as his heart rose. "I hoped so," he admitted. "When you offered to set me up with someone yesterday, I figured maybe you were taken."

"I'm taken in many positions, as often as possible," Aaron countered, batting his lashes outrageously.

Quinn burst out laughing again. He was smiling more than he had in weeks. Just these few minutes talking to Aaron had lifted his spirits. "But you're not against dating?"

"Nah," Aaron said. "But I don't think love is real. If it is, it doesn't last. The best thing to do is find someone who's good in bed and promise to stick it out when the spark fades." He gave Quinn a meaningful grin. "And test the goods before you buy them. Lots and lots."

Quinn tilted his head. Aaron was so free with his words, and every one of them hinted that there was more of a story behind them. "Oh, sex isn't off the table." He shifted, well aware of the hardness in his jeans at this no-holds-barred talk. A nice night in bed with someone he genuinely liked? That sounded like heaven right now. "But I want someone who's open to the idea of more. Even if it's hard to imagine."

"Oh, good." Aaron pretended to be relieved. "On the table, the wall, the back seat, the back room... I'm open to all kinds of ideas, especially when they're big and hard."

Quinn covered his face as his cheeks burned again. He couldn't help the laugh. "You're a handful, aren't you—oh, don't," he added quickly as Aaron giggled.

"That one was too easy. Like me," Aaron hummed, winking as Quinn snorted. "So, is it your turn to proposition me, so I can dramatically accept and fall into your arms?" Aaron asked, tilting his head and fluttering his lashes.

Quinn grinned. "I was still making up my mind whether to proposition you," he countered. "As incredible as it sounds to spend a night with you... I want to take the chance that there might be more between us."

Aaron's eyes narrowed, and then he clicked his fingers. "Oh, I have a brilliant idea."

"Uh-oh," Quinn teased. "Tell me."

Aaron licked his lips and rubbed his hands together. He suddenly looked nervous as he bit his lower lip. "Well... you want something longer than a night, and I want something longer than my own fingers, right?"

The laugh that escaped Quinn was full-throated. "Yes."

Aaron was nothing like the guys Quinn had always dated. They'd been nice, soft-spoken, with ordinary jobs and lives. The most interesting of the lot had collected gin bottles for fun. Nothing compared to vivacious, outrageous Aaron.

"So how about we try it for this month?" Aaron leaned in. "I rescue you from the boring, flaky men you've been meeting in *real life*." He air-quoted with a teasing grin. "We can start with a date. And if we hit it off, then we take it from there. Either you'll see that fuck-buddies rule, or I'll see that boyfriends aren't all drama and bad times. To be fair to you, feelings take time to develop, so we'll give it until the end of December."

Aaron's smirk was cocky, but it didn't deter Quinn. He

caught his breath. That actually was a great idea. Not only did Aaron want him in bed, but he wanted to give this a shot? He wanted to pinch himself and make sure this was real. "That's... that's a great deal."

"It is," Aaron agreed cheerily. "I don't offer it to just anyone, you know."

"Why now, then?" Quinn wanted to know. If Aaron talked about running away from commitment before, why was he willing to date Quinn for over three weeks? Aaron hesitated, and before he could speak, Quinn added, "Honestly, please. No joking for a second."

Aaron gave him a small smile. His tone was softer. "Okay. I've been avoiding dating since my last relationship. It's been a year now. I don't know if there's something more out there for me. I doubt it. But I'll give myself a chance."

Pink spots appeared on Aaron's cheeks as his gaze flickered to the table. He twisted his hands together again on the tabletop.

Impulsively, Quinn laid his hand on top of Aaron's. He wanted to punch whichever jerk had shattered Aaron's heart so much that he'd given up on love. "I'm sorry," he murmured. "Thank you for telling me that."

"Phew. I can raise my deflective humor shields again." Aaron smirked, turning his hand over palm-up.

As Quinn's fingers grazed Aaron's wrist, their palms slid together and ignited something under Quinn's skin that he'd almost forgotten: desire. Fuck, just these sides of Aaron he'd already seen in a few short minutes intrigued him.

"So we have a deal?" Quinn asked, his smile growing. "For the rest of December?"

"You've got until midnight on New Year's Eve to make me fall in love. Hah. As if."

"And you've got until midnight to make me see that true love isn't real and mind-blowing sex is better anyway."

Aaron snorted and stuck out a hand to shake. "It's a deal. I'd spit on it, but I'd rather save it for my ass. We're gonna need a lot of lube this month."

His words made Quinn's brain go full throttle on the dirty images. Aaron wasn't the kind of guy to let Quinn take it slowly and softly in any area of his life... most of all, in bed. Quinn had the feeling he was going to be struggling to keep up with him.

They shook on it, and Aaron's excited smile was a relief. It mirrored the butterflies fluttering in Quinn's stomach.

"So, dinner at Millie's tonight? When does this place close?" No point in beating around the bush. If he was going to persuade Aaron that dating was the best plan, he didn't want to waste a moment.

Aaron beamed. "Perfect. Meet there at six?"

"Six it is." Quinn drained the rest of his latte and set the cup down, then rose to his feet. "I'll see you then."

At the very least, he had a guaranteed date. He might not know Aaron that well yet, but he was already positive Aaron wouldn't stand him up. He just had a good feeling, that was all. A really good feeling.

Please don't let me be wrong about him.

3

AARON

Oh, hell, no.

Bryon was so not allowed to walk into the cafe like he was God's own gift to Aaron.

"Seriously?" Aaron put his fists on his hips and glared as the guy strutted up to the counter. Bryon had proven impossible to ditch even though they'd never actually hooked up. Yet.

"I'm still waiting for your answer, hot stuff." Bryon leaned over the counter, resting his forearm on it. Even with that dominance gesture closing the space, it just brought him down to Aaron's height.

Aaron gritted his teeth, his nails biting into his palms. Customers at the tables were turning to watch. The last thing Aaron needed was his customers thinking this was his personal cruising spot.

But Bryon didn't care. In fact, he probably wanted to leverage Aaron's desire to get him out of there as soon as possible.

Thank God Aaron's last few wild weeks had kept them from hooking up like they'd planned. Bryon was reasonably attractive and clearly used to getting his way. He'd acted whiny and entitled, demanding that Aaron drop everything to get premium dick.

"I'm still pissed about that text," Aaron told Bryon frankly. "I told you I was busy."

Sure, he'd promised to meet Bryon a couple of weeks ago. But then he'd had to work late painting this place, making his fingers bleed screwing together the display cabinets. Getting laid had been the last thing on his mind.

All you have to do is lie there and take it hadn't been the effective sales clincher that Bryon had hoped.

Aaron should have just told Bryon to fuck off. Instead, he'd burst into tears and yelled at his friends. He wasn't great under high stress, and Bryon was trying to dial up the pressure by walking into his place and demanding a date.

Well, he was wrong if he thought that would work. He wasn't going to like the results.

"That was last week." Bryon waved his hand. "You're not busy now. You said yes before. Set a time and date."

Bryon's breath was hot on Aaron's face as he leaned over the counter, his tone commanding, yet quiet. He didn't even look away from Aaron. A younger, dumber Aaron might have mistaken his quickening pulse for attraction.

Now, Aaron was keenly aware that the creep was just trying to get in his pants by applying pressure. Bryon probably thought he was an irresistible power top.

Aaron whipped out his spray cleaning bottle and cloth, then pointed his bottle at Bryon's arm. "Move it."

"Not until you give me a time—hey!" Bryon's tune

changed when Aaron sprayed his arm. He stumbled backward, shook his arm, and gave Aaron a slack-jawed stare like he couldn't quite believe what had just happened. "What the shit, man?"

"I don't want you," Aaron told him flatly. He scrubbed the counter in quick circles.

"But you said yes before." Bryon went to grab his hand, but he read Aaron's flat stare correctly and stopped with his hand midair. Instead, he leaned on the display cabinet, leaving his greasy fingerprints across it. *Great.*

"You're being a giant douchecanoe. I changed my mind. Thank God I did," Aaron hissed. With his hackles up, it was hard to keep his voice down.

It was nearly closing time, so at least there were only a few people left—a table of two, and another of four. But they were all looking over, and the attention made a blush creep up Aaron's cheeks. Those were rare for him, and he hated the feeling.

He didn't do shame. That was bullshit designed to make people afraid of embracing their happy. But having this weirdo here, making him out to be the bad guy for putting his business first?

"You can't just send me nudes and leave me with blue balls. You owe me for that one."

Aaron snorted. "Don't worry. You're never getting a nude from me ever again."

"Don't be like that."

"No," Aaron countered sharply. The pitch of his voice crept up, as it did when he was upset. But he couldn't help that. What mattered was his words. "We're done here. Order coffee or get out."

Bryon hovered on the other side of the counter, and for a

moment Aaron wasn't sure that he wasn't going to stride around the counter and lay hands on him.

But he didn't. Instead, he huffed out a quiet snort through his nose and stomped for the door, a glimmer in his eye.

Aaron had the sickening feeling Bryon was seeing this as a temporary setback. If he could take a hint, after all, he would have given up long before now.

When Aaron's gaze swept around the coffee shop, both the tables were suddenly engaged in conversation again, very carefully avoiding looking his way.

Ugh. Why do men have to be like that? Aaron headed around the counter to polish the cabinet. Once he was behind the cash desk again, he sat on his stool and folded his arms.

Well, there was one guy who wasn't. Aaron had known him for all of a few minutes, but Quinn had already come across as far more sweet and polite. Maybe a little too much so. Aaron was going to persuade Quinn to disrespect him in all the best ways.

That brought a smile to his face, at least. He should have just enough time to get home, shower and change, and head out to Millie's.

A quick text to the house group chat on his phone ensured that he'd have the car they shared this evening.

Thinking about Quinn made the unpleasant afternoon fade in his mind. By the time Aaron kicked his last few customers out with some polite chitchat, he was armed with his smile again.

Aaron had no idea what to expect, and he loved it already.

Aaron anxiously shifted from foot to foot outside the front

door of Millie's. A quick scan of the restaurant had confirmed his date wasn't there yet. So he waited outside, tucking his hands into his pockets.

Even here on the Oregon coast, winter evenings were nippy. He'd had to huddle into clingy black jeans and a billowy blue collared shirt. A dust of bronze highlighter along his nose and cheekbones finished the look off. Aaron couldn't wait for summer, when he could get back to his cropped tops and booty shorts.

Aaron would pay good money to see Quinn's face if Aaron showed up for a date in *that* kind of outfit. Instantly, he put it on his mental to-do list. Quinn was probably the kind of guy who would never knowingly let a dick print show through his jeans. Unfortunately for Aaron.

"Hey!" Quinn greeted him as he briskly strode around the corner of the building and waved at Aaron. His cheeks were flushed and his eyes bright. "It's busy tonight."

For a small town, this was the main eating spot, so the parking lot was pretty big. He'd missed Quinn driving in. "I got lucky, grabbed a spot that just opened up right here." Aaron would never admit he'd been circling the place for five minutes before letting himself park, then waiting out here for ten minutes.

"Are you okay? Not too cold?" Quinn reached out for Aaron's hand and then hesitated, like he wasn't sure if Aaron wanted the touch.

And right there, Aaron saw what kind of man Quinn was compared to a sleazeball like Bryon.

"I'll cope, as long as I have something hot to hold soon," Aaron said, flashing a grin at his date.

"For now, I can offer my hand." Quinn held it out and raised a brow, grinning back at him.

"Already?" Aaron pretended to gasp. "I hope that's not a proposal." He slipped his hand into Quinn's, a pleasant shiver running down his spine.

His date's hand was larger, his fingers thick between Aaron's slender ones, and his grip strong, yet gentle. Standing so close, it was impossible not to notice how much taller he was.

"Not yet," Quinn said gravely, but his eyes sparkled as he gazed down at Aaron. "Shall we get you out of the cold, then?"

"P-P-Please." Aaron's teeth chattered as a cold gust swept them. Quinn stepped in front of him slightly, sheltering him. How chivalrous. Suddenly, Aaron was a little less freezing. He blushed and tried to remember the last time anyone had treated him like that.

The waitress who seated them gave them a curious glance and smile, but brought them over to the small row of tables for two by the window.

Larger groups and friends sat in the tables in the middle or the booths along the walls. Even as a relative newcomer to town, Aaron knew that their seating area was the romantic hot spot of the town.

Quinn slid his jacket off, which showed that he'd dressed up in a collared shirt and tie. Classic date night outfit.

"So, um... how was the rest of your day?" Quinn asked.

Aaron was used to judging men at a glance. Quinn? A gentle, shy giant, without a doubt. He couldn't miss the nervous smile that flickered across Quinn's face or the way he gripped his glass of water.

"It was great," Aaron told him and picked up his menu. "Flew by, with this to look forward to. Yours?"

"I think I tried on every nice shirt in my closet," Quinn admitted with a sheepish grin.

Aaron laughed. It was disarming how Quinn didn't take himself too seriously, yet he was earnest. Unlike Aaron, who was layers under layers of innuendo-laced humor to keep everyone at bay. "I appreciate the effort. You made a great choice," he told him.

"Oh, phew. I didn't want to re-wear a date outfit you'd seen me in before. You've had the advantage of studying me out of uniform."

Not nearly as out of uniform as I'd like him to be, Aaron thought but resisted saying. "Mmm? Who says I've been studying you?" He raised his menu to hide the grin.

A fingertip appeared at the top of the menu and pushed it down. Aaron giggled and looked up, meeting Quinn's gaze.

"The fact you knew my name." Quinn chuckled and picked up his own menu. "I thought you just knew everyone around here. It didn't even occur to me you were waiting to hit on me."

Aaron caught his breath. So Quinn had been watching him at work, too, then. He wasn't the invisible scenery he'd imagined himself to be. "Oh, I've been waiting since last week," he assured Quinn, who laughed. "I don't know everyone in town just yet. I'm working on it." Aaron finally started to actually read his menu. "I'm just glad I finally got an excuse to talk to you."

"I'm glad, too," Quinn told him.

By the time their waitress came to take their orders, they were swapping the basic first-date biographical details. Quinn Powell was twenty-four, had lived here his whole life, and had dinner with his family at least once a week.

"I'm pretty boring," Quinn admitted with a laugh. "Sorry. Average mom and dad with middle-class jobs, lived in one place for my whole life. Running my own business is the most unconventional I get. I'm a personal trainer."

So that explained the muscles on his muscles. Aaron nodded and shifted impatiently. "Are you bored of first-date questions? I mean, you've had a whole year of this crap. Making polite conversation with guys you might not even like."

"A little," Quinn said and smiled. "I guess your way involves less questions."

"Hell, yeah, it does." Aaron grinned, but he was more nervous than he wanted to admit—even to himself—as he leaned forward. "Sometimes I don't even bother with names. Can't call out the wrong one if you never ask."

How would he react? So far, Quinn had been willing to laugh about Aaron's jokes, but some guys got weird about dating a man with notches on the bedpost.

Quinn's eyes grew round for a moment before he grinned. "Smart thinking."

Although Aaron scanned his face, he didn't see any disapproval. Relief made a few knots in his shoulders come undone. *That's one hurdle overcome, at least*, he thought. He didn't have a chance to say anything before Quinn spoke again.

"I don't know you well yet," Quinn said slowly, ice cubes clinking in his Coke as he stirred with his straw. "But you've been up-front about showing me who you are. I respect that. And I respect that you know what you want."

Quinn really did wear his heart on his sleeve. The Grindr mill would chew him up and spit him out. He was the kind of boyfriend anyone would dream of.

If only Aaron could let himself believe it could be real.

"Thanks," Aaron said quietly. He hadn't expected that to mean so much. "I *am* proud of who I am, and what I've done.

Who I've done, I should say," he added with a grin. "But every time I try to settle down and date, I meet guys who try to belittle me for it. Or who want me to be the perfect little boyfriend, not say the first thing that comes to mind."

Quinn scoffed. "Well, that's bullshit. Screw those people—they don't deserve you. Speaking your mind isn't a bad thing. Plenty of people would say it makes you the perfect boyfriend. It took me a minute to adjust, but I like your humor."

"Pffft," Aaron murmured, looking away rather than accept the compliment. "I'm not used to people being so open about what they want. If only dating were like this all the time."

Their food arrived before Quinn could answer, and Aaron just shared a smile with him as they waited. The waitress placed a huge, fully loaded chicken breast salad in front of Quinn, and the parmesan pork chops in front of Aaron.

Once they were alone, they dug into their food and made small talk, but it wasn't long before they were finished and back to talking about deeper things. The waitress cleared their dishes and left the dessert menu, but they hardly noticed.

"So I guess we should talk about what we want?" Quinn suggested. "To make sure we're on the same page this month?"

"Yeah." Aaron pushed back his plate and folded his hands in his lap. "I haven't dated anyone in like, over a year. And that was a live-in relationship, so we didn't go *out* together, if you know what I mean."

Quinn nodded. "It's been even longer for me. But I've been going on first dates, and sometimes even second dates, all year. I don't mind that. I'd just like to stop trying to get to know people who aren't very interesting."

Aaron burst out laughing. "I hear you. I'm open for whatever. I'll even try to be romantic."

What did he have to lose? A few weeks of fun dates, hot

sex, and getting to know someone who could at least turn out to be a great new friend.

Since they were up-front that Quinn wanted more and Aaron didn't believe in it, nobody's heart could get hurt.

"Only if you want to be." Quinn's brows pulled together. "I don't want anyone feeling pressured here. If this is just a fling, and we wind up being friends at the end of this… that's fine with me."

Aaron nodded once, sharply. His heart was soaring with something he couldn't quite place. Fear, yes, but not the bad kind of fear. An excited fear, like there was a real possibility he was ignoring here.

The chance of love.

"That brings me to my only catch, while we're laying down the rules," Aaron told Quinn.

"Oh?" Quinn sipped his Coke, but his curious gaze never left Aaron's. "Tell me."

"You can't pretend to love me," Aaron said, his voice barely steady. He had to say the words without letting them sit in his brain for too long, or the full weight would hit him.

Too late. It did anyway.

Aaron hadn't expected something in his chest to physically tighten as the words left his mouth. It felt like a thick elastic band compressing his heart.

Apparently there was a wound that had never quite healed, no matter how many beds he'd hopped between.

Since the betrayal last New Year's Eve, he hadn't tried trusting another man. It might be for a limited time, but this month did mean trusting Quinn, and the full weight of that decision had suddenly hit.

Quinn's voice was soft and careful as he leaned in. His

gaze studied Aaron, flickering between his eyes. "What do you mean?"

"Don't ever lie to me—or to yourself—just because you want to make the relationship work. Because you want something else out of it." Aaron could hear the thickness in his own voice, but for once, he didn't try to hide it.

Quinn was going to have to deal with *all* of him, including his messy emotional baggage.

"Ah," Quinn breathed, his eyes lighting up. "I understand. Yeah. I promise." He reached across the table to take Aaron's hand. Then he turned it palm-up, his fingers tracing the lines by touch alone, his gaze still on Aaron's.

It was almost hard to handle the way Quinn sat with him and let him feel things—harsh things, things he'd never let creep in for a whole year.

"And in return," Aaron went on quickly, clearing his throat. As Quinn stroked his palm gently, the mist faded from Aaron's eyes. "In return, if I do... you know, magically fall in love and find my fairytale ending... I promise I won't hide it."

Quinn nodded. "That's fair," he agreed. "It's a science experiment, not a bet to win or lose."

"Yeah. It's about the journey we go on in the meantime." Aaron snorted. "Or something like that. I'm a barista, not a poet."

"Perfect," Quinn said. "Dessert? Two spoons? Start our fling off right?"

"Hell, yeah." Aaron offered a weak smile, hardly able to believe he'd bared so much of himself so quickly.

It was easy to show a stranger his dick. Much harder to show his heart. But Quinn was being so gentle and sweet that Aaron felt safe with him.

When the cheesecake arrived, Aaron tapped spoons gently

with Quinn and waited to hear what toast Quinn wanted to offer.

"To our new beginnings."

The smile that brought to Aaron's lips felt like it vibrated through his whole body and soul.

"To our new beginning."

4

QUINN

"Ten more seconds!"

Quinn's heart pounded, even though he wasn't the one pushing his body to the limit. He crouched on the exercise mat next to his client, counting down the seconds with his fingers.

Andrew was flushed red, breathing ragged, and not even cursing now. Every client was different—but for most, that meant they were actually close to their max. As Quinn always cheerfully said, if they were able to swear at it, they were able to bear it.

"Three, two, one... done!"

Andrew collapsed to the mat, arms and legs outstretched. Quinn clapped his back and laughed. "Awesome work, man. Seriously great." Andrew had finally made gains in these last two weeks, after plateauing for months. But he'd stuck with it.

Moments like this, he was proud of his clients—and of his job. Helping people see how much they were capable of was its own reward.

"I'm actually dying," Andrew mumbled, rolling onto his back and wiping his face with his sleeve.

Quinn laughed. "Go get showered. And remember your—"

"Water and protein. Yes, boss. I'm on it." Andrew dizzily pushed himself up as Quinn put a hand on his shoulder to steady him. "Thanks for the torture. See you Wednesday."

"Bye!" Quinn waved, grinning as his last sweat-soaked client stumbled off to the showers.

Every Monday, Wednesday, and Friday, Quinn came here and worked with four regular clients in a row. Andrew was the last, so it was time to take off for home.

As Quinn set the free weights back on the rack, he caught sight of another personal trainer, Troy, walking away from a client.

Troy's client was lifting on a bench, his feet sprawled rather than grounded, which made Quinn twitch. It was inefficient, but it wouldn't necessarily get him hurt. Just a dumb thing that anyone worth his salt should have caught.

His trained eye couldn't help spotting mistakes in fellow gym patrons. It happened every time, however hard he tried to switch off work and lose himself in his own routine.

Normally Quinn didn't say anything unless they were in serious danger. Most people didn't take well to him trying to help, and that went double for their trainers. It was far smarter to have a quiet word with their trainer and pretend they hadn't noticed their client screwing up.

There was no way he could have a word with Troy. The guy was a total meathead. His technique seemed to be copying YouTube videos and speaking in manly grunts. He had a revolving door of clients, and now Quinn saw why.

As Troy's back was turned, his client on the bench flared his elbows, pushing them out to the sides as he lifted sixty pounds. Sure, it looked effortless, but every fiber in Quinn's body cringed at the inevitable shoulder injuries. It could happen at any moment, especially if he kept piling weight on that bar without a spotter.

Crap. Quinn couldn't ignore someone potentially getting hurt. It was a breach of the personal trainers' code, but he wasn't poaching the client—just helping him.

Pretending he hadn't seen Troy training him, Quinn chose a route that took him past the guy's bench and then stopped. "Hey, man," he said casually. "I'm a trainer here. Can I help you for a sec? You wanna keep your elbows tucked in so you don't hurt your shoulders."

The guy set down the bar on the rack and squinted up at him suspiciously. "I'm fine, thanks," he snapped. "Buzz off. I've already got someone."

Quinn bit his tongue and raised his eyebrows. "You have?" He pretended to be surprised and a little skeptical. He already knew he didn't want to work with the guy, but hopefully that would make him think twice about hiring Troy. "Well, uh. Good luck with that."

Before Quinn could take off, he heard a gruff voice. "Hey. Eyes off my guy."

Troy was back, holding a full water bottle and swinging it menacingly from a strap. He looked pissed—which was the extent of his range of facial expressions.

"No sweat. I just spotted his elbows sliding out. Didn't want him screwing up his shoulders," Quinn said, raising his hands in a peace gesture.

"He's taken." Judging by the possessive hand Troy slid along his client's chest as he came to stand next to him, and the way the guy laid his hand on top of Troy's, he didn't mean *just* as a client.

God. Quinn's exes had screwed up his heart before, but

never his joints. One day, this guy would be in for a wake-up call.

"You know the rules," Troy added. "No harassing each other's clients. Desperation is ugly." The sneer was unmistakable as he looked Quinn up and down like he was the class runt.

Okay, now he'd gone from rude to Grade A dick. Quinn didn't have time for anyone who played those kinds of games. Life was too short.

Quinn just raised a brow at them both. "Yeah. It sure is," he said pointedly and smiled to show he wasn't rattled. It wasn't the smartest insult, but at least it was something. He turned on his heel and headed for the shower with a shake of his head. "Not my hospital bill, not my problem."

He couldn't stand when gyms hired trainers who clearly didn't know what they were doing. He'd have to have a word with Marv, the gym manager, about Troy. If he was doing that badly at training his boyfriend, he had to be even worse with his clients.

And implying he was desperate for a date? As if. If only they knew he'd found someone much better than either of them could hope to be.

Even thinking of Aaron made Quinn's blood hot, on top of the adrenaline rush from his confrontation with Troy. It took Quinn several minutes to calm down again as he walked out to his car. This much excitement was rare for him.

Or it had been, until recently. Aaron was a stick of dynamite Quinn was sticking into his boring life, and he was cautiously optimistic.

The date yesterday had gone so well—the best first date he'd had all year, by leaps and bounds. At the end of the night, they'd traded numbers and parted ways in the parking lot with big smiles.

Smiles much like the one Quinn was wearing now just thinking about Aaron.

As he drove the forty minutes back to Hart's Bay, Quinn hit the Bluetooth call button on his phone and waited for his parents to answer.

"Hi, honey," Mom answered as always. He always called them on the drive back home on Monday nights. It was a nice way to brighten up the Monday blues.

"Hi, Mom. Dad there, too?"

"I'll put him on speaker." The phone crackled, and then her voice echoed a little more. "There we go."

"Hey, Dad," Quinn said. "You had some work thing, didn't you? How did that go?"

"Oh, my work party," Dad sighed. "Your mother dazzled everyone as usual. That young upstart—Pascal—ended up facedown in the punch bowl."

"He didn't leave a good first impression on me," Mom agreed. "Hopefully he skips Bert's retirement party."

"I hope so, too. He ate all my favorite cheese at the last birthday party."

Dad clicked his tongue while Quinn hid the snort of laughter. Those were the sort of antics his parents didn't approve of. Any antics, really. No wonder Aaron seemed so rambunctious and irresistible to him.

"And how was your weekend?"

Uh-oh. Here they went. Usually, Quinn didn't have much to say. He worked most weekends, left bars before the party got good, and cooked the same few meals all the time. Everything about his life was simple and... well, boring... to most people.

Except Aaron. He was already a giant thorny mess of

bouncy laughter, deep wounds, inappropriate innuendo, and zero shame. And Quinn was irresistibly drawn to this, even though it was like standing still and waiting for a tornado to rip through his carefully arranged living room.

Just bringing Aaron to a family party would scandalize half of Quinn's relatives—and not just because he was a guy. Aaron wasn't the kind of guy his parents expected him to marry. If Quinn's boyfriend didn't work nine-to-five in a suit and tie and he didn't have an excuse—like being a doctor—his parents would balk.

Quinn bit back a laugh at the thought and cleared his throat. "Actually, pretty cool. I met someone interesting."

"Oh, really?" Dad asked while Mom audibly gasped. The sudden second of silence made Quinn roll his eyes and grin, picturing their silent conversation in gestures as they debated how much would be polite to ask.

It was best to cut this conversation off before they got too nosy and started the interrogation. "Anyway, I gotta go," Quinn said. "Talk to you tomorrow."

"Okay, bye!" It sounded like she couldn't wait to phone everyone she knew and ask for details. No doubt someone had noticed the two of them at Millie's. It would be the talk of the town before he knew it.

With another twenty minutes or more left in his drive, Quinn bit his lip and took the chance on calling Aaron's phone.

"Hello?" Aaron sounded startled and vaguely worried. "Quinn?"

"Hi. Sorry I couldn't text to warn you I'm calling. I'm driving. I just wanted to say hi. Is this a bad time?"

"Oh," Aaron breathed out. "No, it's not. I thought... something was wrong for you to be calling. With an actual phone call." With relief in his voice, he added, "Hi! How are you?"

Quinn laughed. "I'm good. How are you?"

"Great, now that I know you're not getting cold feet and breaking up in the second most gentlemanly way," Aaron said with a breathy laugh.

"Oh, no!" Quinn tapped the wheel thoughtfully. "Are you that much of a phone hater?"

Aaron groaned. "Ohhh, yes. I wouldn't survive if I had to drive around as much as you. Texting is the way of the future."

"Sorry," Quinn said, biting his lip with worry. Some people were like that—he had clients who would answer a text message in seconds but never pick up their voicemail. "If you're more comfortable, we can hang up and I'll text you once I'm home."

"No, no." Aaron chuckled. "Now that we've broken the sound barrier, I don't mind it."

"You're a visual man, then." Quinn could work with that.

"Totally. I live on WhatsApp. I'd rather throw myself into the harbor in January than make a phone call to most people," Aaron said, laughing.

"Brrr." Quinn shivered. "I only use WhatsApp when clients want to text me progress photos and accountability."

"Strictly work, then. Boring. I could text you much more interesting things," Aaron said, the teasing notes lifting his voice. "But I'll deal with calls for your sake, because you're hot and I've always wanted to try phone sex."

Without the over-the-top deadpan facial expression, it was hard to tell if Aaron was joking. And Quinn wasn't sure if he wanted him to be.

No, scratch that. He was sure, all right. Sure that he wanted it to be far more than a joke between them. Sure that he wanted to find out what pleasure Aaron's way had in store for them both.

His whole body sparked until, for just a moment, he felt Aaron's narrow hand engulfed in his own again. What those soft fingers might feel like trailing down his body, igniting nerves from his cheek down to his chest and belly, and even farther...

"I guess I should add that it was a joke," Aaron interrupted before Quinn's imagination could get to the good part. He giggled softly. "But if you're not ready, I don't want you to feel any pressure."

How sweet for a guy who seemed to spend nine of every ten seconds thinking about sex. There was a lot more to Aaron than met the eye—or than Aaron wanted to let meet the eye, Quinn suspected.

Quinn lowered his voice to a playful growl. "That's a disappointment. I like a bit of pressure in the right places."

Just because he wanted a long-term relationship didn't mean he couldn't enjoy the here and now. Flirting with a guy who turned him on was fun. Getting in bed with him? Yeah, that was already on the table.

Or the wall, as Aaron would say.

Aaron gasped and giggled. "Oh, Mr. Powell," he purred in return. "Do go on."

Quinn licked his lips as heat coiled in his belly and deeper down. The post-gym shorts he changed into, no matter the time of year, were loose.

Then there was a faint clunking noise in the background and a voice, followed by laughter. In the foreground, Quinn picked up a huff from Aaron. His voice was back to normal—annoyed, even. "Scram, you nosy little fuckers," he called out.

Quinn laughed. "What?"

"Sorry. My roommates are trying to listen in. I'm out on the porch and"—Aaron pointedly raised his voice to finish —"they think I won't notice the window opening."

"Ohhh," Quinn said. "We'd better press pause on this if we're giving your friends easy gossip."

"Oh, no. Since they're *apparently* a bunch of voyeurs all of a sudden, they deserve whatever they overhear," Aaron added. Then he softened his voice again and laughed. "Friends. Who needs enemies, right?"

He didn't sound seriously annoyed, though. It sounded like they were good friends teasing each other, rather than anyone picking on Aaron.

Good. Quinn would have a thing or two to say to anyone who made fun of Aaron—whether for his supposedly free sexual habits or for anything else. He'd hardly known the man for two days and he was already ready to go to bat for him.

"You live with them?"

"Yeah. Most of the time, it's awesome. They all work in that art gallery downtown on the square. It's an art co-op, more or less. Initially, I was the one with the day job to help pay the bills while they got it up and running. Then they've been covering *my* bills while I get the cafe running. Give and take."

"Oh, that's great," Quinn murmured. He admired Aaron even more already.

He didn't have any close friends of his own. Some of his childhood friends were moving back to town, spurred by the economic upswing in Hart's Bay.

But he'd never been close to many people even as a kid. He was the reliable friend that everyone called for help but nobody knew very well. Mostly because he was also the boring one—or so he'd been told.

"They're a fun bunch. You wanna come over tonight and meet them?"

Quinn sure as hell hadn't expected that suggestion. But the meaning behind Aaron's offer made him grin. Anyone who wanted him to meet their friends was serious. "Are you sure? It wouldn't make them even nosier?"

"It will, but I don't care." The firmness in Aaron's voice dissuaded any argument. "It'll be fun to make them wonder what's going on. I never introduce them to guys. Well, sometimes over the toaster in the morning, but that's it. Supper would be much more civilized. You have supper plans?"

"No," Quinn said, grinning to himself. Then he winced at the thought of the carb count. At this rate, he'd have an entire cheat month. But his heart told him that this was more important—that Aaron didn't care about him only for the number of abs he had.

Plus, if all went well, he'd get some very physical workouts in with Aaron, one-on-one, and soon. His shorts stirred again, and he bit his lip, curling his toes in his sneakers. His car jolted forward as he stepped on the gas a bit too much.

He'd have to stop by his house first and change into something nicer, obviously. And take a better shower, since he'd only given himself a half-hearted scrub at the gym. Maybe wear cologne, too.

"Come at six. What about breakfast plans tomorrow?" Aaron asked, the implication hard for even a distracted Quinn to miss.

Quinn chuckled. "Nope. I'd love to come over for at least one of the above," he told Aaron. Good thing Aaron couldn't see how hard he was beaming. His cheeks already hurt. "I'll bring the wine."

"For breakfast or supper?" Aaron giggled.

"Why not both?"

"You're perfect. I'm keeping you around," Aaron declared cheerily before they said their goodbyes. The casual declaration made Quinn's heart soar until it joined his head, lost in the clouds.

Hopefully Aaron was right.

5

AARON

"You're inviting a *guy* for dinner?"

"No, I thought I'd bring home an alpaca. Yes, a *guy*. Tsch." Aaron tutted and rolled his eyes as he checked the wine provisions. Quinn might be bringing a bottle, but no way would that supply the whole household.

It was hard to count the housemates anymore. Technically, the only ones living here were Aaron, Ross, Ezra, Beau, and Benji. But the potential dinner crowd didn't stop there.

Jesse had once lived here but now lived next door with his fiancé, Finn. Both of them came and went as they pleased. Then there were guests like Finn's cousin, Rain, and his boyfriend—no, fiancé as of last week—Colt. And Rain's best friend Justin had promised to visit sometime with his own boyfriend, Harry.

Not to mention housemates' boyfriends: Ezra's new boyfriend, Rusty, came around a lot. With Aaron, Ross, Beau, and Benji all single, it wasn't uncommon to run into a guy one of his housemates had brought home. None of them tended to stick around, though.

Despite his jokes to the contrary, Aaron rarely brought guys back. This house was his own little sanctuary. He only invited men home with him when they couldn't host and it was too cold for a quickie in the forest.

"I can't believe it. Aaron, bringing a *boy* to supper," Jesse teased with a wicked glint in his eye. "I'll make sure you get a small portion tonight. *Are* you eating? Or just living off ice?"

Of course they were going to be like this. Aaron pretended to gasp and swatted Jesse's shoulder. "Amateurs. I can bottom after Taco Bell." He made a break from the kitchen to hover by the front door and wait for Quinn.

The rest of them were setting the table, grabbing wine bottles, and chatting at full volume in the large kitchen/dining room combination. A large table stretched the length of a wall, with a bench along one side and chairs on the other. It normally seated about nine or ten with elbows tucked in, but some days that wasn't quite enough now.

Ezra smirked and called after him, "We have so much payback in store for you."

Aaron had earned every bit of it. He always mercilessly tormented his friends about their crushes and provided sexual commentary. This was going to be a trial by fire for Quinn.

Quinn was going to show up at exactly six, wasn't he? Aaron could tell he was just that conscientious. He perched on the arm of the sofa and listened to his friends laughing about something. And sure enough, at six on the dot, he heard tires crunching by the road.

Aaron sprang to his feet and then sat down again. No, he didn't want to seem eager by hovering on the other side of the door, ready to yank it open. But he also didn't want anyone else to get to the door first.

Wait, maybe it's not even Quinn, he realized. *It could be any of the other guys.*

Aaron bit his lip and nudged the curtains aside just enough to peek through the gap. It was dark outside by now, so it took a moment for his eyes to adjust.

That was definitely Quinn stepping out of his car, carrying something. Hopefully the wine... or a king-sized lube bottle. He peered up at the house, and Aaron quickly let the curtains fall back into place.

Oh, man. He was suddenly nervous. He glanced down at himself, smoothing a hand over his tight black T-shirt with a gray-and-white floral print. His dark blue jeans were the nice skinny ones that showed off his ass. Simple and elegant. He'd nearly added a collar before deciding to go easy on Quinn tonight.

Beau popped his head into the room and gave him a friendly grin. "Hey. You want red or white?"

"Neither, thanks." Aaron forced himself to stand up slowly, casually, and saunter toward Beau like he wasn't aware that Quinn must be at the top of the driveway. "Quinn's bringing wine with him."

The corners of Beau's eyes crinkled. "Which you're waiting to share with him, romantically..."

"Oh, shut up," Aaron scoffed.

They both heard steps on the porch and glanced toward it. Before Beau could move a muscle, Aaron slid between him and the door. "I've got it. Shoo."

"Oh, okay, then." Beau laughed, raising his hands as Aaron flapped his hand at him. "Look at you, all cute and eager—okay, okay!"

Aaron leveled his glare at the guys who had overheard

Beau's teasing and were now peeking around the corner of the kitchen doorway. They ducked away with more laughter.

The old doorbell wired into the house rang in a harsh, flat note. It made Aaron jump, suddenly aware of his pulse racing. He strolled across the entrance hall and opened the door, smiling at Quinn.

The object of his December fling was standing there with his hands behind his back, looking far too respectable. His hair was neatly slicked back and still damp, obviously freshly showered. Musky aftershave met Aaron's nose. In the gap at the top of his not quite zipped-up black jacket, Aaron spotted Quinn's usual collared shirt—this time, dark blue.

"Well, hello." Aaron beamed and stretched onto tiptoe to kiss Quinn's cheek for the first time.

Quinn bent at the knee slightly to make it easier, which made them both laugh. His lips brushed the warm, smooth skin of Quinn's cheek.

Aaron had kind of hoped Quinn would touch his shoulders as they kissed, but before Aaron could be disappointed, he stepped back and presented—with a flourish—a bottle of red wine and a bouquet in one hand.

Well, he'd found a way to make Aaron blush. All he could think to say was "Oh, that's so sweet!" He took them both and stared as Quinn presented him with another bottle of wine, which he'd been holding in his other hand.

"For your friends, to smooth the way."

Aaron laughed and took it, too, cradling it in the nook of his arm. He stretched up to kiss Quinn's cheek again. "Oh, you didn't have to." This time, Quinn's hand came to rest in the small of his back. It felt nice there. "Thank you. Come on in."

"Let me just get my shoes off," Quinn said, leaning on the

wall to pull off his black dress shoes. Then he took his jacket off and looked around for a hook.

Every little moment was laden with anticipation and suspense. This wasn't the kind of suspense Aaron was used to, either. It made him feel a little clumsy, overeager, like it was his first-ever real date all over again.

"Right there." Aaron showed Quinn where to hang up his jacket. As he did, he took a moment to admire the perfectly creased gray slacks and subtle, shimmery black floral pattern laid into the deep blue shirt. "You look so nice."

"So do you. Look, we match," Quinn pointed out, grinning.

The shout from the kitchen of "Supper's almost ready, lovebirds!" came with a round of giggles.

Aaron snorted. "I'd flip them off if I had a free hand."

"Here," Quinn said, taking a bottle back from him and winking. "Wouldn't want to leave you unguarded."

"Thanks." Aaron grinned and led Quinn through to the kitchen and dining room combo.

Time for introductions.

But first, someone whispered, "*Flowers,*" in a tone of shock, like they couldn't all see Aaron carrying them.

Aaron felt himself going red again. "Okay, guys, this is Quinn," he said as he set his bottle of wine on the counter. "You can introduce yourselves, since you're gagging to do it." Meanwhile, he grabbed a vase to pop the bouquet into.

"Hi! Welcome. I'm Jesse. I don't know why I'm welcoming you in—I don't live here anymore," Jesse added with a laugh.

His fiancé snorted. "We're just next door. I've never lived here, but some days I'm sure I do. I'm Finn."

Beau, Rusty, and Ezra introduced themselves, too, while

Quinn dutifully hugged everyone. He clearly wasn't used to all this physical contact, but he also wasn't being rude about it.

By that time, Aaron had the flower vase set up on the windowsill, so he rejoined Quinn. "Let's sit down."

He'd hoped to save a spot for Quinn on the end of the table so Aaron could crowd in next to Quinn and insulate him. Judging by the full glasses on the table, it looked like the guys had shifted them around, though. Now the vacant seats were next to each other in the middle of the table.

Beau gave Aaron a cheeky grin once Aaron had looked at the table and then at his friends. He shrugged, fluttering his lashes innocently. "I had to be on the end since I'm taking off early."

"Sure," Aaron snorted, picking up the bottles. "Dibs on the white wine. You guys can have the red, if you're fast enough."

Despite Aaron's fears, the teasing had already faded. Either they all knew better than to tease him, or they couldn't make up their mind on who was in charge of doing it. Aaron was usually the one making all the inappropriate jokes.

Everyone's stomachs growled at the smell of chicken pot pie with salad on the side, plus a smaller tofu version for Ross. The pie wasn't quite done, but they were all waiting on the timer.

"So, what do you do for work?" Beau asked as they started dishing out food. As usual, he was the one trying to make everyone feel comfortable.

"I'm a personal trainer. I work from a few gyms upstate and in Portland," Quinn answered like he'd had the script ready.

"Oooh. You two can talk about strong things." Ezra leaned into Rusty and beamed up at his new boyfriend. The timer went off, and Jesse sprang to his feet to get the pie.

Rusty laughed. "There's not a lot to talk about, hon," he said but smiled anyway. "You ever get out to do outdoor sports?"

"Not as much as I'd like," Quinn admitted. He took the salad bowl as it was passed around. "I'm mostly inside."

"That's a shame. If you ever want to get out on the water, let me know. Uses a whole bunch of different muscles."

Quinn nodded. "Yeah. A rowing machine doesn't have surprise waves," he said, which made Rusty laugh.

Jesse interjected, "Move, move, 'scuse me, hot dish!" He reached between Quinn and Aaron with the hot pan and set it on the trivet in the middle of the table.

"Oh, God, that looks good. Who's in charge of cooking for all of you?" Quinn asked.

"Everyone takes turns," Aaron answered, straightening up again and leaning into Quinn. "We try to RSVP for supper on the house WhatsApp chat, or make flexible suppers we can scale up. It's hard sometimes, though," Aaron admitted.

"You have a house chat?" That sounded like way too much work for Quinn.

"Two. One for the housemates only, and one for us, boyfriends, frequent guests—anyone who might show up for supper."

"Plus the secret chat we don't tell Aaron about," Jesse deadpanned.

"Fuck off," Aaron told Jesse with a cheerful grin, which made Quinn laugh in surprise next to him. "I know you can't keep a secret that long."

Finn was busy talking with Ross about barbecuing tofu, so Jesse rolled his eyes and served his fiancé before elbowing him. "Let the poor guy eat, and he'll get you recipes later. He's even more emo before food."

"*Thank* you," Ross sighed.

"Oh, Benji says he'll be here in a few minutes," Beau said, looking up from his phone. "And on the other chat, Rain said he'll drop by later with Colt for a word with you, Aaron."

"Oh, yeah?" Aaron spoke around a mouthful of pot pie, checking his phone. Sure enough, they wanted a word about sales numbers as they tried to judge the foot traffic in the units so far. "Thanks."

Conversation soon got back to Quinn. "I knew you in school, didn't I?" Finn asked, scanning Quinn's face. "You're a little younger...?"

Four or five years, in fact. He had a good memory, if he noticed Quinn. "Yeah. I grew up here," Quinn said. He smiled crookedly. "But I stayed pretty quiet. Always back of the classroom."

"That explains it," Finn said with a good-natured smile. "Have you stuck around here?"

Quinn nodded. "Couldn't get much work around here, hence the freelance job."

"Good for you." Finn nodded with a sincere smile. "Not a lot of us have stayed. My brothers had to move for work, too. One of them's back now, though. Dash. He's a teacher now, or working on it."

"Mmm." Aaron spoke around his mouthful. "Is he gonna teach nearby?"

"He wants to. There's word of a new school, but nothing confirmed." Finn reached for the salad bowl to dish out some more greens for himself.

Before they'd finished eating, Beau shot to his feet, excused himself, and headed for the back room of the house that served as a mini studio. He had some last-minute Christmas orders to fill.

Rusty rushed through his meal, too. "I've got to catch low tide. See you, babe," he told Ezra, leaning in to peck his lips while the others made *awww* sounds and wolf whistled.

"You're all right by yourself?" Ezra murmured, bringing a momentary still to the table.

Everyone remembered that Ezra had nearly gotten himself into trouble just over a week ago by heading out in bad conditions. It had turned out fine, but Aaron didn't blame Ezra for worrying even more about his boyfriend now.

"Yeah, it's a clear night," Rusty told him, waving at everyone and winking at Quinn. "Good to meet you. See you all tomorrow."

Just minutes later, Benji got home and thundered upstairs. He shouted, "Down in a minute! Save some for me!"

"Hurry up, then, or I'll go for seconds," Ross called back. "Did you lock up?"

Benji's voice was faintly audible from upstairs. "Yeah, I was the last out."

Quinn shook his head. "Is it always this crazy?" he asked in a murmur as he leaned into Aaron, wrapping an arm around him.

Oh, that hold felt good. It washed away the worries that had filled him over the last hour: that Quinn wouldn't get along with his friends, or that his friends wouldn't like him, or that Aaron himself would be clumsy and weird about it all.

With Quinn's strong arm around him, Aaron's brain thrummed with a thick, honey-like pleasure.

"Yeah, it can be. It's gotten pretty wild over the last few months." Aaron grinned. "People moving out, moving in, making friends..." He tried to sum up the history of housemates, but he wasn't sure Quinn would remember anyone's names anyway.

Quinn smiled. "That's nice. I like it. I'm so not used to this, though."

"Oh?"

"Yeah. At family dinners, there are... *rules*." Quinn rolled his eyes. "Like someone will kick a puppy every time someone stands up without a formal announcement."

Aaron wrinkled his nose. Gross. He knew all too well what that was like. How had Quinn survived?

"Hey, everyone." Benji bounced into the kitchen and stopped dead as he spotted Aaron cuddling into Quinn's side. "Oh. Hi?"

"Quinn, this is Benji," Aaron introduced them as they shook hands. Then Benji grabbed a plate and took Rusty's vacant seat, kissing Ezra's cheek in greeting. It made Aaron smile to see.

The two of them had clashed not long ago when Benji tried to hit on Rusty, but now that Ezra and Rusty were openly together, they'd obviously made up.

Jesse cleared his throat. "Sooo," he said, leaning over the table. "Inquiring minds want to know..."

Here they went. Aaron glanced at Quinn, wondering how much he wanted to say. His heart raced with excited antic-ipation.

Quinn shrugged at him and grinned, leaving it up to him.

"He's my December fling. I'm rescuing him from first-date hell for the holiday season," Aaron told them, leaning into Quinn again. He snuck a glance to make sure that had gone over well.

"Yeah," Quinn confirmed with a nod. "And I'm trying to convince him that long-term relationships are a good idea."

A chorus of *Oooohs* went around the table.

"Good luck with that," Ross muttered. Beau must've

kicked him under the table, because he snorted, and then Ross jumped and glared at him.

Quinn laughed. "I understand I've got my work cut out for me. But so does he, putting up with me." He gave them all a grin.

"So, fill me in on the Quinn-and-Aaron-related gossip," Benji told the table, winking at Quinn. "What did I miss?"

When Aaron looked around the table, Ezra caught his gaze and raised his brows. He gave Aaron a look that said he was going to catch him for a talk later.

And for good reason. Not that long ago, Aaron had counseled Ezra through his relationship woes, letting slip more than he'd meant to about his loneliness. Ezra was probably wondering if Aaron had been hiding Quinn from them already.

It was strange to think that Quinn had walked into his life at practically the moment Aaron had admitted he wanted more. *Right time, right place. It's like it's meant to be*, he thought.

No, Aaron knew that was crazy talk. People didn't just fall into each other's lives for a good reason. That was the stuff of cheesy movies and power ballads. Relationships took hard work. Which, to Aaron, sounded like settling for less than he could get.

But as Quinn gently rubbed Aaron's back while talking with Beau about his fitness regime, Aaron wondered for a moment if it couldn't be both: hard work and fate.

After all, there were plenty of guys he'd shared a bed with but wouldn't dream of introducing to his friends. And guys he couldn't imagine falling for after three *years*, much less three weeks.

The fact was Quinn didn't feel like a stranger, even if he

practically was. Some part of Aaron felt like this was the hundredth time Quinn had sat next to him at a dinner table to talk about training anecdotes.

What was happening to Aaron? He'd promised to set aside his skepticism and give love a chance, and suddenly he was getting swept away?

No, he reminded himself, he wasn't going to date a guy just because. There had to be a good reason to entangle his life with someone else's for the foreseeable future, swear off other guys, and hand over his heart—and all the risk of heartbreak.

"Should we move to the living room?" Beau suggested, coming back in from the studio with a box of addressed padded envelopes. "I'm all done with work, and I could use another drink."

It was Ezra and Aaron's turn to clear the table. Quinn tried to wait for Aaron, but he shook his head. "You're the guest. Go on, I'll be with you in a minute," he promised.

"Don't forget your wine," Beau told Quinn and grinned as he led him off to the living room.

Aaron glanced after them, his chest tight. It was hard to be out of Quinn's sight when he was meeting everyone for the first time. Quinn was doing great so far, but his housemates could be overwhelming. He wanted to protect him.

"Don't worry, Beau of all people won't interrogate him," Ezra murmured. He gathered plates into his arms and nudged Aaron with his hip. "So...?"

"So?" Aaron echoed, nodding back at Ezra. "What do you think?" He took the empty casserole dishes and serving utensils.

"I like him a lot," Ezra told Aaron with a frank smile. "He seems like a sweetheart."

Ezra had got it in one. "Opposites attract, then," Aaron

said. Ezra cast him a confused glance, so he clarified, "Choosing *me*, the least sweet guy here."

"No," Ezra said simply. He clicked his tongue and pinched Aaron's arm gently. "You're very sweet. Having the dirtiest mind of anyone I know doesn't preclude sweetness. Your heart's always in the right place."

Aaron blushed to the tips of his ears and shoved dishes into the dishwasher so he didn't have to look at Ezra. Somehow, he felt even more vulnerable now.

After a few moments of silence and clinking dishes, Ezra bent next to him to poke cutlery into the basket. "It's okay to be sweet, you know," he murmured with a knowing little smile. "Not hold everyone at arm's length."

Aaron swallowed hard, waiting his turn to put the last few bowls in. "Yeah. I'm working on it." A shaky little laugh escaped as he tried to breathe through the nervousness. The last thing he wanted was to get stressed and lash out at people. "God knows how it'll go, but at least we only have three weeks. Then I can go back to never letting men in."

And what if we get to the end of the month and he wants to keep going and I don't? Or... I do, and he doesn't? Aaron bit his lip.

"Hm," Ezra mused. "Well, I have a good feeling about him." He took the dishes out of Aaron's hands. "I'll get the rest. You go be with him." He shooed him away.

Aaron thanked Ezra, then took his wineglass and the bottle to join Quinn on the couch. They were in the middle of a discussion about TV.

"So you don't watch reality TV? At all? Even in the middle of the afternoon when nothing else is on?" Beau solemnly shook his head. "I don't know about this one, guys."

Ross pretended to clutch his chest. "I will live and die for storage unit auctions. That's all I'll say."

Aaron tensed up protectively as he came to sit next to Quinn, but Quinn was just grinning at them both. He casually slid an arm around Aaron's shoulders. "None of that stuff is *real*," Quinn countered. "I'm not going to reward them for being too cheap to credit their script writers."

"Oooh," Jesse laughed. "He's got a good point."

Aaron smiled and relaxed as Quinn tucked him against his side. He rested his hand on Quinn's knee and listened to them make fun of Ross's TV habits.

It was fun to let down his guard around his friends for once and let them see a side of him they hadn't in over a year—and for the newer friends, ever. Quinn made him feel safe to do so in his completely disarming way.

In fact, it was easy for Aaron to rest the side of his head on Quinn's shoulder and close his eyes. It was impossible to ignore the way the simple, affectionate touch instantly calmed him.

Excited him, too. He wanted so badly to press his body against Quinn's and take his time to explore the energy that was building between them.

They weren't under any pretenses that this would be a long-term thing. So Aaron wasn't going to let his nerves get in the way of a good time. As long as he could keep himself from blowing the whole relationship up by being his usual self, he was in for a good December.

But did he even remember how to have fun that didn't end in someone blocking someone else's number?

Aaron's grip on Quinn's knee tightened. God, he desperately hoped so.

6

QUINN

It was impossible to be nervous around Aaron's housemates.

They were an eclectic bunch—from Ross, who rarely smiled and only seemed to tell dark jokes, to Beau, who was bending over backward to make sure Quinn felt comfortable. But though people came and went so freely their names blurred in Quinn's mind, they all had a friendly smile and word for him.

He did remember Rain and Colt, who showed up not long after supper. They chatted briefly with Aaron about foot traffic and marketing plans for Christmas, and then they took off again, too. They both made sure to say bye to Quinn, though.

Jesse and Finn eventually headed home, and Ezra snuck off to Rusty's house. As the other guys started heading to bed, one by one, Aaron pouted. "I'm so not ready for sleep. Should we go out?"

"Well, I'm not driving after this much wine." Quinn chuckled and held up his empty glass. "I'm trying not to think about the sugar in this."

Aaron giggled and put aside their glasses, then pecked his

cheek. It made him prickle with pleasure. "How about a walk? I could use the fresh air."

"Perfect." Quinn waved slightly to catch Beau's attention, since he was busy debating Ross about tomorrow's dinner. "Sorry to interrupt. We're heading out for a walk, but it was great to meet you. Thanks for having me over."

They both hugged him, and Beau even kissed his cheek. "Make sure you come back anytime."

"Will do. Thanks."

Then Quinn headed for the entrance hall with Aaron. They shrugged on their shoes and jackets, and Aaron huddled into a hat and gloves.

"We can walk around the neighborhood and look at the lights. Then head up the path if it's not too cold?" Aaron suggested.

"Sure." Quinn would walk anywhere that Aaron wanted if he got to spend more time alone with him.

Once they were alone together on the sidewalk, Aaron slipped his gloved hand into Quinn's. "Thank you for coming over tonight. I hope you had fun."

"I really did." Quinn gave him a smile. "I thought it would be a lot more scary than it was."

"They're not bad," Aaron agreed. He swung their hands lightly. "And this isn't, either."

"*Not bad?* I'll take it. Slowly, we'll get to *awesome*," Quinn teased. "And then you'll fall hopelessly for me, right?"

Aaron pretended to recoil. "I don't know about that, mister." But despite Aaron's comical expression, his hand stayed firmly in Quinn's.

The houses between their neighborhood and the ocean were decked in lights. They stretched along fences, outlined houses, and lit up trees. Some people had inflatable Santas tied to the front lawn, or wire reindeer lit up in shimmering blues and whites.

It was a pretty sight, but more impressive to Aaron than Quinn. It was pretty much the same view every Christmas, with few new people moving into town—until this year, anyway. A good dozen new households had formed, and it was nice to have fewer empty houses and dark yards.

Soon, they were wandering up the slope and into the forested clifftop path. The smells of cedar and salt grew thick around them. It was a great night—crisp but not too biting cold, and there was practically no wind.

As soon as they reached the coast, the view opened up to a steep slope. The moonlight barely lit the drop to the water, so Quinn stuck to the path. The darkness beyond was the only visual clue of the vast expanse of the Pacific Ocean. The waves sounded soft, lapping against the beach below.

"So, what's your ideal relationship look like?" Aaron murmured at last, peering up at Quinn as they picked their way slowly along the dark path. "Do we go on dates every day? Call each other on the phone, like it's the age of the dinosaurs?"

Quinn laughed. "Oof. Let me see..." He squeezed Aaron's hand tightly and guided him around a stump. "I'd like to talk or text most days, and see you at least a few times a week. Doesn't have to be every day, since we don't exactly work nine to five. By the way, what are your hours?"

They were almost at the top of the path now. From this exact spot on the point, in the daytime, they'd be able to see both bays below. To their left lay the sheltered rocky cove where the town held bonfires from time to time. Beyond that lay the harbor and downtown. On their right was the sandy beach, stretching into wilderness and the open highway up the coast.

Quinn decided to loop around through downtown rather than keep walking up through the wilderness at this hour.

"Yeah," Aaron sighed. "Right now it's just my head barista—Yolanda—and me. I open the cafe on weekdays, and she opens on weekends. I'm usually off sometime between noon and never."

Quinn smiled at the quick wit, which even a few glasses of wine didn't touch. "Okay. I work weekday mornings and evenings, and most weekends... kind of weird shifts. Some of my clients are flexible, so I can rearrange things going forward."

"I hope they're all flexible," Aaron countered. "Or what are you doing?"

"Training for strength—or worse, for show." Quinn groaned. "I hate it when guys get so wrapped up on showing off that they forget the basics."

"I'll show off my flexibility for you anytime." Aaron giggled playfully.

"Speaking of which, what are *you* looking for?" Quinn asked, anticipation quickening his breath. "If you're going to win me over by persuading me that sex is everything..."

"I... well..." Aaron hesitated. Then, he turned to face Quinn and took his other hand, too. "I want to make sure you know we don't need to rush into it."

"I thought you wanted to get laid as much as possible," Quinn teased, pulling Aaron in with a short, sharp jerk of his hands. Their bodies pressed together as he wrapped his arms around Aaron's lower back.

God, Aaron fit so nicely against him. Quinn could feel his hot breath under his chin. Without the bulky winter clothes in the way, he'd definitely reveal the excitement that had stirred in his pants at the question.

"I do," Aaron moaned, his hands resting on Quinn's chest. They ran slowly up to his shoulders. "God, yeah." He rose onto his toes and suddenly, his lips were on Quinn's.

Oh, that kiss was worth waiting for. Alone in the forest on a crisp night, only the moon shining down on them, the waves washing onto the shore below... it was everything Quinn had ever dreamed of.

But it was also as hot as a campfire, this energy that had been smoldering between them all evening. It burst through suddenly, uncontainable and utterly addictive.

Heat rushed from head to toe as their warm, wet lips slid together, hands groping through outerwear across each other's arms, sides, and backs.

When Aaron grabbed Quinn's ass, Quinn gasped and scolded him with a bite of his lip. Aaron just whimpered and pressed closer, his hardness pushing into Quinn's thigh.

It was impossible to breathe, or think straight, or even remember the conversation they'd been having. The connection that had suddenly opened was utterly intoxicating.

"But," Aaron finally whispered, pulling back and gripping Quinn's shoulders.

His breath tickled Quinn's cheek. It was hard to resist kissing the words away from him.

"But?" Quinn murmured. He locked his arms around Aaron's lower back and playfully pushed his thigh into Aaron's groin, letting him grind against it.

"Nnnh." Aaron's breathless moan made Quinn grin with satisfaction. "You big distraction."

"Wait 'til you see my even bigger distraction."

Aaron gasped and then giggled. "I knew you had a filthy

mind under the respectable *boy next door* act. Where was I? Oh, right. I wanna screw you six ways from Sunday. But I don't want you to rush if you don't want—"

"I want you," Quinn growled quietly, pressing his mouth against Aaron's until Aaron stopped trying to talk him out of it. Until Aaron's mouth was pliable and gasping against his, begging for more. "I need you."

It had been so long since he'd been with anyone, and he was done trying to ignore the chemistry between them. They were writing their own rulebook, and Quinn was eager. He wanted to explore every inch of Aaron's body and find out if sex really did make a good basis for a relationship.

"Take me, then," Aaron moaned. "Here, your place, my place, I don't care."

"It's a little cold here. I'd rather impress you," Quinn chuckled deeply. He grabbed Aaron's hand. "Come on. Walk fast."

The night felt colder without Aaron's thighs slotted between his. They set off at a rapid pace, apparently both as eager as one another. Quinn's legs were longer, so Aaron trotted at his side.

It didn't take long to head down the path that snaked to Quinn's street. He strode briskly down the sidewalk toward his house, then held the gate open for Aaron.

It seemed to take years until they were on Quinn's front porch, even though it was probably a five-minute walk. Almost twitching with impatience, Quinn let them both in. He kicked off his shoes, stripping his jacket and throwing it on top of the chair near the door.

Aaron barely had his gloves and hat off. He nearly stumbled over their shoes, so Quinn grabbed him by the waist, lifting him out of the hall.

He practically slammed Aaron against the wall, the sudden heat around them nothing compared to the heat deep in his body. "Is this what *you* want in a relationship?"

"Oooh!" Aaron gasped. He rolled his head back, looping his arms around Quinn's shoulders. "Yes. As often as possible, please."

Quinn grabbed Aaron's ass and hoisted him up. "Noted." The openmouthed kiss they shared next was dirty and full of promises, and Quinn lingered in the moment as long as he could.

They made out hot, hard, and heavy, and it was everything he'd been waiting for. They were still far too clothed, but already, nerve endings Quinn had forgotten about were pulsating deep inside.

God, this was perfect.

"Show me to your room," Aaron whispered. The need dripping from his voice made Quinn's already-hard dick twitch in answer.

"I'll do one better." Quinn hoisted Aaron even further into his arms, firming his hold even though he was light as a feather. Then he turned and carried Aaron straight to the bedroom.

"There's another dream come true," Aaron giggled breathlessly, his face tucked into the crook of Quinn's neck as his arms and legs looped tightly around him. "I bet you're strong enough you can fuck me standing up!"

"Can and will," Quinn growled. He dumped Aaron on the bed and hovered over him, pressing kisses along his jaw, neck, and ear, until Aaron was whimpering.

Then he pulled back, keeping his lips just out of reach however much Aaron strained upward. "What do you need in bed?" Aaron had talked about starting from sexual compatibility, but they'd never really discussed it. All he knew was Aaron was a total bottom.

"Total honesty," Aaron whispered back, his gaze flickering across Quinn's face. Then he relaxed and smiled. "And being willing to handle me. It takes a firm hand."

"I've got two of those." Quinn gripped Aaron's wrists and pulled them above his head. He bit his lip at the gorgeous sight under him, Aaron's body stretched out and quivering.

"Be loud," Aaron continued, breathless. "Forceful. Bold. It's just us, and nothing else matters. Show me who you are. That's what I love about sex."

Each word resonated somewhere deep inside Quinn. This was no five-minute pump and dump. A little piece of his soul was already naked and vulnerable. Meanwhile, all of Aaron's joking and defenses were gone. Quinn had never known what he needed, let alone been able to put it into words, but Aaron had just done so for him.

"I want that, too," he whispered. "I want to lose myself in you."

Aaron's cheeks rounded into adorable dimples as he beamed up at him. "Then do it."

It was a challenge, and Quinn rose to meet it—in every sense.

As he stood up, Aaron shifted. Fluid as a puddle, he flowed down off the bed until he knelt in front of Quinn, gazing up at him in the light of the bedside lamps.

"Yes," Quinn gasped. His world narrowed in a split second until it was just Aaron. He needed Aaron's hot mouth on him more than he needed to breathe.

Aaron fixed his gaze on Quinn's as he slid the zipper down with his teeth and unfastened the button of his slacks. Vibrations shook through Quinn with every accidental brush of

Aaron's palm on the tent of his cock in his slacks—or was it an accident?

His slacks fell to the floor, and he stepped out of them, bracing himself on Aaron.

Even through his underwear, Aaron's mouth was skilled. He gripped Quinn's cock between his lips and flicked his tongue along the skin, each sensation dull and soft.

Even so, Quinn's fingertips tightened around Aaron's shoulders. "Fuck!" Quinn needed to be naked right now.

Aaron sensed the urgency. He didn't delay, pulling back and hooking his thumbs through Quinn's underwear. As he pulled them down and off, his gaze stayed fixed on the erection that sprang free.

"I think you mean fuck *yes*," Aaron breathed out, pressing his lips against the underside of his cock, his nose tickling along sensitive skin. Already, the tip of Quinn's shaft was dripping wet. At last he sat back on his heels and looked up. "I want to suck you off like this. That okay?"

Quinn gulped. "I... I'm tested. All good if you are."

"How lucky. Me too." Aaron's gaze slid back to his cock. He wrapped his fingers gently around the base, sending sparks of pleasure through Quinn's whole body. Then he nuzzled it against his cheek before kissing all over, his admiring gaze making Quinn stand even taller over him.

His licks turned into openmouthed kisses, and then his lips smoothly slid over the head and down the shaft in one smooth gulp.

Quinn cried out sharply, his nails biting into Aaron's slender shoulders as Aaron took him into the hot, tight wetness of his mouth so fast. The sensation overwhelmed everything else, so raw it was almost painful. But quickly, as Aaron pulled back and then swallowed him again, Quinn adjusted and it built into a steady, pleasurable crescendo.

Until Aaron pulled his mouth off him with a quiet popping noise and rested his hands on Quinn's thighs.

"Oh, fuck." Quinn wasn't sure he could handle any more teasing from Aaron tonight. He clenched his jaw as hard as he could as he met Aaron's gaze, trying to convey the desperation he felt.

The more Aaron teased him, the more he caught Quinn's interest. Already, he knew that if this was all he got from Aaron, he was going to be sad.

But there was no time to think about that. With the tip of Quinn's stiff erection resting along his cheek, Aaron batted his lashes. His voice dripped with honey innocence. "Would you bend me over and fuck me until I scream your name? Please?"

Fuck, would he *ever*. Aaron was driving Quinn out of his goddamn mind. He knew exactly what he was doing to him.

"Anytime you ask," Quinn growled. He grabbed Aaron's arms, yanking him to his feet. It was effortless to turn Aaron around and bend him over. One arm went around Aaron's waist, and the other pressed down on his back. His cock jutted between Aaron's denim-clad thighs.

Aaron rested his hands on the bed, spreading his legs while Quinn grabbed lube from the bedside table. He practically ripped the rest of his clothes off, followed by Aaron's.

"Yes," Aaron panted, squirming out of his underwear and kicking them away. Now Quinn could admire the hot-as-hell view of his cute little ass poking up in the air, his narrow back, and Aaron craning his neck to see over his shoulder.

Aaron was slick and ready for him in just moments, pushing back eagerly into Quinn's fingers and begging for his cock instead.

"Please, Quinn. I need you in me," Aaron whimpered. "You have no idea how much."

So Quinn gasped and pulled out, adding a little more lube. "Just a moment, baby," he whispered.

They both moaned as Quinn pressed into Aaron's body, sliding past the ring of muscle until Aaron took him in.

The tightness was almost too much at first. Inch by inch, fiery pleasure danced along the surface of his shaft and deeper, straight up the core into his belly. Quinn's heart pounded, his muscles tight and breathing strained.

But within moments, he had control again, the lightning storm subsiding into sparks of pleasure that shot along every nerve.

"Fuck me hard," Aaron begged, tightening around him and twitching. "Please."

Quinn guided himself into Aaron until he was balls-deep. Then he pulled back and thrust hard, his hands rising to Aaron's shoulders to press him into the bed.

"Yes!" Aaron panted. As their bodies drove together, Quinn filled him up and stretched him open with every push of his hips. Aaron's gasps turned to moans and then cries of pleasure.

Being deep inside Aaron was more than Quinn could ever have hoped for, and he was instantly addicted. Aaron was hot and tight around him, yet pliant and squirming under his hands. Every time his cock hit that spot deep inside, Aaron let him know with a throaty sound.

Time became irrelevant, minutes sliding by into one another until they were sweat-soaked and gasping for air. Quinn's whole body was taut and needy, his climax nearly impossible to fend off.

Beneath him, the slightest touch of Aaron's cock made

tightness ripple around Quinn. He jerked his hand along the sensitive skin slowly at first, spreading wetness from the tip with his thumb.

Soon he couldn't help it, stroking him harder to pull him along the unstoppable path to climax. Quinn already felt like he'd glimpsed Aaron's spirit here, irrepressible and defiant and proud. And he wanted more. So much more.

At last, at the edge of his endurance, Quinn pulled out of Aaron. He hoisted Aaron up the bed, rolling him over and nestling between his thighs.

He wanted to be face-to-face. No, *needed* to be.

"Kiss me," Aaron breathed out.

Quinn leaned down to catch Aaron's mouth, showering him with tender kisses. Then he gripped both their shafts in one hand and jerked them both off together, whimpering with pleasure. The hard ridge of Aaron's cock head made heat pool in his stomach.

"Yes... don't stop!" Aaron begged him. "Please, Quinn!"

Blackness closed in, and all Quinn cared about was Aaron. Keeping him safe, guiding him to his end, giving him every ounce of pleasure he deserved, making him scream with pleasure just as he'd asked for.

Aaron bucked off the bed, giving a sharp, keening noise as his nails bit into Quinn's shoulders. They were long past the point of no return, frantically sharing gasps and moans against one another's lips. Skin slid against skin until, at last, Quinn felt bliss crashing into him.

Aaron shivered and arched under him, his cries music to Quinn's ears. They spilled their loads together in a hot, sticky mess that made every stroke slicker and more sensitive.

Quinn fought for breath when the fog finally lifted, slowly uncurling his hand and gripping Aaron's hip instead.

Aaron curled into him, rolling onto his side and pressing tightly, skin-to-skin. He buried his face into Quinn's chest with a whine of pleasure.

Quinn chuckled quietly. They didn't need to exchange words to understand how good they felt. "Mmhmm."

They lay together for a few long minutes, sweat cooling and hearts slowing. Aaron's hands smoothed Quinn's skin as Quinn finger-combed his hair.

Finally, when they could move again, Quinn stretched. "Let me clean this up. Staying for breakfast?"

A part of him wondered what the response would be to that question—if it was too romantic for him. If he drove him away now, Quinn would be devastated.

Not that he had any right to be. It was only a temporary arrangement anyway. Just a few weeks, some dates and casual sex, some friendly rivalry to see who was right.

Would love win? Or would Quinn's needs clash with Aaron's already?

But he needn't have worried. Aaron's smile was surprisingly shy but excited. "You bet I am."

"Good," Quinn breathed out. He leaned over and kissed Aaron's forehead. "Just the way I like it."

Aaron yawned and sprawled onto his back as Quinn left to get a washcloth. "Ditto."

7

———

AARON

As Aaron stretched, half-awake, his toes brushed someone's legs.

Quinn, he instantly remembered and smiled. That made a wonderful change. Aaron was used to awkwardly searching his memory for a name or just slipping out the door. But it was easy to remember his night with Quinn.

In the unfamiliar room, Aaron's phone wasn't in the usual spot on his bedside table. It took him a few moments to find it under his pillow, groping around in the darkness.

It was twenty past five. Shit. He'd slept in without an alarm. But it had been a deep, restful sleep—the kind he hadn't enjoyed since before the grand opening.

As Aaron gingerly sat up, Quinn shifted and yawned. "Where are you going?"

"Crap, sorry," Aaron whispered. One foot touched the ground, and he wriggled with displeasure at the cold floor but slipped out of bed. "I didn't want to wake you up. Gotta get to work for six."

"Story of my life," Quinn sleepily chuckled. He rubbed his

eyes and sat up. "Don't worry. I'm usually awake at this hour." Then a slow grin spread across his face. "I don't usually have this view, though."

Aaron was still naked, morning wood and all. He smirked at Quinn. "I really wish I hadn't slept in now. You'd get me up early like nothing else."

Usually, Aaron would find a way to cram in one more quickie. But things were different with Quinn. He didn't have to rush to get whatever he could, whenever he could.

They had time—a luxury Aaron could get used to.

"How late are you? Can I make you toast?" Quinn sounded so hopeful that Aaron couldn't help smiling. "I bought bread, in case... in case."

"That would be nice. Thanks." Aaron untangled his jeans, grinning at how hard it was to find all his clothes from last night. That was a sign of a good night.

"You bet!" Quinn dressed with incredible speed, still hopping from foot to foot and wrestling on his socks as he thumped down the hallway to the kitchen.

Aaron laughed, gazing after Quinn as he sat on the bed to pull his jeans on. "Be careful!"

"I'm always careful. Perpetually careful. If anything, *too* careful."

Aaron shook his head to himself. "That's not a bad thing. Sometimes impulsively shaking everything up is tiring."

"Yeah. The most excitement I get in a week is watching someone lift weights dangerously and get pissy at me for pointing it out," Quinn said, laughing.

Aaron followed the sound of his voice down the hallway to the kitchen. When he reached it, Aaron glanced around. It looked like a farmhouse kitchen, complete with a framed picture of a rooster on the wall.

"This is a cute little house." So very white-picket-fence. Like a place he could nest.

Aaron swallowed hard. A year ago, he'd lived like that—with an apartment in central Portland and a handsome boyfriend.

Everything, outwardly, had been perfect. They'd been on their way to becoming a power couple. And then...

Well, Aaron had moved onto his friends' couches and then found his own crappy little place. No more cozy Netflix nights and picking out picture frames together.

"It's a nice place to lay my head. What do you want? Butter? Peanut butter? Jam?"

"Oh, on my toast? Butter, please." Aaron grinned. "I thought you were offering to lie down while I butter the rest of you up." He swayed into Quinn's side, resting his chin on Quinn's shoulder and kissing his cheek.

"Next time," Quinn promised and grinned. "But it's better for your macro counts if the protein goes inside you."

Aaron nearly choked as he took the plate Quinn handed him. "Oh, I'm planning to mainline your protein," he assured him.

Quinn jolted and then blushed, covering his face. "I can't say anything innocent around you, can I?"

"It's never too early for a sex joke." Aaron devoured the toast in a few bites, not even caring if he looked like an animal. He needed to get a move on.

"You want me to walk you? I have to pick up my car anyway."

"Sure." Aaron bounced over to the door and got his outerwear on, then stepped outside to wait for Quinn to join him.

It was a misty, drizzly morning much like any winter morning in the Pacific Northwest. The smell of the fog rolling in from the sea—salt and a metallic sort of heaviness—made him breathe in deeply.

Life was better in Hart's Bay. Even if moving had been a stressful change for a lifelong city boy, Aaron loved it here. No more stressing about paying rent or finding parking. The neighbors knew him, and not just the ones his friends were dating. And nearly everyone had been so supportive of the art gallery, the cafe, and the other new businesses in town.

People seemed to be making a point of shopping at the little knickknack boutique that shared Aaron's building, or stopping by Howya Bean for their morning cup of coffee. A lot of people had shopped at the art gallery for their Christmas gifts. And that money went back into the community as the guys all shopped at the hardware store or grocery store, or hung out at Cher's bar.

Quinn stepped onto the porch and locked up, then slipped his hand into Aaron's gloved one and led him carefully down the wet steps to the sidewalk. They both pulled up their hoods as the rain met them.

Aaron set a brisk stride that warded off the chilly early morning air. They were nearly alone—few people were awake at this hour. As much as Aaron loved being around people, he also loved having early mornings to himself.

A car passed and then slowed just as Aaron's house came into view. A familiar face popped out the window—Gregory, one of the older town residents. Once a fisherman, he'd spent most of his days at Cher's bar until recently.

Now, he was Rusty's business partner, which meant heading out on the water at all hours to check on their experimental seaweed farm.

"Hope my coffee will be ready on time, boys." Every

morning since Aaron had opened, Gregory had shown up good and early at Howya Bean for his fix.

"Working on it!" Aaron promised. He bit his lip as Gregory pulled away, nervously drumming his fingers on his leg. He couldn't start letting people down now. Especially since he'd earned a good review in the town newsletter. People had high expectations for him to meet.

Quinn laughed. "Look at you go. There's a crowd beating down your door already."

Aaron shivered. "Hopefully not literally, if I'm late."

"You're popular already." Quinn squeezed his hand. "It's a good thing."

Aaron took a breath and drew strength from his cool confidence. "Yeah. A lot of the construction crew stops by. And Cher, and Victor, and all my friends from the art gallery, and... well, a lot of people."

"Single-handedly fueling the revival of the town." Quinn was teasing him, but not completely.

Aaron blushed and let go of his hand to swat him. "Oh, shush."

"I won't," Quinn insisted. "Can you take a compliment that's not about sex?"

Aaron opened his mouth for a few moments and then shut it again, his cheeks flushing. When he thought about it, Quinn was right. "I don't think so."

"Okay. So I'll keep trying." Quinn touched Aaron's back lightly as they reached the driveway. "But I'd better let you get to work so Gregory doesn't kick the glass in and try to make his own coffee."

Aaron grinned at him. "Thanks. Catch you later, yeah? I'll text once I've opened up."

Before he let Quinn go, though, he grabbed the front of his jacket and pulled him in and down for a bold kiss.

Quinn gripped his biceps tightly as he kissed Aaron back, his mouth hot and insistent. It was no polite peck on the lips.

Yet, at the same moment, it was oddly romantic kissing in the winter rain, the darkness sheltering them, alone but for the hum of car engines in the distance and the ever-present thrum of the sea.

Aaron grinned as he broke away breathlessly. If he didn't stop this now, they'd be here all day.

Quinn raised a hand and got in his car as Aaron sprinted for the house and its shelter from the rain.

Well practiced at the art of changing for work as fast as possible, Aaron was back out of the house just moments later.

He nearly took the car, but the shortcut between houses that led to Hart Square was just as quick. He usually left the car for the other guys since he was the first up by far. They had supplies and art pieces to transport, unlike Aaron.

Even taking the path as fast as he could go and cutting through the square, Aaron spotted Gregory's car waiting outside the converted warehouse and his heart sank.

Shit. It was two minutes past six, and his professionalism was in question. He couldn't let this happen again.

Aaron was flushed and out of breath by the time he made it across the parking lot and over to the cafe on the far end. "Sorry," he panted as Gregory climbed out of the car. "Can I... offer you... one, on the house?" He unlocked the door and held it open for Gregory, then flicked on the lights.

Gregory looked at him like he'd sprouted another head. "Not on your life. Now, if you make a habit of this, we'll talk."

"I won't, sir." Aaron ducked behind the counter and switched the machines on, working as fast as he could.

Minutes later, thanks to the wonders of machines, Gregory had his black coffee and change. As he left, Aaron sagged onto the counter to catch his breath and dab the cooled sweat from his forehead.

When he didn't feel like a human Jacuzzi, he finished opening up and then flopped onto the stool behind the counter.

But there was no rest for the wicked. A dozen little tasks ate up the next few hours, from dusting to learning how to operate the window blinds he'd never figured out before launch.

When the morning rush kicked in, it was all he could do to keep up. Working alone, he could put out a coffee every two minutes or less, but people never came one at a time.

The steaming machines, constant back-and-forth shuffle between the machines and the counter, and the few rude customers were worth it. More people from out of town were stopping in Hart's Bay for a refuel on their drive up the coast. That was good for business, but they tended to treat him like a faceless barista from a big chain.

Though his feet and back ached by the time Yolanda came in, Aaron was always satisfied by a hard morning's work.

She was great at rolling up her sleeves and jumping into the fray without being briefed. Working together, they could turn out more drinks and even have a moment to breathe now and then.

Things settled down at about quarter past nine, and Aaron could finally say good morning to Yolanda properly.

"Thanks for saving my neck as always. You're the best," Aaron told her.

Yolanda held up a hand to high-five him. "I am. But I've got a pretty cool boss."

For now, it was just the two of them versus the caffeine-starved Hart's Bay hordes.

If business was steady in January, Aaron would hire another employee and scale up very carefully from there. He had to build a customer base first among folks who hadn't had a local coffee joint in many years.

"So..." Yolanda glanced around, and Aaron followed her gaze. A few customers were sitting at tables. Nobody was looking their way.

"So?" Aaron wiped down the counter briskly. Instantly his mind raced. It was probably about her time off over Christmas.

"How did things go with that guy?"

"Which guy—*oh*." Aaron had nearly forgotten coming in on Sunday to find Quinn waiting to talk with him. He smiled to himself. That felt like a long time ago, strangely.

"Yeah, *Oh*," Yolanda echoed, grinning. "Is that his nickname, or does he have a name?"

Aaron snorted at her and moved out from behind the counter to wipe down the display cabinet. There was no harm in telling her. After all, hopefully he'd be in a lot. "Quinn. There's a... a thing going on."

He spritzed the glass of the display cabinet.

"I could tell. You and him?" Yolanda gestured between him and thin air with her pen, leaning on the counter. "Whew."

"What's that mean?" Aaron laughed, stopping with his cloth in midair, droplets trickling down the glass. Then the innuendo hit him. It was impossible not to laugh as he started rubbing them away in circles.

"It means," Yolanda laughed, "that you looked like a whole different guy when you were talking to him."

Aaron frowned to himself. The last thing he wanted was to

lose himself. He'd fought hard to figure out who he was and stand up to the slut-shaming, the judgment, and maybe worst of all, the entitlement.

"In a good way," Yolanda added softly. "Don't worry."

"Getting laid is good for me. Who knew?" Aaron deadpanned, flourishing his cloth and heading for the door to wipe it down.

His phone was burning a hole in his pocket now. He'd felt it vibrating with text alerts during the rush but hadn't had a chance to check it yet. So as soon as he was behind the counter and Yolanda was busy in the stockroom, he peeked.

Oh, God. It had been a Grindr alert, not a text message. And not from someone he wanted to talk to again. The handle was unmistakably Bryon's.

His mood sank as he tapped it and opened the app to see what that sleazy jerk had to say now.

It was a picture message. Aaron prepared to fling his phone into the nearest boiling water, but luckily it was just a photo from the internet of a guy holding a gift-wrapped box in front of his crotch.

What does the slut get for Christmas if he asks very nicely?

Aaron worked his jaw around. Not only did Bryon think he could charm his way into Aaron's pants, but he thought Aaron *wanted* him to. The idea he'd beg for that prick to be anywhere near him made him snort.

The ego on that man was insane, and he still wasn't the weirdest hookup Aaron had gotten to know this year. God, men were exhausting.

Aaron tapped out a quick response. *A boyfriend who respects him. Which I have. Go away, forever.*

The response was almost instant.

WTF?? You stood me up but you had time to meet someone else? Go choke on his dick you whore you'll regret choosing him.

Then there was a stream-of-consciousness rant of swear words without any punctuation, all implying that he was missing a good thing by turning down Bryon.

Aaron laughed, relief making his shoulders sag. There were no more attempts to convince him that Bryon was better for him. In his own twisted way, Bryon seemed to respect another guy's claim on him—even if he hated Aaron for choosing him instead.

For that matter, he didn't need this shit. Any of it.

He carefully pressed the block button, confirmed it, and closed the app. No more holding himself back, filtering bits and pieces of himself for public consumption. He didn't want to do that. Not with Quinn, who had his whole heart on the table.

It was funny—on an app, he wouldn't have picked Quinn out of a lineup of profiles. Well, maybe he would on appearance alone, but Quinn was the type to write up a detailed profile. And more to the point, to specify that he was only looking for a boyfriend.

Aaron would have run the other way, screaming and blocking Quinn as fast as possible. But now look at him—dating the romantic and blocking the sex addict.

"Everything all right?" Yolanda caught him looking at his phone and paused on her way by, rolls of paper towels in her arms.

Aaron smiled as he tapped out a quick text to Quinn. "Yeah. Couldn't be better."

The drizzle outside had stopped, which was almost the same thing as sunshine in the depths of winter. The rush had settled down, and it was a new day in Aaron's life in every sense.

Good morning, sexypants. Aaron grinned at the thought of Quinn squinting at that word. *Hope you have a great day with your clients. Drive safe & call me on your way home.*

He had no idea when to expect a response yet, so he placed his phone on the counter and poked it on his way by as he refilled the bakery cabinet and cleaned the machines.

Every time it lit up with a notification that wasn't a text message, his heart lifted and sank again. It had been a long time since he'd felt that.

Last night had been wonderful, and Quinn was sweet to get up with him—even walk him home. He really was the whole package. And he *had* the whole package.

Maybe Aaron didn't have to compromise on anything at all. All he had to do was trust a good thing when it was standing in front of him with an eager smile and a sweater vest.

A ray of sunshine burst through the clouds and shone straight through the front windows, and Aaron snapped a quick photo for the cafe's Instagram account.

He had the perfect caption, too: *Come on in and find your sunshine. We did!*

8

QUINN

Quinn couldn't stop smiling on his drive home from work. He and Aaron talked the whole time, right up until he parked in his parents' driveway.

Even then, he lingered in the car for another minute, transferring the call to his phone to keep going. They'd each said some variation of "I should let you go" twice by that point.

But it was hard to be the first one to hang up when Aaron's free-spirited laugh filled up the empty car on the long drive back along the coast.

The porch light turned on, and the front door opened. His mom was standing there, shading her eyes against the artificial glare as she looked out at him.

"Crap. Mom's spotted me. I gotta head inside," Quinn said with a laugh.

"Good luck! Don't think of me naked," Aaron told him, giggling. "Bye!"

"Oh, you…" Quinn huffed as Aaron hung up. He waved to Mom and cleared his throat as he stepped out, pocketing his phone. "Hey!"

"What are you doing out there in the cold? Come in!" She glanced back to the car and ducked her head like she was checking for someone else.

Quinn trotted through the evening's finest raindrops toward the porch. "Sorry, had to finish up a phone call."

"You didn't call to say you were coming. Good thing you're as reliable as you are. We knew you'd come for dinner," Mom told him with a smile, leaning in to kiss his cheek as she ushered him in.

The place smelled great. It was definitely soup tonight. "Oh, what kind of soup?"

"Stew with dumplings. Your favorite, of course," Mom told him, taking his coat. "Come on, sit down."

After the usual round of greetings with his dad, swapping stories about their days, they were all settled at the table.

Quinn had barely started eating before Mom leaned in. "So, we've heard the news."

"Um..." Quinn hastily swallowed his bite and set his spoon down. "About?"

"The date, of course. At Millie's!"

Well, there went Quinn's thunder. He deflated a little and ate more of his soup while he waited for the questioning to begin.

"It's the talk of the street. Fiona—you know, Forester—was there with her daughter—just back from college, can you believe it? How time flies! Anyway, she was talking to Patty, who said she talked to the fellow who runs the gazette. The newsletter. What's his name?" She clicked her fingers.

Quinn held in his sigh, since he'd only get told off for it. "Scott."

"That's right. Scott said he saw the fellow who's opening

the coffee shop—or, I suppose, already has—down by the water. Anyway, he was there with someone else, and apparently—rumor has it—"

Here she came, to the point at last. Quinn braced himself to confirm it.

"It was *you*. How haven't we heard about him before? Anyway, your father and I haven't been to his cafe yet. We thought we'd give you space until he's ready to meet us."

"Thanks," Quinn told her, his lips twitching. That was something, at least.

Dad asked, "What does he do? I suppose he owns the business? That's respectable enough." He stroked the ends of his mustache down as he always did when deciding whether Quinn was behaving suitably.

"That's right. And he works there most of the time, but he has his first staff member already." Quinn smiled. "He's new to town. He moved here with that artist co-op. But he's got lots of friends, and he's really friendly. He fits in already."

"Well. That's good." Mom put her cutlery down. "Oh, no."

"What's that?"

"The family Christmas card. He won't be in it." Mom put her hand on Dad's arm. "No, that's just rude. Honey, could we get it reshot and printed in time? I haven't sealed the envelopes yet."

Soup splashed off Quinn's spoon, and only by luck did it fall back into the bowl. "N-No, I really don't think he'll mind."

He hadn't planned to mention yet how very far from traditional Aaron was.

"No, dear. It's been so very long since you've been on a real date with anyone. You must be serious about him." Mom's hint wasn't subtle. "Everyone will be so excited for you."

"Thanks, Mom," Quinn mumbled. He wanted to slump over the table at the reminder that he'd been sad and single for years now. His mouth burned as he gulped soup, hoping to bring an end to this torture soon.

Dad nodded gravely. "And he should feel welcome. Otherwise, that's no way to build a future."

Okay, it might have been a mistake letting them think the two of them were serious. But Quinn couldn't exactly explain the terms of their December fling without scandalizing his family.

His parents had met the traditional way, through friends. Everything had been by the book. Internet dating was alien enough to them. The idea he might be relaxing and finally letting himself have some fun hadn't even occurred to them.

In fact, how much of his stress this year had come from these subtle hints? It wasn't just that he wanted a relationship —but he felt like they expected one from him. Not because they didn't care. Quite the opposite, unfortunately. That made the situation more delicate.

"Whoa. We're not talking *future* yet." Quinn set down his spoon. "Like I said, it's early."

Dad frowned at him, swapping glances with Mom. "That's not like you."

They were right. Quinn had never dated a boyfriend he hadn't planned to eventually marry, which was why he'd only had two boyfriends.

He'd hooked up a handful of times, mostly in college, but much less than most of the men he knew. No-strings-attached sex just didn't hold any appeal for him. And all the one-off dates hadn't gone anywhere.

"And how well has that worked so far?" Quinn countered, smiling despite his frustration. "I'm trying something new. I don't want to ruin this, so *please*... don't scare him away."

Mom went still and silent for a moment, her face crumpling.

Ah, shit. Quinn hated hurting anyone, least of all her. "No, Mom, I didn't mean that..."

"Like we're the difficult in-laws?"

Well, they're sure acting like it right now, Quinn thought. He didn't have to say it out loud for his frustration to show on his face. "No, just... he's a flight risk. And I want to make sure he's the right one before I get everyone excited."

"Well, why are you dating someone if you don't feel like he's the right one? You should know that straightaway," Dad told him. "Your mom and I did. Deep inside, you'll be able to feel it."

Oh, God. Quinn didn't need another lecture about how the right man would walk into his life and he'd just *know.*

This man in particular wouldn't appreciate hearing that Quinn was utterly smitten and prepared to do anything to make him happy. Quinn could already tell that if Aaron knew how fast he'd fallen, he'd run a mile.

The best thing he could do make Aaron happy was give him space and let him stumble into love in his own time. Which was also the very hardest thing for Quinn to stand back and do.

"I *do* know," Quinn burst out, standing up. "I want him in my life, and I need to make sure he's as committed as I am, and I'd *really* appreciate you guys not making it even harder."

Silence rang for a moment before the tension broke. His mom slowly stood up and patted his arm. "I'm sorry, honey."

"We'll leave the subject alone," Dad told him with a solemn nod. "But... your aunt Maggie already knows. She's setting an extra place at lunch next week. I'm sure we can make excuses for him."

"Oh, for..." That meant everyone else in his extended family knew, too.

"But if it's not too much trouble," Mom said quietly, that sting in her voice, "we'd still like to meet him. Just to make sure he feels welcome."

Well, there goes any hope of it being low-pressure. Quinn rubbed his face. "Okay. I'll ask him."

There was only so long he could hold off his family before they started to post a watch on the cafe to find out more about Aaron.

"I don't know where this is going," Quinn warned them. "We might end up just friends."

Mom swapped glances with Dad. "If he doesn't want to be *on* the Christmas card... well... would you call him your boyfriend?"

Despite himself, Quinn laughed. "You've been saving up a *To our son's boyfriend* Christmas card, haven't you?" As she blushed, he shook his head and pinched his nose. "Maybe. I'll ask him that, too."

Thankfully, Dad interrupted at this point to ask Quinn what he thought about them redecorating the kitchen next year. Quinn had done a lot of the work on his own house, so he'd been telling them for years he'd help when they were ready to do it.

Everyone was much happier talking about tile colors and cabinets than Quinn's love life. They'd almost gotten past it by the end of the evening when he hugged both his parents and headed out to his car.

But hell, no—he didn't feel like heading home and rattling around alone, second-guessing himself.

So Quinn drove home and parked, and then walked down to the town square even though it would take a little bit longer.

Since his walk through the neighborhood with Aaron, Quinn had remembered how nice it felt to take life at a slower pace. He did enough driving during the day.

Plus, it made him appreciate that Cher's was actually open tonight. She seemed to be keeping more regular hours now. With more people in town, it was more worthwhile—and she did seem to enjoy the company. Still, there was always the chance that she'd kick everyone out and lock up at a whim.

He pushed the door open and headed into the little bar, glancing around at the seating areas for people he knew.

"Well, hello." Rusty was standing at a table with Colt and Gregory. "How's it going?"

"Oh, hey. Great." Quinn scratched his head, acutely aware that they all knew Aaron. So much for coming here and anonymously venting about it with Cher.

"Wanna join us, or did you have something else in mind?" Rusty grinned, glancing around as if checking for Aaron.

"Oh, no. Thanks. I'll grab a beer and be right back."

Cher leaned on the bar. "Hey, Quinn. How's life treating you?" Quinn blew out a sigh, and she laughed. "That well, huh?"

"No," he said quickly, looking around to see who was in earshot. "Lots of good stuff. Just all at once. Can I get a beer?"

"Mmhmm." Cher headed for a pint glass and took her time pouring his pint. "You and Aaron, huh?"

Quinn groaned. "Et tu? I just got the third degree from my parents. I think they're picking out baby names."

Cher cracked a grin. "Ouch. You're telling me you haven't tried for one yet?" She winked.

It took Quinn a moment to catch the implication. His cheeks flooded with heat. "Well..." He laughed sheepishly.

"Good on you." There was a faint worry line between Cher's brows, though, as she took his money and grabbed change.

"You think? I don't know much about him, but everyone else seems to. I've been living under a rock since he and the guys moved to town. Always driving to gyms and stuff, I haven't felt like I'm really spending time here. And I guess I haven't been going out much."

"Mmm." Cher nodded. She handed back the change. "Well, what's worrying you?"

Quinn glanced toward the table, but the guys were excitedly talking about something, hands waving. They wouldn't miss him for a few more moments.

"I like him a lot, but it's hard to tell what he wants." Quinn shrugged. "I don't think even he knows. So we're taking it easy. Except my family wants me to be settled down and serious, like, yesterday."

"Don't let anyone else tell you how to feel," Cher told him, slapping the counter before she grabbed a cloth. "That's your free advice. Five bucks if you want any more, but no guarantees it'll be good."

Quinn grinned. He swigged his beer. A contented sigh escaped him at the cold, refreshing taste. Just what he needed after his hour in the hot seat. "Thanks for listening."

"It's my job." She winked. "That and keeping my mouth shut."

Quinn laughed. "Yeah. I guess you and Aaron hear it all."

"I wouldn't breathe a word. You're not an asshole like Floyd Hart. I'll spread his business all over town. That asshole tried to call me." Cher scoffed. "Apologizing for being an ass last week. Like I'm gonna let him in again. Let Aaron know he'll be trying to suck up, won't you?"

"Will do," Quinn promised.

The once-patriarch of the town had fallen from grace sharply in the last six months, culminating in his ban from Cher's—the town's living room. Thanks to Quinn's mom, he had heard most of the details—or some version of them.

After a few more minutes' chat about all the things Cher would do to Floyd if he tried to weasel his way into her good graces, other patrons distracted her, and Quinn escaped to the table.

Okay, Quinn didn't usually hold with gossip, but this was relevant. Floyd had been a dick to Colt before, after all. "Guys, did you hear about Floyd?"

"That he's trying to save face?" Gregory snorted. His accent was noticeably thicker now, betraying his feelings about Floyd instantly. "That chancer's as useless as tits on a bull. Time he faced up to that."

"Every bit of progress in this town is in spite of him," Colt muttered, his expression thunderous. "I can't believe he hasn't slunk out of town yet. Why's he staying for Christmas?"

"We sure don't want him down our chimneys," Gregory chimed in, setting his Guinness down hard. "Or up them, even for whatever gold he offers."

Quinn chuckled. "I've got better options than him," he agreed.

"Speaking of progress—" Rusty nudged Colt. "You were just saying?"

"Oh! There's word of a new school opening." Colt grinned. "Just a big land purchase and gossip so far, but that would be phenomenal. The old place shut down ten years ago."

Quinn smiled, nodding and agreeing with most of the things they said.

He was still processing everything from dinner with his parents, and he'd just jumped from one political soup to another.

His family had been on Floyd's side in the early days of the rift between the Harts. They'd both worked for him, and they'd earned great money. They'd been certain that he was bringing their town prosperity. That illusion had slipped when they'd both had to commute out of town to find work.

Mom had retrained as a dental hygienist, and they'd actually ended up better off than they had been. They'd never struggled financially like a lot of those in Hart's Bay, but it had been a blow to their egos.

Then he snapped back into real time as he heard his name mentioned.

"—Quinn's fella wouldn't mind the extra trade from the builders," Gregory was saying, elbowing him with a grin.

Oh, shit. That made him grin like an idiot. Quinn loved Aaron being called *his* by these guys, without expectation and pressure. They just wanted to respect the fact Quinn had something going on with him.

What he wouldn't give to feel like this for years to come. To be able to call Aaron *his*.

"Yeah. I know he's in the early days," Quinn spoke up, his chest inflating with pride. "He appreciates all the business he can get."

Quinn had spent enough time with Aaron to know there was something there. His whole spirit had told him from their first conversation to pay close attention to him.

By now, he'd happily give Aaron his heart. But he had no

idea if that was just infatuation talking—and if so, was that a bad thing?

If anyone was worth taking a chance on, it was Aaron. But Aaron wasn't going to make the first move to turn this into something more serious. So Quinn had to do so, and hope that he wouldn't scare Aaron off.

With pressure from all sides, it looked like Quinn didn't have much choice.

9

AARON

The old Aaron would have laughed at himself for spending Friday night in. They were being such homebodies that Aaron was stirring risotto rice in Quinn's kitchen, a glass of wine in his hand. Being *civilized.* And after the meal, they were going to cuddle up and watch some rom-coms together.

Well, the old Aaron could go suck dicks. *This* Aaron was pretty damn happy stirring a pot of oil and rice instead of stirring up trouble on the town.

"Do you have the whole deconstructed meal ready?" Aaron asked with a laugh as Quinn set a chopping board down next to him—one of three. All were loaded with their respective ingredients, neatly chopped. Even the broth was already made up.

Apparently opposites did attract. On nights when it was Aaron's turn to cook, he often found himself frantically chopping vegetables and turning down the heat to avoid charring everyone's supper. It pained Aaron to wait so long to get started with the actual cooking, but Quinn had finally given him the go-ahead.

With the rice toasted, the onions went in first, and Aaron poked them around to soften before stirring in broth.

"I haven't cooked risotto in so long," Quinn said with a laugh. "I don't want to screw it up. Chicken's defrosted, what else? Oh, peas."

"Gay chicken?" Aaron puckered up for a kiss and then pouted when Quinn took the chicken out of the fridge instead.

"Later," Quinn promised and winked. He opened the freezer to grab the peas.

Aaron raised his eyebrows at the contents he saw over Quinn's shoulder. Identical packages—down to the labels—filled the top two shelves. "Is that your emergency backup chicken, in case this one goes horribly wrong? I'm getting worried now."

Quinn burst out laughing. "If there's one thing I can cook, it's chicken. Don't worry."

"Obviously you have plenty of practice handling peckers." Aaron widened his eyes innocently when Quinn stared at him.

Quinn opted to try to ignore the innuendo, though he looked flustered and nearly tossed the peas on top of the chicken. "Uh, yeah. I buy in bulk, because it's pretty much all I eat."

"So risotto and dinners out at Millie's aren't your usual fare?"

Quinn laughed. "Not at all. Most people I know can't stand eating like I do. I don't mind—it's one less decision to make, and I know the macros are all balanced."

"Macros, micros, protein." Aaron waved a hand. "I much prefer my way."

"Me too, actually." Quinn gave him a light smile. "I've been thinking of taking it easier, now that I have plenty of clients. My body was my best ad while I was getting started."

Aaron paused his stirring. He hadn't even thought of that. "Oh. Because of my delicious cooking?"

"In part," Quinn said, handing over a cup of peas. "In part because I'd like to be more normal around you. Here. Peas."

"Thank you. I'll treasure them always."

Quinn snorted and smacked Aaron's ass gently. "I don't know what to do with you," he said, his voice warmer and quieter—almost fond.

"I have plenty of suggestions." Aaron poured some more broth in and stirred the pot.

"I have something to ask you," Quinn murmured, his brow furrowing as he arranged the chopping boards with broccoli and diced avocado next to Aaron.

He looked so worried that Aaron leaned his hip against the stove to face Quinn while he stirred the broth, adding a little more. If this was a conversation about safe sex or boundaries or something, he wanted to show he was taking it seriously. "Yeah?"

"You know how I was visiting my parents last night?"

"Mmhmm?" Aaron certainly remembered lying on his bed on his phone, talking to Quinn for almost an hour.

It had felt like he was back in school, trying to figure out how to hint to his first crush that he liked him, and instead ending up just listening to him rambling for hours on end.

Except Aaron was a lot older and wiser than he had been all those years ago. No straight guys, no fooling around without talking about expectations. Everything was on the table now. They couldn't possibly cross wires.

"Well..." Quinn hedged, rubbing his palms on his thighs like he was about to tell Aaron some huge deal breaker. God, maybe they were long-lost stepcousins. The suspense was awful.

Aaron nudged Quinn's leg with his foot. "You're killing me."

"Sorry." Quinn rubbed his face as he laughed. "Okay, so Mom and Dad want to meet you. And invite you along to all the family holiday parties."

The blood rushed to Aaron's ears, and he only heard his own heart pounding for a few moments. He left the spoon in the pot and straightened up, his arms folding.

Meeting the parents?! His thoughts raced a mile a minute. *But that's, like, moving-in-together stuff. Not "we're seeing each other for three weeks" stuff. Unless he's trying to make the most of it while we're together…*

"It only has to be once. You know, to prove my boyfriend exists," Quinn said quickly, his grin distracted like his thoughts were elsewhere.

Bingo. Aaron's suspicions were confirmed, and his spirits crashed. He stared through the TV, trying to stop himself from biting Quinn's head off.

His ex, Kasey, had sprung the relationship status on Aaron without ever really asking, too. Aaron had just spent a week straight at Kasey's place, enjoying all the great sex, and Kasey had casually said, *"So, we're dating, right? If you're moving in?"*

It was hard to argue with Kasey—and Aaron had been happy to finally feel tied down. So he'd moved in, given Kasey his heart, and picked out throw cushions with him.

Until New Year's Eve.

Things had been fizzling out for a while, but Aaron had had a plan to get them closer again. The best-ever New Year's party. Kasey always had his friends around, but now, Aaron could help him impress them.

So Aaron had spent the afternoon cutting cheese wedges,

baking brownies, and arranging chairs. He'd even looked up how to fold napkins into peacocks. A few of them looked more like lumpy whales, but the general effect was there.

And then Kasey had walked in, tossed his jacket over the back of a chair, and loosened his tie while blurting the words that were etched into Aaron's brain.

"So, it's over. I want to see in the new year alongside someone I've got a future with."

Aaron didn't remember most of the rest of the night. Just furiously packing, the floods of tears on Jesse's shoulder, and a lot of Fireball. A *lot*.

"Is that off the table for you?" Quinn's voice, gentle and calm, brought him back to reality. His big hands suddenly closed around Aaron's narrow shoulders and steered him to one side. He added more broth and picked up the spoon, quickly stirring.

Aaron breathed out a sigh and pressed the heel of his palm into his forehead. Why was he being such an ass?

It ought to be nothing to just show up and smile at Quinn's parents. Except that he'd been there, done that, for years of his life. But he didn't want anyone to know that part of him. He sure as hell wasn't telling Quinn.

Then Quinn set down his spoon and took Aaron's hand, squeezing it tightly between his palms. "Are you all right?"

"I..." Aaron's throat felt tight. "I don't want to let you down at the end of the month. Let everyone down."

Quinn's eyes widened abruptly. He stepped closer and wrapped his arms around Aaron, and Aaron buried his face into Quinn's chest. The tears he'd never let himself cry flooded out.

Tears of anger, of injustice. Of grief for the younger, dumber Aaron who had thought he could just love someone *harder* and they'd come around. Who had thought he could be *more* himself and win over the very people who hated that he had the strength to be himself unapologetically.

Quinn's strong arms wrapped around Aaron, and he rocked him gently. "You won't let anyone down," he promised. "But you've already given me what I need."

Aaron gulped for air, his eyes burning and chest tight. He wasn't sure if he liked that more or less. "Yeah?"

"This is supposed to be fun. If it's not, then we're not doing it right," Quinn reminded Aaron.

Aaron blew out a little sigh and finally pushed back so he could dab his eyes. "Yeah. I'm sorry. It's just my first time meeting parents in a long time. I told you, right? My rotten ex kicked me out."

"Out of the house, too." Quinn's voice darkened. "Asshole."

Aaron sighed and waved it off. "Yeah. And I'm not good with parents. Who am I without the dick jokes and inappropriate gestures?"

"Well, I like you the way you are," Quinn said, winking.

"So did my ex. He liked having me around because I'm always up for it," Aaron mumbled, his gut tightening. "Until the sex wasn't enough and he wanted a future."

"Baby, I do," Quinn reminded him gently. The simple words cut through the heart of Aaron's fear.

And he was right. Quinn was a traditional kind of guy through and through. He wouldn't just invite Aaron along to Christmas parties or parent meetings for no reason. For Quinn, those were things he'd do to see if there was room for a future to thrive.

Aaron had to pull himself together, or Quinn really would

think he was broken beyond repair. And at the end of the three weeks, Quinn would be the one running away.

Aaron pouted. "Can't you avoid your parents for the next few weeks?"

"Not over Christmas. I can tell them no—"

Aaron didn't want to let Quinn down. He *wanted* to give him what he needed. So he shook his head. "No, let me think about it. I'm sorry," Aaron mumbled, resting the side of his head on Quinn's shoulder so he could wipe his eyes. "I just... I can't imagine why you want *more* with me."

"More than...?" Quinn groped for the spoon and carefully added broth, but when Aaron tried to pull away, he kept one arm around Aaron's waist.

"More than everyone else wants." Aaron chuckled bitterly. It hurt to say out loud. "A quick fuck. Ditch me in the morning. Hit me up after midnight when nobody else is answering. That's what I'm good at. Not... meeting parents. You can find plenty of nice guys next door for that. Who can make decent conversation without dick jokes."

Quinn shook his head. "But I don't want them. I want *you*. Inappropriate and all. As a friend, or a boyfriend. Is that the problem? The label?"

Aaron blew out a quiet sigh. "Maybe," he admitted quietly. "It's been so long, and now I have all this baggage attached to the idea of being someone's boyfriend. Especially if we're only committing to these next few weeks."

"That makes sense," Quinn murmured. "It feels strange to call each other boyfriends for just a couple of weeks. But I don't really want to say you're my..."

"Boy toy?" Aaron suggested with a grin.

Quinn shook his head. His hand gently slid up Aaron's back, cupping the back of his neck. His fingertips traced circles in the hair at the back of his head. "How about we use our own word?"

"Like what? *My beau?*" Aaron managed a grin. "Beau will be so confused."

"My fella?" Quinn's grin was lighthearted, but he was serious. "I don't think I'm Irish enough to pull that off. My guy?"

Aaron stood a little straighter. "I like that," he said instantly. It was hard to explain to Quinn, but it felt right. "Can we?"

But Quinn didn't make him explain. He just smiled and took Aaron at his word. "Okay. I'll tell people you're my guy, and you can do the same."

Aaron nodded. "And I'll meet your parents, since apparently you're reckless enough to want *that* to happen. I have warned you, after all."

Quinn grinned and ruffled his hair. "Thanks, babe."

"Now, let me do that," Aaron ordered, plucking the spoon out of Quinn's hand. Before Quinn let him pass by to get to the stove, though, he blocked his way and leaned down for a kiss.

Aaron dabbed his eyes and tilted his chin up, letting Quinn softly press his lips against Aaron's. The kiss lingered for a few moments, until the storm in Aaron's stomach had calmed to a few gentle waves.

Working together, they finished the risotto and chicken. Quinn even surprised Aaron by setting the table with candles and fancy placemats.

"The special place settings for my special guest," Quinn said, flourishing a mat as he laid it on the table.

Aaron grinned. "Also new for me. I usually eat out."

Quinn went bright red, and Aaron cackled as he added the last of the broth and stirred it around.

It was nice and domestic. Now that his fears had subsided,

Aaron found himself startled at the pleasure he took in cooking for just the two of them. He hadn't realized how much he'd missed this vibe—it was completely different from cooking for his friends.

"So, is tomorrow good for supper with my parents?" Quinn finally asked as he loaded the dishwasher.

"Why not?" Aaron shrugged, laughing to himself. Better to get this over with. Quinn was inviting disaster, so that was exactly what he'd get.

"Awesome," Quinn said with a naive grin, wiping the kitchen counters and putting everything back in its place.

After supper, they headed to the living room. Aaron stretched along the couch, his head in Quinn's lap while a rom-com played. It wasn't Netflix and chill—it was Netflix and cozy.

Time flew by when he was with Quinn.

"I still don't see why they have to compete for the trophy," Aaron complained. The baking contest didn't make sense to him. Why did she have to be a small-town girl versus the big, corporate baker, anyway? "They can just work together. His ovens, her recipes."

"Shhh, don't spoil the ending," Quinn said with a grin. His fingers paused their languid strokes through Aaron's hair. "But first, they have to kiss."

"Hmph." Aaron snorted and peered up at Quinn. He fluttered his lashes. "Because of the irresistible, magnetic attraction that makes them hate each other because they're afraid to admit they love each other?"

"Bingo."

Aaron stuck his tongue out. "Gross. They're missing out on hot sex, you know. I prefer our way."

"So do I." Quinn's voice was a low rumble that Aaron

already knew meant he was making a silent promise. He kept stroking Aaron's hair, but this time he let his fingertips trail down across Aaron's cheek, down his jaw, to his neck.

Aaron squirmed against the couch, hoping he could cash that check as soon as possible. Quinn's fingertips just barely brushed his skin, making his hair stand on end and his dick bolt upright in his pants. Every touch made him whimper softly.

But then Quinn rested his hand on Aaron's chest and gazed toward the screen. "Shh. This is a good part."

Aaron pouted to himself but looked over at the screen. If anything made Quinn happy, he was willing to give it a chance.

Even coming to dinner with Quinn's parents, perish the thought. Whatever Quinn said, sooner or later, he was going to regret asking Aaron to be his guy in public.

Might as well be sooner rather than later.

10

QUINN

"Right, so they're Mrs. and Mr. Powell," Aaron muttered under his breath. "An accountant and a dental hygienist."

Quinn reached across the central console of the car to take Aaron's hand. They were close to his parents' house already—the residential areas of Hart's Bay were all within a few minutes' drive of each other at most. "That's right."

"And they know what I do?"

Quinn chuckled, rolling his eyes. "Yeah. Apparently one of your friends spoke to one of their friends or something."

"God, Finn always said rumors around here spread like it's *Days of Our Lives*." Aaron huffed and squeezed Quinn's hand, then let go to fiddle with his sweater again.

"They're going to be surprised you're not some stuffy trust fund kid in a suit and tie, though," Quinn said. He smiled at the thought. "Opening your own business after working in Daddy's firm. They've tried to set me up with that kind of guy before."

"Oh, God." Aaron pressed a hand to his chest and fanned

himself with the other hand. "Why the fuck didn't you tell me? I could have worn a suit and tie. Or at least a tie…"

Quinn snuck Aaron a glance. "What? Do you even own a tie?" Aaron was always in tight-fitting, trendy clothes.

Aaron deflated. "Well, no. I mean, somewhere in my closet, probably. I'm going to be so out of place."

Quinn took his hand again. "They were happy to hear you own your own business. That's respectably middle-class. Probably the most average thing about you," he added with a wink.

"Ew, average," Aaron joked. "Best for weather forecasts, not men. In any department." Quinn easily picked up the tight note in his voice, though. He was anxious—anyone could tell that.

It made Quinn's heart swell. He was touched that Aaron cared about getting this right. That meant something, didn't it?

"So they're expecting me to be a nice, respectable young man," Aaron said to himself as the car came to a stop. "That's what dating is about? Meeting people and being respectable? Thanks. I hate it."

Quinn laughed and turned off the car. He unbuckled to take both of Aaron's hands. "You're going to be fine," he assured Aaron, who didn't meet his gaze. There was no convincing him, was there? "Come on, let's do this before they wonder if we're hiding out here."

"We *could* hide out," Aaron mumbled. When Quinn leaned over the seat for a kiss, Aaron tried to pull him in and deepen the kiss. "Go park on the beach and get our supper from each other."

Quinn smirked at him and pecked his lips again before sinking back into his seat and opening the door. "Dessert?" he countered.

"Fine," Aaron sighed and climbed out, heading for the door like he was marching into battle.

Quinn caught up with him and grabbed his hand, shaking it lightly to try to get him to relax and smile. But the closer Aaron got to the house, the stiffer he looked.

Maybe this isn't such a great idea, Quinn thought. But it was too late to do anything about it.

The door opened before they were even on the porch. Mom again, standing in the doorway shielding her eyes as she peered at them. "Come on in. This must be Aaron? Oh, we've heard so much about you!"

Quinn laughed. *Hardly*, he thought as he glanced at Aaron. He'd tried to avoid the interrogation. But Aaron still blanched and shot him a frantic sideways glance.

"Have you? Uh-oh," Aaron joked, his smile tight.

"Not that much. Just that I've got a guy," Quinn interjected. He squeezed Aaron's hand hard and got a flutter of fingers in return.

"I hope the drive was okay today," Mom told Quinn as she kissed Aaron's cheek. "And how about you, Aaron? Did you get any time to relax, or is it all duty all the time?"

They had to let go off each other's hands to get their jackets and shoes off.

Aaron kicked his shoes off. Luckily, instead of leaving them untidy, he turned back and nudged them together before facing Quinn's mom. "Mostly work, ma'am. The shop closes at four, but Saturday is payroll time."

"Oh, don't you have people to do that?" Mom laughed. "Enjoy yourself. It's the weekend."

Quinn rolled his eyes and rescued Aaron, putting a hand on his shoulder. "She tells me this all the time. Just because dentists don't work weekends, Mom..."

Aaron managed a smile, but Quinn could see the walls in his eyes. They looked a lot like they had when they'd first met—only without the humor to deflect, all Aaron had was ice.

Now his father was approaching. "Pleasure to meet you, son."

Oh, God. He doesn't mean son as in son-in-law, Quinn tried to convey mentally to Aaron, but it didn't work.

It didn't get any less painful. In fact, it only grew worse.

Quinn's parents peppered Aaron with questions that made it clear they expected him to live a very different lifestyle—a house and car of his own, and an ordinary hobby like watercolor painting at night.

The fact that he lived with four of his best friends, shared a car with them, and certainly didn't have a 401k just confused Mom and Dad. They didn't seem to know what to do with him. He was nothing like the med school student Quinn had brought home last, three years ago.

Instead of coming out of his shell and asking them questions, Aaron mumbled answers and focused on wolfing down supper, as if keeping his mouth full would mean no more questions.

It sort of worked. They all fell into silence before long, pausing only for occasional compliments on the food. Aaron knew all the right cutlery and kept his elbows off the table, his manners impeccable.

Somehow, Quinn had expected him to be more reckless, maybe even deliberately snub etiquette. But Aaron wasn't himself—not in the slightest.

"This really is a good quiche," Quinn found himself saying. "You'll have to send us the recipe. We cooked risotto together yesterday, you know."

"Mmm." Aaron clutched his water glass to his chest like he was hoping it would turn to wine.

Quinn's heart sank. He'd seen Aaron at work in the coffee shop. He always had a kind word for his customers and a joke to tell. Starting conversations came more easily to him than it did to Quinn. He'd never seen Aaron this quiet before.

And Quinn was painfully aware of his parents' body language. The way Mom smiled and spoke at a higher pitch, and Dad took his time ponderously stroking his chin before he spoke.

They thought Aaron didn't fit into their neat little life and shouldn't fit into Quinn's, either.

The conversation dragged on through town events, and briefly, Quinn perked up. Aaron's cafe was the new center of town life before Cher's opened for the evening. Surely he'd have something to contribute.

But even as they talked about Scott, the newspaper editor who had written up Aaron's place in the paper, Aaron seemed half-afraid to open his mouth.

"That photo he took of Aaron in front of the cafe was great." Quinn put a hand on his shoulder. "You should frame it and put it on the wall. All the cool little indie places do—they frame their publicity."

Aaron offered him a strained smile. "That's a good idea," he said quietly.

"Oh, speaking of photos!"

Oh, no. Quinn tried to shoot his mom a warning glance, but she carried on anyway.

"We spoke to the photographer, and he said yes. So," Mom said, and Quinn could hear her bracing herself like she didn't actually want to do it.

Then don't, Quinn begged her mentally. Hadn't he made it clear enough that this was a casual dating situation?

Or, it struck him with growing horror, were they trying to make it clear what was expected of Quinn's boyfriend? From the determined look on their faces, he had the suspicion it was more the latter.

"If you'd like to be in the Christmas photo, I'm sure all our relatives would be charmed. We've written out all the cards, but it's no trouble to change things."

"The... Christmas photo?" Aaron echoed, glancing at Quinn and looking utterly lost.

"Oh, we always do a Christmas card with a family photo," Quinn said, resisting the urge to roll his eyes. "Like it's the '90s. I told them you might not want to." He tried to give him an out. "It's a weird tradition."

"It's a perfectly ordinary tradition, isn't it?" Dad looked at Aaron, clearly hoping for agreement.

Aaron's laugh was quick and breathy. "Yeah. Lots of people do it, but... um. Thanks, but no. I don't do photos that other people take. Unless my hands are full..." He trailed off, his cheeks flushing pink.

It was all Quinn could do not to gasp. The ending of Aaron's joke was obvious to him, but luckily his parents were so oblivious they'd never know.

Before anyone could say anything, Aaron stood so fast his chair almost fell over. "Do you have a washroom I can use?"

"Yeah, it's just that way." Quinn pointed down the hall. He was torn between laughter and crying a little bit.

Everyone involved just needed to hit the reset button and pretend that today hadn't happened.

Once he was gone, Mom and Dad looked at him. Their expressions were as one: *Why him?*

Quinn gritted his teeth and sat up straight, listening until the door closed.

The moment it did, Mom spoke up. "We don't mind who you date, or how different he is."

Oh God, can I just disappear now and skip the rest of this? Quinn thought. He heard the implication clearly: they didn't like him.

"As long as he treats you right," Dad said, gathering up the dishes. "That's what matters."

Yeah, they disapproved, all right. They couldn't choose stronger words to do so.

Quinn couldn't disagree that the guy he'd chosen was different. But how could he possibly explain that this very difference was what drew him to Aaron?

Aaron was smart and funny and likable when he was being himself. Quinn had no idea what had made him shut down so badly, but he just wished he could make them see what he saw in Aaron.

When they were alone together, with none of this crap, Quinn felt perfect with Aaron. Like he'd never felt with anyone else before.

"I think we're going to go for a drive before the rain comes back," Quinn announced, loud enough that Aaron could probably hear.

Sure enough, Aaron scampered back into the room just a minute later, his eyes red. Quinn ached to hug him, but he knew Aaron had to be dying of embarrassment already. He wasn't going to add to that heartache.

Mom and Dad also politely pretended not to notice as they shook hands and wished him well—even more formally than they'd introduced themselves.

The moment they left the house, silence fell. It held for the entire distance between the porch and the car, and Quinn winced more with every step.

The moment they were in the car with the doors closed, Quinn let out a breath and turned to Aaron. "No more parties, I promise. I'm sorry I dragged you into doing this. Thank you for seeing it out with me."

"I'm not exactly *seeing it out,*" Aaron mumbled, buckling up and rubbing his face, hiding it in his palms. "I think we're running away."

"A tactical withdrawal. There's a difference," Quinn said with a gentle smile, hoping to draw a smile from him.

But Aaron didn't even look up at him. "Don't drag it out. Are we still... doing this?"

"The beach drive?"

"*Us,*" Aaron snapped, looking up at last. Deep wrinkles in his brow and pinched lips hid his anxiety behind anger, but Quinn could tell the difference already. "You and me. Being each other's guy for the month. After all that." He folded his arms.

The storm didn't scare Quinn. Neither did Aaron's glower, or the quick breaths he took, like he was ready to chew Quinn out. He'd figured Aaron out better than that by now.

Every time he got angry, he was really just overwhelmed, and he needed a minute to gather himself.

Quinn reached out for Aaron's hand, watching him patiently as his heart pounded. This felt like an important moment, and he didn't want to fuck it up.

Aaron glanced at Quinn's hand, his shoulders softening and arms going less rigid. He still hesitated, hands against his chest as he looked back up at Quinn.

"Come here," Quinn murmured.

Aaron sighed, but finally a smile touched his lips as he took Quinn's hand and squeezed it. "Yeah?"

"Good." Quinn raised his hand to his lips and kissed it gently before setting it back down to start the car. "Yes, we come from different places. I see that better now. But I still love spending time with you—romantic or sexual. And I love being around you. I just wish you'd introduced the real you to them."

Whatever he'd said, it hadn't worked to cheer him up. Aaron's expression closed off again as he glanced ahead. "Can we go home?"

"What, to your place?" Quinn hoped Aaron had meant Quinn's house, but he didn't want to assume.

"Yeah."

Crap, Quinn thought. "Yeah, we can."

The drive there was silent between them, and for the first time, Quinn didn't know what to do. All he felt from Aaron were waves of feelings he didn't know how to handle or help with.

"I'll see you soon, though?" Quinn prompted as he put on the parking brake and Aaron unbuckled.

"Yeah." Aaron hesitated, then plunged over the console and pressed one quick, salty kiss against Quinn's mouth before he shot out of the car, up the sidewalk, and into his house like a bat out of hell.

Quinn finally let a sigh escape and rolled his head back against the car seat, closing his eyes.

What had he done, and was there any way of fixing it? He hoped like hell there was, because the thought of a life without Aaron in it suddenly hurt far deeper than he'd thought possible.

A small, crazy part of him wanted Aaron to run back out

and ask to drive to the beach. He wanted to fumble around like clueless teens in the dark of the back seat and forget all of this evening had ever happened.

But the door remained closed, and he finally took the parking brake off to make the drive by himself.

If Quinn's eyes reacted to the salty air that met his nose minutes later, alone in the parking lot, nobody had to know.

11

AARON

Well, that couldn't have gone any worse.

Aaron didn't dare look back over his shoulder as he tested the handle of the front door. Thankfully it was unlocked, so he could stumble inside without awkwardly digging out his keys while Quinn watched, probably making sure he got inside safe.

Damn it, why did he have to be so *sweet*? Worse, why did Aaron have to care about what Quinn thought? If he were just another one-night stand Aaron could cut loose, this would all be a million times easier.

But instead, Quinn wanted to make his parents happy, and Aaron had wanted to make Quinn happy, so he'd said yes to an awful idea, knowing perfectly well how it would go.

Aaron would accept any and all praise in the sexual department—but he knew perfectly well he wasn't the kind of guy parents liked. Not even his own.

A lump rose in Aaron's throat, and he gulped it hard, hoping the sick, hot feeling in the pit of his stomach would stop. *Anytime now, please.*

His senses numbed by regret, Aaron's shoes were off before the scent of pine broke through the haze like smelling salts.

"Huh?" Aaron swiped at his eyes, grateful for the distraction. Thinking about disapproving parents was not his favorite hobby—no matter whose they were.

It hurt the most to know that they didn't like him for who *he* was. If they'd known about his own parents' career, they might have changed their minds. But that wasn't the kind of approval Aaron wanted.

He wanted to be loved for himself. Who didn't?

"Whoa...! More this way—don't crush Jesse!"

Aaron stepped into the entrance of the living room and covered his mouth with both hands.

An enormous, bushy Christmas tree had invaded the corner of their living room. They'd taken away the table that had sat there, between the two sofas, leaving a square space for the tree to go.

Ezra and Benji each stood on the arm of one sofa next to it. Jesse sprawled on the floor underneath the tree. As the tree lurched toward him, Jesse covered his face with his hands and shrieked.

Ezra grabbed at the branches and saved it, though he wobbled himself. "Please don't snap!"

But the flexible branches held firm, letting him and Benji straighten it again.

"Okay, Jesse, screw it in. Crap, wait. Go check if it's level this time," Benji panted.

"No, I've got it," Aaron called out and joined them at a trot. "Um... a little more toward Ezra." When the top spike looked vertical, he called out, "There!"

Jesse tightened the screws in the base of the Christmas tree stand and then sprang to his feet, which tripped Benji as he jumped down from the couch.

"Oh, my God. Leave you guys alone for five minutes and you're a disaster!" Aaron scolded, grabbing for them both.

Benji flopped onto the couch with a breathless laugh. "It was fine! You should have seen us with a saw."

"Jesus wept," Aaron moaned. "How many limbs are missing?"

"On the tree, or us?" Jesse grinned. He waggled all ten fingers. "Oh yeah, and then we tried to tie it to the top of the car, but we ran out of rope, so we... actually, I probably shouldn't admit to that. I'm sure our insecure load citation is in the mail."

Despite himself, Aaron laughed. He sat next to Benji and finally took in the rest of the living room, and Ezra collapsed in a pile with Jesse on the other couch. There were lights strung around on hooks and a cheesy set of plastic Santas on the table, along with candles on the mantel.

"What do you think?" Ezra beamed. "For our first Christmas in this house."

"Which needs a name," Benji pointed out. "Especially if you're going to have people moving in and out."

Jesse gasped. "Oh my God, you're right! I can't believe none of us thought of that before."

A tidal wave of relief hit Aaron as the debate began over names, because he didn't have to say what he honestly thought —that Christmas decorations made him squirm. He'd rather not acknowledge his uncomfortable feelings about the holiday.

But it didn't take long for him to be the center of attention again. "Sooo, how was the date?" Jesse asked, grinning at him.

Aaron hadn't told anyone about the parental dinner, but

he didn't have the heart to bluff. "Awful, let's never talk about it."

There were quiet gasps, but Ezra stood up and offered a soft smile. "Okay. Wine?"

"Please."

Ezra disappeared to get glasses, and Benji put his arm around Aaron and leaned into him. "Let's talk about Christmas instead."

"He hates Christmas," Jesse supplied, but he couldn't stop the train wreck in this conversation. "All the hot guys are busy, he says."

"It's true." Aaron mournfully shook his head.

"And Quinn...?" Benji prompted.

"Ugh," Aaron mumbled. He managed a little smile so he wasn't acting ungrateful that Benji was trying to cheer him up. "Probably busy with his parents. I'll spend the day at the shop, I think."

Benji gasped. "Oh, no. You can't be alone for Christmas. I'm sure you're not the only one here who would be. What about your family?"

Benji had no way of knowing, since Aaron had found out about the cruise long before he'd moved into the house and met everyone.

"Well, my family are rushing off to do a Christmas cruise, and I can't leave the coffee shop..."

"A cruise? Without you?" Benji scowled. "My parents will adopt you."

"Now we're circling back to tonight's horror show," Aaron groaned, taking the glass of wine from Ezra with a nod of thanks as he reappeared. "I met Quinn's parents, and they think I'm some weirdo."

"We all think you're some weirdo," Ezra teased, but he sat

on Aaron's other side and put his hand on his knee. "Was it really that bad?"

"Tragic," Aaron declared. He kept a deadpan face, kind of hoping everyone would think he was being overdramatic as usual. "Please distract me."

"All right." Jesse turned up the speaker, which was playing Christmas music. "Let's finish decorating this tree! And we saved the best part for you."

Aaron squinted at the sprig of greenery Jesse held out to him. When it finally clicked, he managed a chuckle. "Is that mistletoe?"

"Yup! No hanging it at waist height," Ezra said with a wink.

Although Aaron laughed, he wasn't really in the mood. If he were feeling like himself, he might have made a raunchy joke about it. But tonight, he couldn't bring himself to try.

Aaron hung lights and tinsel, handed hooks to Benji for little baubles, and smiled, but it never quite reached his heart.

His parents' house was probably color-coordinated right now. The base color was always silver, and his mom alternated accent colors between blue, green, and red. The better for his dad to take the obligatory politician's Christmas photo with his successful family.

Well, his wife. Dad didn't consider his only son a success by any means.

He'd made that very clear to Aaron a few years ago when his parents got home two days early from a party fundraiser to find Aaron on the couch, sandwiched between two hot, naked men.

A disgrace, Aaron distinctly remembered hearing his dad spit at him, razor-eyed and coldly furious. And *You're just asking for a scandal.* Something about attention seeking, and people thinking his dad had failed as a parent, ending up with a kid like Aaron.

And then the worst word of all: normal.

Why couldn't I get a normal American boy? Instead, I got... you.

The son his dad wanted had only ever existed as a figment of his imagination. From his first steps, Aaron had pranced; from his first craft projects, he'd covered himself in glitter and twirled around the house.

His parents weren't opposed to having a gay son. But that position was miles away from *accepting* it, and conditional on Aaron being someone he wasn't.

Playing baseball, schmoozing at country clubs, going to law school. Definitely not getting spit-roasted by strangers on his weekends off from studying to be a barista.

Normal. The word had hung over him for his whole adolescence, been drilled into him. He had to be normal, to show the public that his father had good morals and could be trusted in the mayor's office.

And for the first time, the word had cracked through the numbness that froze his heart.

The only person he knew who didn't give a crap about being normal was his grandma, and she'd been the happiest of them all. Gramma had always accepted him for exactly who he was without even treating it like a big deal.

And then she'd passed away, and the walls of his life had closed around him. She'd always supported him learning more about coffee. Over long Sunday breakfasts, Aaron had talked to her about what he was learning, and she'd never treated his job as any lesser than his dad's.

Gramma had been as far from normal as it was possible for a woman in her generation, and she'd been proud of him for following in her footsteps. So Aaron had snapped. He wasn't going to put up with that shit anymore.

"I'm normal, and if you can't see it, that's your problem." Aaron had moved out the next week. In two and a half years since, they'd seen each other a handful of times, but always at a distance, like there was a glass wall between them.

Aaron had expected them to be relieved when he'd announced the spur-of-the-moment move to Hart's Bay. They'd just been pissed off that he was throwing away his chance at a future by moving to the beach to pour coffee.

Whatever. *He* knew the skill and dedication that his job took. People like Mom and Dad never would.

But it did choke him up, walking into a house like Quinn's that represented everything he'd run away from. Only this time, it was his potential future he saw melting away in front of him, not his past.

"So can we help patch anything up?" Ezra finally asked, quietly, once the tree was decorated and the other guys were busy in the kitchen cleaning up from supper.

Aaron blew out a sigh, taking a sip of wine and letting it roll across his tongue. When it touched his palate, he savored the kick to it. "No. I need to apologize to Quinn tomorrow."

Ezra only looked more worried.

"I don't think so," Aaron murmured at last, finishing his glass and setting it aside. "He seemed to think his parents would like me. But I don't *do* parents."

"Oh, hon." Ezra put his arm around Aaron's shoulder and pulled him in for a hug, which Aaron leaned into. "Anyone would be lucky to have you in their son's life."

Aaron's lips twitched into a sad little smile. *Their sons get lucky with me. That doesn't make them lucky*, he thought. But there was no point in opening those wounds. He was tired of feeling like shit for tonight. "Thanks, babe," he said instead. "I think I'm gonna head to bed. Early morning, as always."

Ezra wavered, looking like he wanted to shadow Aaron and talk to him one-on-one, but Aaron shook his head.

He loved Ezra, and they understood each other pretty well most of the time. Ezra had lost his brother years ago, though he rarely talked about it. That event had shaped him, just like Aaron's loss had molded his life direction. They understood one another without needing to explain.

But this wasn't just about Quinn, or Quinn's parents, or Aaron's parents, or his grandma, or even his own choices. It was all of them, all at once, and that was something he had to bear alone.

Aaron tried to ignore his vibrating phone, too, as he climbed into bed. He was too tired to feel the guilt that tried to gnaw at the edge off his consciousness.

But he couldn't. Even convinced that Quinn hated him and that he deserved better, thinking of him on the other end of the line had Aaron reaching for the phone.

"Hello?" Aaron shut off the bedside lamp and nestled into his bed, closing his eyes against the sudden darkness.

"Hey." Quinn sounded uncertain, and Aaron felt bad that he'd left him doubting everything. "Are you all right? Do you need company?"

"It's hard to explain. But I'm fine for tonight," Aaron answered. Might as well get it out of the way with. "I owe you an apology."

"No," Quinn tried to say, but Aaron wouldn't let him dismiss it.

"I do. I wasn't myself tonight, and I let you down. All you

wanted was a nice guy who'd make your parents happy for you. I could have played that role. I *should* have."

"That wasn't part of the deal," Quinn said softly. "I pressured you into it."

Aaron chuckled. "Equal fault, then?"

"Yeah." Quinn blew out a sigh. "So you're not running away from me yet?"

"No."

There was a rustling sound in the background, like Quinn was settled on the couch and leaning back into the cushions. For a brief, intense moment, Aaron's whole chest ached with the desire to be nestling into him, skin-to-skin, his face pressed into Quinn's chest.

Quinn's soft voice came through the line again. "Do you wish you could?"

"Run away from you?" Aaron nearly sat upright. "What? No." After a moment, he managed a grin. "The sex is too good."

"Okay." Quinn's laugh sounded more confident now. "Just making sure."

"And I like hanging out with you. I even like this... fling we've got going on. Being your guy. I just don't like being a..."

"Son-in-law?" Quinn's voice was dry. "Yeah, I get it. There's no in-between with my parents. You're either all in or all out."

"They definitely think I'm weird now," Aaron muttered. "Good. No surprises later."

Quinn didn't deny it, which told Aaron everything. He just wished it didn't feel so crappy.

"Would you come over tomorrow?" Quinn asked softly. "I'd like to hit the reset button. No more getting family and friends involved. Me trying to win your heart, you trying to win my... um..."

"Dick?" Aaron supplied, a giggle escaping. Why did talking to Quinn make all the knots in his chest unwind, one by one? It was so subtly he hardly noticed it until he found himself nestling into the pillows with a smile.

"Yes," Quinn laughed.

Aaron hummed, but there was no questioning what his heart wanted: just the two of them, alone together. "Okay."

"Okay, good." Quinn sounded excited again. "Afternoon? My client wraps up right when your place closes. I could pick you up from the coffee shop at four?"

"I won't be out of there until four thirty," Aaron warned him.

"No problem. I'm patient," Quinn said. "I can sit there and watch."

Aaron giggled. "I'm not, when a hot guy is sitting there and watching me."

"Oh, now we're getting back to phone sex territory," Quinn said. He dropped his voice to a hoarse whisper. "And I wouldn't want to leave you wanting tonight."

Aaron gulped. Too late. There was already a tent forming in the sheets. Just Quinn's sexy voice was enough to get him hard. "I'll forgive you, as long as you don't leave me wanting tomorrow."

"Never," Quinn promised. "Sleep tight, baby."

"I will. Tighter than my cute little ass is right now," Aaron shot back, grinning at the stifled gasp from the other end of the line. "Bye, baby!"

Aaron hung up, grinning into the darkness. He could just picture Quinn's face—the one he wore when he was shocked but more than a little bit turned on by Aaron's boldness. He turned onto his side and squirmed, trying to ignore the blood rushing south.

Save it for tomorrow night, he told himself. It would be worth the wait.

For now, Aaron closed his eyes and prayed he wouldn't dream of red baubles glinting on a cold silver tree.

QUINN

The weather was beautiful, and Quinn's spirits soared as he drove along the coast toward home. For once, he wasn't drowning out the clatter of raindrops on his car roof with loud music.

No—the window was down, the open horizon lay to his left, and all he heard was road noise and the ocean. With less than an hour until sunset, the clouds were tinged orange and pink, like a bright veil laid across the waves.

The phone call with Quinn's parents had gone quickly today. He'd been done before he even hit the highway. When they'd asked about his evening plans, Quinn had told them the truth: that he was going to pick up Aaron for a date. They'd wrapped up the call quickly after that.

Quinn was excited for another evening with just the two of them. It was just what they needed after the chaos of the last few days.

This was his and Aaron's relationship, nobody else's.

Quinn sighed and muttered, "I'm always chasing rainbows, watching clouds drifting by..." The words carried the hint of a tune, but no more. It was more a true statement of fact.

But was it so bad to be a dreamer? Sometimes, dreams had to come true.

As Hart's Bay drew closer, Quinn drummed his fingers on the windowsill of the car. He'd showered at the gym and changed into a nice date night outfit to save time.

It was after four o'clock when he arrived, parking as close to the warehouse as he could. Howya Bean was already closed. Hopefully he wasn't too late.

Quinn considered texting before realizing Aaron might be counting cash in the office or something. He got out of the car with another appreciative glance toward the calm harbor, then approached the glass-and-steel converted warehouse.

For years, this building had sat empty. Quinn remembered years of neglect and decay, in step with the rest of the town center. He'd never been that kind of troublemaker, but other kids had tried to smash the tiny windows high in the eaves at each end.

He shaded his eyes to peer through the front door. The place was empty, apart from Aaron behind the counter.

Quinn rapped softly on the glass, then waved when Aaron looked at him. He tried to mime, *Should I wait outside?* by pointing at himself, then the sidewalk, then folding his arms.

Aaron grinned and shook his head, coming around the end of the counter to unlock the door. He'd already changed out of his work clothes, and was now wearing gray skinny jeans and a bright purple oversized knitted sweater. "Hi there. Don't wait in the cold. I'll let you in as long as you promise not to rob me."

He beamed and tilted his chin up, a clear invitation for a kiss.

Quinn laughed and leaned down, pressing his lips against

Aaron's for a long moment. "I'm only here to steal your heart," he promised.

The shiver that passed through Aaron didn't go unnoticed. But Aaron rolled his eyes at Quinn and stood aside, gesturing for him to come in so he could close and lock the door again. "You're not Canadian?"

"What? No." Quinn squinted his brow at Aaron.

"Well, you should be a maple tree, with all that sap." Aaron winked at Quinn and went back to counting his cash.

Quinn laughed, taking a seat at the counter. "It was worth a try. Anything to win our bet." His compliments and flirting might roll off Aaron, but he was going to keep trying anyway. One day, he hoped, he'd break through.

"How was your day at work?" Aaron asked, coins clattering in the cash register tray. His lips moved silently as he watched the coins.

"Ugh, don't remind me." Quinn stuck out his tongue. "This meathead trainer keeps getting clients injured, and I said something to one of his clients last week. Who turned to be his boyfriend, of course. So the jerk talked to the gym manager, who told *me* off for trying to steal his client."

Aaron gasped. "Can they even do that?" When Quinn nodded, he scoffed, "Well, that's bullshit. They should be thanking you for saving him. My knight in shining armor."

"I am," Quinn said with a serious nod. "The armor is my skin and it's shining from sweat."

"Ah, shit. Now I have to start over." Aaron groaned at his cash tray and dumped the nickels in his palm back into the tray. Then, he leaned over the counter for a kiss. Quinn's hands were free to roam, so he cupped Aaron's cheeks.

They got distracted with this kiss, lips seeking the heat of each other's mouths. To be exact, whenever

Aaron tried to come to his senses and pull away, Quinn softly lapped at his lower lip or sucked it between his teeth.

Aaron finally whimpered, still on tiptoe as he rocked backward. "I could do this all day, but you'll get a crick in your neck. And my hands are disgustingly covered in money germs."

"Is that a *please stop distracting me?*" Quinn laughed.

"It is." Aaron held out his hands palms-first and wiggled his fingers. "Unless you want a germ attack. And I warn you, some of my customers today had winter colds."

"Oh, God!" Quinn swayed backward, out of Aaron's reach, and grabbed the counter to steady himself. "That's gross, now that you mention it. Thanks for that. My appetite is much better."

Aaron beamed. "You're welcome!" He finished counting nickels and then pennies before bringing the cash tray to the office.

When he reemerged, Aaron ducked behind the counter and washed his hands. "Just for you," he told Quinn as he dried his hands.

"No, it's so you can hold hands with me and stay warm while we watch the sunset."

Aaron paused midstep behind the counter. "Oh, is... is that the plan?" He sounded flustered.

"It is. Unless you object." Uncharacteristically for Aaron, he only shook his head, no sassy comeback in sight. "Then it's the plan," Quinn said. "Come on."

Aaron set the alarm and locked up after them, and Quinn led him down to the pier which stretched even farther than the marina tucked into the coastline beside it.

From here, they could look back at the town square, the

warehouse, and over to the point that hid the sheltered bay on the beach where town barbecues were held.

"Brrr." Aaron snuggled into Quinn's side as a cool sea breeze swept in.

"Here." Quinn stood behind Aaron and wrapped his arms tightly around his waist and chest, resting his chin on the top of Aaron's head. "You won't block my view."

"How are you so tall?" Aaron murmured. "Not fair. You must have drunk a lot of milk."

"Or you have short parents."

Aaron didn't say anything, just rested his arms on top of Quinn's and laced his fingers. They were already cool, so Quinn held on tight, willing his body heat to help.

A minute later, Aaron's shivers subsided. He hummed, a contented note. "You're a sauna. I like it. I might climb onto you more often."

"I hope you do," Quinn said. He smirked and let one hand wander south.

As Quinn should have expected, Aaron didn't stop him or scold him. "Mmmm," he approved, squirming against Quinn's front. "Yes, please. Bet I can come before the sun goes."

Quinn just laughed and ran his hand back up to Aaron's chest, rubbing gently. "You're absolutely impossible," he murmured and leaned down to kiss the side of Aaron's neck.

"Not impossible. Just improbable," Aaron giggled softly. "Oh, here we go."

The sun was sinking rapidly toward the horizon as waves lapped gently against the edge of the pier. The bottom of the orb touched the perfectly straight line that divided burnt orange from dusky, warm-hued blue.

Aaron shielded his eyes, while Quinn stared just to the side of the bright light.

It felt like Quinn was holding his breath, waiting for the ending of something. What that was, he had no idea. But he went still, and so did Aaron in his hold. Even their breathing fell into sync. The chilly air didn't seem to matter anymore.

Orange glinted off the sea directly below the sun, lopsidedly filling in the missing circle, and the light danced along the tips of the gentle waves.

For a few moments, they were part of something bigger than themselves, knitted into the tapestry of life that soared, sailed, swam all around them.

How long had Quinn lived here, and how few days had he done this? He'd taken for granted the sun setting over the horizon every night, sometimes enjoying the view from his car window while blaring his favorite music. Rarely had he stopped to bear it witness—and never with company like Aaron's.

It was so fast Quinn barely wanted to blink, the disappearance of the sun across the horizon. The orange trail along the water receded, and all light seemed to draw together at the horizon, like cloaks the sun was gathering after her.

Just as Quinn was drawing breath to say something to mark the final sliver of light, he gasped.

An emerald flicker appeared around the top of the last streak of light, bright and bold against the sienna sky. It only appeared for two, three seconds at most as it drew together on itself and vanished.

Aaron spoke first, in a rush, turning to look up at Quinn. "Did you—"

"Yes!" Quinn gasped. He kept his gaze fixed on the horizon, but it didn't return. "I've heard stories about that. Gregory told me, down at Cher's one night. Sailors have all kinds of legends about the green flash."

"Good luck?" Aaron murmured, hope in his voice.

So Quinn smiled, finally letting go of Aaron so he could turn around in his hold. "Very."

He bent and pressed their lips together. For one more perfect moment, it was just the two of them.

Then Aaron's stomach interrupted with a long, deep growl that made Quinn burst out laughing.

"Sorry," Aaron muttered, a pink flush creeping up his cheekbones. "Didn't have a chance to stop for lunch today."

"You poor thing." Quinn wrapped his arm around Aaron's shoulders. "Let's get you to Millie's and fix that."

He cast one more look over his shoulder at the darkening sky before leading Aaron back along the pier to his parked car for the short drive.

Darkness set in by the time they were seated along the windowed wall of the restaurant. There wasn't much ocean to be seen yet, without the moon to illuminate it, but knowing it was there made Quinn smile. And when Aaron caught him looking, he shared that smile.

Like that one precious moment was their very own secret.

Quinn was less nervous this time as they placed their orders and settled down to chat. It felt easy and familiar with Aaron, like this was a weekly routine. What he wouldn't give to make that the case.

And any anxiety that Aaron might run away again vanished when Aaron leaned in. "After this, how about we take that drive I bailed on? Since it's such a nice evening?"

Quinn beamed at him. "Yeah, I'd love to."

As Aaron talked about his funny customer stories, his roommates' antics, and the cuteness of the newest couple in his household, Quinn was happy to sit and listen. Even the cadence of his voice was adorable.

But the more Aaron talked, the more Quinn started to notice little signs: scratching his neck, tapping his toes, chewing his lip. It was like he was talking to distract himself from what was really on his mind.

"Are you all right?" Quinn finally asked after dessert, as they waited for the check.

Aaron blinked, and then his eyes went big and round. "Me? Oh, yeah. Why wouldn't I be?"

Quinn just raised an eyebrow at him. "That's not the most convincing answer I've ever heard. Want to try again?"

"How about I tell you on the drive?" Aaron asked. "Somewhere more private. You know how the walls have ears around here."

"I sure do," Quinn agreed, patting Aaron's hand. "I've got this one."

"Then it's my treat next time," Aaron said.

Quinn beamed to himself. That meant there *was* a next time, and the relief made him suddenly able to draw a deep breath for the first time since he'd noticed Aaron's nervous tics. "Deal."

They headed to the car hand in hand, and Quinn smiled as people who knew his parents stared at them. Whoever wanted to report back that they'd had another successful date was welcome to do so.

"Want to drive down to the sand beach?" Quinn suggested.

"Perfect," Aaron said.

With any luck, they'd be alone. There might be a few people walking their dogs at this hour. Hopefully, no high school kids necking in cars.

It didn't take long to reach the turnoff for the parking lot, and then they cruised into view of the broad, flat expanse of sand that opened up past the rocky points that sheltered the cove and harbor.

The shores around here were usually rocky, so back when Hart's Bay was still a tourist haven, the town had created a sand beach. It was still recognizable from the dated advertising posters hanging in the town's grocery store.

It made Quinn smile, the vision of how it must have been once: people in old-fashioned bathing suits with inflatable life rings. These days, the beach didn't fill up with towels at dawn, but on good days, surfers still ventured here.

The parking lot was empty, so Quinn half-expected to have an Aaron in his lap as soon as he parked.

Instead, Aaron unbuckled and drew his knees up beside himself on the seat, reaching out for Quinn's hand. "So, I think I owe you an explanation for the other night."

Oh, no. He wasn't still feeling bad about that, was he? Quinn's gut clenched with sympathy. Sure, he'd come off as distant and awkward, but there were worse ways to make an impression. "No, you don't."

"It's more of a life history." Aaron's voice was surprisingly quiet and calm. There was no joking around, and it made Quinn go still.

"Go on," Quinn said once he'd unbuckled and taken Aaron's hand. He rested it on one palm, stroking the back of his knuckles.

Aaron looked out over the ocean and then drew a sigh. "Okay, so... I'm sure you noticed I don't really talk about my parents."

Quinn swallowed hard. He had noticed, but he didn't want to bring it up and reopen Aaron's scars. "Yeah?" Oh, man. If he was about to hear that Aaron had been thrown out at an early age, he was going to add to the list of people he wanted to punch on Aaron's behalf. "Don't tell me they're homophobic assholes."

"No," Aaron said, smiling a little. "They're a lot like yours. They mean well, they just want me to be someone I'm not."

Quinn sucked in a quiet breath. That hadn't been what he expected. "Oh."

"So I drifted away from them a couple years ago, and I've been a lot happier ever since. More myself. I met my friends, back when we all lived in Portland."

"And then you moved here together?" Quinn stroked Aaron's hand lightly.

"Yeah. Jesse impulsively decided he wanted to move, and the rest of us said, *why not?* We're all artists and creative types —Portland is too expensive for what we were getting out of it."

That made sense. "And you chose Hart's Bay. I'm glad you did. One little ripple can make big changes." Quinn smiled, raising Aaron's hand to his lips.

Aaron giggled quietly. "Oh, you flatterer."

Quinn didn't know how to tell him it was the truth. Not just because the town was picking up again, but in his own life —he'd smiled more in the last week than ever before. The future seemed rosier now, no matter how the month played out between them. But there was no denying what his heart wanted.

"But I'm sorry about your parents," Quinn added, a frown forming. "I had you down as being from some hippie family. Free love, all that stuff."

Aaron sighed. "I only wish. I used to think I was switched at birth."

"I think we all felt that way at one point or another," Quinn mused, glancing out over the ocean as Aaron's phone went off.

He squirmed to get it out of his pocket, and there was no missing his gasp then.

"What?" Quinn asked, quickly looking over. "Is something wrong?"

"I... I don't know." Aaron's lips tightened. "Benji was on his way home and he saw some guy near the coffee shop door."

"Right...?" Quinn wasn't sure where this fit in with Aaron yet.

"Toward Howya Bean. He's worried it could be Floyd."

Quinn sucked in a quick breath. "Oh!" Though nobody ever confirmed it, rumor had it that Floyd had been responsible for the fire that nearly stopped the fledgling art gallery in its tracks.

For a former patriarch of the town, he seemed to waste a lot of his time now trying to keep progress from coming. Anyone starting a small business—especially a young gay guy —had to deal with his meddling.

"Let's go," Quinn said instantly. He buckled up and started the car. "We'll drive by the place. If he's up to no good, we'll catch him at it. If not, it'll put your mind at rest."

"Thank you," Aaron breathed in a sigh of relief. "I was worried it would sound crazy."

"Of course not. That place is your life now," Quinn said and offered him a smile.

In a few tense minutes, they were parking on the edge of the lot closest to the warehouse. Quinn gestured for Aaron to stay in the car as he checked the back of the building. With nobody in sight, he waved for Aaron to come join him.

Aaron looked nervous, his fists curled by his sides as he strode in front of the building toward the end unit. "If it were a break-in, the alarm would have gone off. So there's that."

There weren't many places to hide beyond the warehouse

—just a large, grassy meadow leading into trees and more coastline. So once they came to the edge of the building and Quinn had circled around to check it out, he gave Aaron the all-clear nod.

Then he spotted the manila envelope taped to the door. "Ah. This must be what he was up to."

Aaron peeled it off in one swift motion, and then unlocked the front door and deactivated the alarm when it chirped. "Yeah, this hasn't gone off, either. Phew."

"Oh, good." Quinn squinted at the envelope in Aaron's hands. "A resume, maybe?" Before he could see it, Aaron shuffled it under his arm, his laugh loud and a little forced.

"Oh, God. You're right. That was all it was. Someone dropping off their resume. I'll put that in the office for tomorrow."

As he did, Quinn wandered back to the counter and took a seat, running an admiring hand over the reclaimed wood surface. Aaron had taken his time with the details, despite the rush to open the place. Being here felt like being surrounded by him—modern, fresh, sleek, yet friendly.

When Aaron emerged from the office, Quinn smiled at him. "Feeling better now?"

"A million times," Aaron admitted and then grinned as he sauntered closer. "I think I owe you a reward."

"I don't need a reward to look after you," Quinn told him.

It just came naturally, in a way he couldn't explain. Maybe it was because Aaron was small, delicate, and full of life. Whatever the reason, something deep inside Quinn wanted to wrap his arms around Aaron and never let anyone near him.

"Oh?" Aaron turned Quinn's stool around and pushed his way between his knees, running his hands up the outsides of his thighs as he gazed at him.

Quinn gulped at the thickening air between them—and the thickening in his pants, too. Aaron's narrow hips between his thighs felt so incredibly right.

Aaron caught Quinn's gaze and slowly, deliberately, licked his lips. Then, his hands still running along the outsides of Quinn's legs the whole way, he sank down.

"Aaron!" Quinn gasped as he knelt in front of him. He cast a quick glance over his shoulder, but it was utterly deserted in the darkness. And even if it weren't, with the lights off in here and Quinn's back to the door, nobody could see a thing.

It was still the most daring thing Quinn had ever done, and his breath came fast and hard. Aaron's nimble fingers plucked the button from the hole in his slacks, then unzipped them.

"Look who likes my good ideas," Aaron whispered, drawing Quinn's half-hard shaft into the open air, his fingers warm and ticklish against the sensitive skin.

Quinn gulped, his thighs tightening to hold himself in place. He grabbed the counter with one hand and Aaron's shoulder with the other. "More than I should."

"Who says you shouldn't?" Aaron's fingers curled tightly around Quinn as arousal thrummed deep in his bones. "Because I'm in charge right now, and I say you should like all of my ideas."

Quinn gulped. "So far, I do."

From the first moment they'd met, he had. And he could easily see himself getting sucked in. But for now, he'd settle for being sucked off.

AARON

This was what Aaron had been picturing when he'd suggested their deal just a week ago. Just fun, no strings, no history, and no future to worry about.

And Quinn's orgasm in his hands—and mouth.

As Aaron kissed the rounded tip of that big, gorgeous cock he was cradling in one hand, he relished every one of Quinn's stifled sounds.

There was no time to waste, though. The excitement hummed through the air between them, and Quinn kept catching his breath and looking back over his shoulder.

Aaron focused on his job—stretching his lips around the tip of Quinn's needy shaft and swallowing it inch by inch.

He soon ran out of tongue to slide the silky warm skin across, but Aaron hadn't practiced so much to be an amateur at this. He let Quinn's cock slide into his throat until his lips teased the base of the shaft.

"Fuck, that's hot. How do you do that?" Quinn gasped.

Aaron had plenty of smart-ass answers, but his mouth was

too full to give any of them. He just moaned and started to bob his head like he was desperate for Quinn.

And he was—he craved the salty taste exploding across his tongue, and the desperate passion written across Quinn's face.

Fast and hard was the way Aaron liked it, especially when giving head. No time to think, to second-guess himself, to worry. All he could do was be present and pour every ounce of himself into pleasuring Quinn.

"Yes," Quinn growled, his thighs spreading as he hooked his toes around the lower bars of the stool. "Suck me, baby. Take it all."

Aaron groaned louder this time, appreciating every filthy word. Quinn was losing his inhibitions, and he loved it. With his length throbbing in Aaron's mouth, he had to be desperate to take control.

Sure enough, Quinn's hand tangled in Aaron's hair like he wanted to do so. Aaron laid his hand on top of Quinn's and squeezed hard to get Quinn to tighten his grip. Then, Aaron pushed his mouth all the way down on Quinn's cock until he choked. He stayed there for a few long moments, breathing in tiny, desperate pants through his nose.

As hot as it was to be in control, it was even hotter when Quinn took over.

Quinn got the message. His nails dug into Aaron's scalp as he braced himself and started to thrust slowly into Aaron's mouth. "Oh, yes. You want to know how your mouth feels on me? It's incredible," he whispered. "So hot and wet. I could watch this all day."

Yes, please, Aaron thought as he held still in Quinn's grip. He moaned and whimpered when his throat wasn't full, and gazed up at Quinn through his long lashes when it was.

Quinn's breathing was harsh and desperate now, his

thrusts more erratic. Gone was the caution and gentleness of his first few moments. Instead, there was need in the way he held Aaron's head tightly, hair tangled around his fingers. Quinn was blinded with pleasure, desperately careening toward the edge as he took matters into his own hands.

Quinn pushed himself to his feet, bending his knees and gripping Aaron's shoulders. Now, he was fucking Aaron's mouth, fast and raw, deep grunts escaping each time his hot skin smacked Aaron's swollen lips. "Any moment now, baby. I'm gonna shoot my load in your mouth. Is that okay?"

Aaron moaned in the best *yes* he knew how, grabbing Quinn's hips. He was making Quinn lose control, and he loved every moment of it.

Then Quinn tensed, all at once, even his breath seemingly rushing from his lungs. His strangled cry echoed off the walls of the empty coffee shop, thrilling Aaron from head to toe.

Quinn's thick, hot load shot across Aaron's tongue and down his throat, making him gulp over and over. He held Aaron in place as he thrust in quick shallow movements, his dick throbbing between Aaron's lips until it finally started to soften.

He let go of Aaron's shoulder and head then and hooked his hands under his armpits. Like he weighed nothing, Quinn pulled Aaron up and gently set him on his feet.

"Thank you," he whispered, leaning down to press his lips on Aaron's in a soft kiss.

"Mm!" Aaron squeaked with surprise. Guys didn't often do that, but Quinn didn't seem to care. "Welcome?" he mumbled when Quinn finally let go of him.

"Now, it'll be a few minutes before I can give you *your* reward for that," Quinn said with a breathless grin, tucking himself back in his pants. "Sorry."

"Huh?" Aaron's brain spun around but only landed on the words *your reward.*

"But I have other ideas in store for you before then. Ideas that I'd like to take my time with, so we should probably stop tempting fate and head to my place." Quinn just kept smiling at Aaron until his sex-addled brain understood.

Of course he was going to be all sweet and not just take a freebie. Indeed, the way Quinn's eyes roved over Aaron's body, he was just as eager to please as he had been for his own release.

Aaron gulped, his toes curling into his shoes as he plucked at the sleeves of his sweater. "I'd appreciate that."

"Oh, we'll see if you appreciate it afterward," Quinn said with a laugh.

I want him to make me walk funny tomorrow. If it took a few minutes, Aaron could wait. His body suddenly burned with need—the need to have Quinn's hands on him, his strong arms wrapped around him, and most of all, his perfect cock buried deep inside him.

Aaron bit his lip and sprinted for the alarm, his run a little awkward with the giant tent in his pants. Suddenly it was a good thing for a whole different reason that nobody was around. "Let's go."

Quinn laughed, heading outside to the car to wait for Aaron, who had never been more thankful that the drive was so short.

When they got to Quinn's place, Aaron didn't even wait until the car was off before he unbuckled and flung himself up the sidewalk toward his door. The impatience was impossible to rein in, and he wasn't going to try.

Quinn followed at a maddeningly normal pace, walking

around the car and up the stairs to the porch. "Look at you go. It's like I wound you up and set you loose."

"You're going to wind me up even more if you stand here talking." But before Aaron could keep complaining, Quinn suddenly pressed close, nearly crushing his chest against the door as Aaron squeaked. He pushed his ass back into Quinn's crotch, grinding against him shamelessly.

"What's that?" Quinn whispered in his ear. One of his hands ran up Aaron's front, under his jacket. With his other hand, Quinn rummaged in his own pocket. They were pressed so tightly together that Aaron could feel it behind his ass.

"Fuck," Aaron whimpered. He needed that body blanketing him, only on the other side of the door and with way fewer clothes. "That's just mean."

Quinn chuckled again in a deep tone meant just for him. "Is it?" He gently moved Aaron to the side so he could unlock the door, the key scraping around and around the lock in circles until it slid into the keyhole. "There we go."

Aaron bit back another moan as his brain worked overtime to remind him that his own hole was sadly empty right now. "So unfair. If that's intended to turn me on, it worked."

"It wasn't, but I'll take it," Quinn said and kissed the top of Aaron's head. He turned the key, and Aaron pushed open the door for them both to stumble inside.

This time, Aaron kicked off his shoes and peeled off his jacket, then stepped free of the entryway. "Bedroom?" He tried not to make his tone *too* needy, but just urgent enough. If Quinn insisted on stopping for a glass of water and a chat first, he was going to lose his mind.

"Yes," Quinn growled and smacked his ass.

Aaron squealed and danced away from his hand, trying to race him down the hallway, but Quinn won—he hooked a finger through Aaron's belt loop and yanked him back suddenly, scooping him up with an arm around his waist.

Suddenly—Aaron wasn't sure how it happened—he was over Quinn's shoulder, and then they were through the doorway and he was bouncing onto the mattress, the ceiling above him.

"Yes," Aaron panted, reaching for the hem of his sweater.

But Quinn caught his hands and pulled them over his head. "No."

Then he let go so he could crawl over Aaron, lightning-quick as a predator. How did he move so fast when he was so much bigger?

"Just my shirt," Aaron panted, thinking Quinn had figured he was going to get his cock out then and there. And honestly, that was a real possibility right now.

He tried again, but this time Quinn slapped his hand away. "Not so fast."

Aaron pouted up at him. "But I'll overheat. I'll literally die, actually and literally, right here."

His best puppy eyes and quivering lip didn't work. Instead, Quinn grinned at him. "Now, I don't think that's true."

Aaron moaned, long and low, but obediently laced his fingers behind his head.

Quinn had better make this worthwhile. He'd already held himself back for that whole blowjob. He'd been aching hard in his pants, twitching with every moan and grunt that escaped Quinn's throat.

"Good," Quinn whispered, pressing one hand firmly over his stomach against his oversized, knitted sweater as if molding him to the bed. He ran his hand slowly up the center of Aaron's body. His touch became gentle as he flipped his hand over and brushed the backs of his fingers across Aaron's throat.

Skin on skin—wherever it was on Aaron's body—was enough to send prickling lightning bolts of heat through his nerves. These tight jeans were going to be the death of Aaron. He shifted this way and that, but there was no relief. "Please," he whispered. "I'm so hard."

"Oh, fine," Quinn said. The teasing lilt in his voice matched the twinkle in his eye. As he reached for Aaron's waist, his hands went up instead of down to push Aaron's sweater over his head.

"Damn it," Aaron mumbled. He moved with Quinn to help him yank it off. "I see why you thought I wouldn't appreciate it."

Quinn chuckled. "Was I right?"

"Unfortunately." Aaron stuck out his tongue.

But Quinn just leaned down and sucked Aaron's tongue into his mouth, the tip of his own tongue mingling and dancing with it. For that moment alone, Aaron's hardness pressed into Quinn's thigh, and he gasped with relief.

But Quinn quickly straightened up, denying Aaron even that. "We've had hot, rough, no-time-to-waste fucking. Now it's my turn. If you're showing me your best tricks, it's only fair that I do the same."

"Where *best* trick means *longest*," Aaron mumbled, pouting as Quinn's hands came to rest on his chest. His T-shirt was still in the way, but it was silky smooth, so he felt each individual finger grazing along his body.

"And longest *is* best sometimes." Quinn smirked. "I'm sure you'll agree."

When Aaron tried to retort, Quinn pinched his nipples—both at once, and not gently.

All Aaron could do was cry out as pleasure-edged pain shot through him from head to toe. When he caught his breath, he swore at Quinn, but his maddening, sexy, and totally-in-charge guy only chuckled and leaned over him.

Quinn's mouth was hot against his cheek and jaw, and each kiss he pressed on the way to Aaron's ear made a different part of his body tingle.

Aaron couldn't hold back anymore. He grabbed Quinn's shoulders and ran his nails down his back until he gripped that firm, round ass. He couldn't wait to feel it flexing under his hands again.

Those strong palms glided across his torso, from chest to stomach and back, and around his sides. He didn't miss an inch of Aaron's body, like he was waking up every nerve he could possibly find.

"Kiss me," Aaron breathed, and Quinn's mouth was suddenly there, hot and tender against his lips. The way Quinn kissed him, looked at him, held him, was a soft promise to look after him.

Quinn might drive him to the very edge first, but he wouldn't leave Aaron behind. After all, he was here.

Aaron drew a shaky breath when Quinn resumed his torment of his neck and ears. He squeezed his eyes shut, grabbing at Quinn's shoulder blades. "I need you so much," he whispered. "I haven't taken this long to come in ages. Maybe forever."

"The longer you wait, the better it'll be," Quinn promised hoarsely. "I'm not asking anything of you that you can't do. Just let me show you how good it is."

Aaron bit his lip hard as Quinn's hands found his shirt hem. With each layer removed, the feeling grew more intense. Even bracing himself didn't prepare Aaron, though. This time, his rough palms gliding along Aaron's skin made his whole body spark into an inferno of need.

"Yes!" Aaron gasped, arching clear off the bed.

Fuck, Quinn was right. Aaron was used to a guy feeling him up a little, then spinning him around and having his way with him. Not taking his time to explore every inch of skin until Aaron's body quaked with desire.

"That's it, baby," Quinn whispered. "Let me know what feels good."

There was a wet spot on his jeans already, right over the tip of his cock. He could feel himself straining against the fabric, his thighs shaking as those big, strong hands and surprisingly nimble fingers worked over the same ground.

By the time Quinn was done pinching and rolling the sensitive nubs of Aaron's nipples between his fingers, Aaron was gasping for air.

Finally his T-shirt came off, and Quinn's hot mouth followed his hands. Kisses burned their way along his neck, up his throat, around his collarbone, down the middle of his chest...

For just a moment, Aaron let himself hope that Quinn's mouth would keep going. But instead, he doubled back and licked from his hip bone to a nipple.

Quinn's mouth closing around a nipple felt divine—and somehow, Aaron felt it in the head of his cock, even as he felt himself straining against the denim prison.

"Fucking fucker fuck," Aaron hissed at Quinn, who just reveled in it. "Your way is going to make me come in my pants."

"Good," Quinn chuckled, and Aaron almost hated that his whole body quivered with pleasure at the reaction. "Then I'll get you naked and keep going until you come again."

"Oh, God," Aaron moaned. "You have a filthy mouth now. I almost regret unlocking this part of you."

"*Almost*," Quinn echoed his word, grinning at him.

Aaron gulped. It felt strangely vulnerable to admit this, but it felt right, too. "I haven't been this blissed-out in years."

"Good," Quinn whispered. This time, the word sounded very different. It was tender and soft, almost unbearably so. So much of Aaron just wanted Quinn to rip off the kid gloves and go to town. To rough him up, use his body for his own pleasure.

But Quinn was forcing him to stop and enjoy himself, and Aaron... found that hard to handle.

Maybe he could read Aaron's face, because Quinn smiled at him. "You've been waiting long enough, though." He leaned over Aaron's stomach and kissed his hip bone, finding the spot right in the hollow of the edge of his stomach and groin that made Aaron's whole body light up like a Christmas tree.

Then he kissed along the waistband, every inch closer making Aaron's body sing out with still more pleasure. Finally, he licked the wet spot that lay across the tip of the hard bulge.

Even though Aaron could barely feel the warm, wet pressure, the sight alone made a strangled cry escape as his whole body throbbed and twitched.

Quinn peeled off Aaron's jeans and socks, but of course, he left his underwear on. Aaron was almost too exhausted to protest, except that every fiber of his body was still tense. Still, his boner was so obviously pleased with the extra room, springing free the moment it could.

"You're so fucking hot. Look at you. You're dripping wet," Quinn breathed out, his eyes wide in awe. He kissed back up to Aaron's mouth and settled his weight on top of him, one palm tenderly cupping Aaron's cheek.

Aaron's hardness pressed into Quinn's hip. He ground against him desperately as they kissed, hot and dirty and openmouthed. The sensation went from overwhelming to manageable, and barely had time to start feeling blissful before Quinn pulled back again.

Once Aaron could speak instead of just gasping for air, he managed to moan, "I've made a monster."

Quinn chuckled softly and kissed Aaron's nose, the affectionate gesture making him lose his breath for a moment.

Aaron's every muscle was tense and desperate now. He was so on edge that tears quivered at the corners of his eyes. He was taut as a bowstring, waiting for someone's fingers to dance along it and shoot his load.

Kiss by kiss, Quinn worked his way down Aaron's body—his jaw, throat, and then farther.

"No teasing," Aaron pleaded. He wasn't sure he could hold back anymore.

"No teasing," Quinn promised solemnly. He only paused to pull down Aaron's underwear and toss it aside, and then he unzipped his own slacks and worked his cock out into open air.

He was hard again, swollen and beautiful. But he crouched between Aaron's thighs, so all Aaron got to see was his forearm moving up and down. He could hear what Quinn was doing, pleasuring himself, and feel the bed shifting under him.

"Fuck," Aaron hissed. Before he could beg for a better view, Quinn gave him what he'd been waiting for.

His mouth, hot and wet and perfect, closing around the tip of Aaron's pulsating shaft.

Aaron just about screamed as he pushed upward into Quinn's mouth, his feet scrabbling against the bed for purchase.

The suction of Quinn's mouth wrapped around the head,

and his strong grip curled around the base, and then they met as Quinn swallowed him.

His tongue lapped around the head, teasing the skin around the slit until Aaron lost his breath completely. Every bob of his head made the most sensitive parts of Aaron's cock slide across the wet, tight ring of his lips. Now and then, Quinn gave him an appreciative moan that vibrated through him like the chime of a bell.

Just watching his own hardness disappear into that gorgeous mouth was enough to bring Aaron to the edge. But the best part of all was watching Quinn's arm at work, knowing he was jerking himself off just barely out of sight, hard and fast.

"I can't stop it," Aaron gasped, squirming under Quinn. "I'm too close. Please, baby...!"

All other thought slipped away as his body drew impossibly tight and then, uncontrollably, let go. And Quinn was there to stroke him onward, swallow every drop, and suck him clean.

Aaron came hard into Quinn's mouth, writhing under him and moaning his name like a prayer. He needed him in ways he couldn't fully understand—every inch of him, body and soul. The wave of bliss swept Aaron away beyond all reason.

Gradually, as the last few drops trickled out, that hot mouth and hand let go of him. The bed shifted on either side of his hips, and Aaron managed to open his eyes.

Quinn knelt over his stomach, that hard length disappearing into the tight ring of his own fingers. He pumped up and down his shaft, his eyes fixed on Aaron like he was a starving man and Aaron the last meal left in the world.

And oddly, he looked like he was... waiting for permission?

"Yes," Aaron panted, still out of breath from his own release. "Baby, yes."

A grin spread across Quinn's lips for just a moment, wild and beautiful. Then it was gone, his gaze intense as he smoothed a hand over Aaron's hair and gripped him tightly again, pinning him to the bed. Mercifully, he didn't roll Aaron's head back, letting him watch.

"Yes," Quinn growled, and just as he had not long ago, he lost himself in the moment. His brain shut down, his instincts took over, and Aaron tried to memorize every second as he watched.

Desperately thrusting into his own hand, Quinn's body arched and he threw his head back, letting go of Aaron as he bared his throat and cried out.

Jets of sticky, hot passion streaked Aaron's stomach and chest. One even landed on his chin as Quinn's aim faltered without his eye on the target.

Aaron giggled breathlessly as Quinn looked back down at him and then grinned, too. "Sorry," Quinn breathed out.

"Don't be. Just get more of it on my face next time," Aaron challenged Quinn with a wink.

Quinn bit his lip hard, his gaze roving along Aaron's naked body like he wanted to make that next time happen right now. "I will," he breathed out, and Aaron heard the promise in his voice.

After a few moments, Quinn's hand slowed and stopped. He squeezed himself gently, then let go and looked back at Aaron.

The way Quinn watched him, like he was tenderly committing him to memory, made Aaron squirm.

"Okay, I'll grab cloths. You lay there."

"I... didn't plan to go anywhere," Aaron whispered. "Not for a long time."

Quinn chuckled deeply and cupped Aaron's cheek, his thumb grazing Aaron's jaw before he let go. "Good. That saves me asking about breakfast plans."

Aaron swiped his finger along his chin and sucked it clean. "I thought breakfast in bed."

So worth it to see the look on Quinn's face—disbelief, arousal, excitement, like a hundred emotions were clamoring to get to the front of the line.

"I really..." Quinn trailed off and then breathlessly laughed. "I like your way."

"See?" Aaron beamed at his retreating back.

But, once Quinn had gently cleaned them up and turned out the light, Aaron's thoughts still raced. He nestled back into Quinn, resting his arm along Quinn's as Quinn's foot slid over his leg.

Maybe Quinn's way wasn't so bad, either. Aaron could get used to this. Dangerously used to it.

For the first time, Aaron let himself seriously daydream. What would it be like to do this every day? To wake up in Quinn's arms, and go to sleep snuggled against him? To share more than hot nights and nice meals out?

"Thank you for tonight," Quinn murmured. His voice was soft, sleepy, and frankly adorable. "That was amazing."

It was worth asking. Just in case. So Aaron injected a little cheer into his tone. "You bet it was. I'm great for a good time, if not a long time."

He carefully avoided holding his breath, or tensing up, or giving Quinn any sign that he wasn't just joking around. And he waited.

Quinn gave a breathy chuckle, but he didn't say anything.

Didn't disagree. Didn't ask Aaron if *a long time* was on the table. Didn't even jokingly say *we'll see* or tell Aaron he'd win the bet yet.

Ouch. Aaron swallowed back his feelings and nuzzled into the pillow with a deep sigh.

If not even the self-admitted romantic wanted to make this official, where did that leave him? But Aaron put the disappointment that threatened to swamp him where it belonged: on a shelf in his mind to deal with later.

Aaron had what he'd always said he wanted: great sex. The best of his life. That had to be enough for him, right? Anything more, he'd just screw up.

And he couldn't risk that. Not with Quinn.

1 4

QUINN

Success was bittersweet.

Without ever planning it, the light-hearted deal between them had turned into something more for Quinn. He could see clearly that he was in too deep to back out.

In just a few short days, Quinn had fallen harder and faster than even he had thought possible. Even as a bet, he hadn't expected to fall for Aaron's humor, strength, and cheerful determination in the blink of an eye.

He was Aaron's now—whether Aaron knew it or not. The only problem was, Aaron clearly didn't feel the same way.

At least he'd been able to stop in for coffee and a kiss before setting off on his drive to Cannon Beach, but then he had a whole hour to daydream about Aaron with nothing else to distract him but the open road. The more he thought about their situation, the more his heart ached.

Worse still, a client in Portland wanted one last training session before Christmas. If only he could keep just the easy clients and the nice ones. People like Andrew, who lived halfway between Hart's Bay and the closest gym they were both forced to go to. He got on great with Quinn, and he worked hard. More clients like Andrew, and Quinn would be happy.

But he wasn't there yet. So next weekend, he'd have to drive all the way there instead of spending one precious Sunday morning sleeping in with Aaron.

Quinn wasn't a whiner, but it was hard not to feel dejected. Every sign said he only had two more weeks to enjoy this fling. The days had already slipped by since the weekend and their fantastic reconnection—both emotionally and physically.

All he wanted was to break through whatever wall Aaron insisted on putting up between the two of them. But Quinn knew that the moment he tried, he'd lose him forever. He was lucky to get another chance after making Aaron sit through such an awful family dinner just a few days into their bet.

Even tomorrow, over his usual Thursday evening supper with his parents, things were going to be awkward. Everyone would be too polite to talk about what had happened last week, but Quinn carried around a resentment he'd never felt toward his parents' narrow-mindedness.

He had to respect Aaron's boundaries, and that meant not putting his heart on his sleeve. Even if it made his chest physically ache every time Aaron pulled away from him—literally or not—he'd keep his feelings to himself.

And he'd enjoy every moment of Aaron's cuddly, affectionate nature whenever he managed to catch him off guard. In those moments, Quinn let himself daydream that perhaps this could be a good sign.

Aaron was so much more than he presented himself. Quinn just wished he could help everyone see what he saw in him. But most importantly, if he could only show Aaron himself that he deserved to be looked after and cherished, and seen as more than a willing warm body for a night.

Quinn ached thinking about Aaron going back into the dating minefield in January, being treated like crap by random guys all over again.

As he turned down the radio and pulled into the parking lot of the gym, Quinn tried his best to shelve thoughts of his lover and focus on work. It seemed like an impossible task.

"Hey, Marv," Quinn greeted as he walked past the front desk. The gym manager was a beanpole with a prickly mustache and a round pair of glasses. He looked like he'd never seen a weight in his life. Still, he'd let Quinn join the roster of trainers working from the gym about six months ago, and it had allowed Quinn to pick up more clients here in northern Oregon.

Instead of a greeting smile, Marv crooked a finger at him and stepped away from the desk. "Can we talk?"

"Uh... yeah. Sure." Quinn was suddenly awake and more alert than a German shepherd at dinnertime.

Marv ran a scrutinizing gaze down Quinn's body, like he was on display at a meat market. Quinn shifted uncomfortably on his feet and folded his arms while Marv pressed his lips together.

Couldn't the guy hurry up with it? He wasn't going to wait forever, and his first client would be here any minute.

"So," Marv finally said, "I hate to bug you this early in the morning, but I've heard some stuff about you poaching other trainers' clients."

Quinn felt the blood rush to his cheeks. His temper was usually slow to heat up, but the idea that Meathead had gotten to Marv first... Suddenly, he struggled to breathe without gritting his teeth.

"Whatever that asshole's been saying—pardon my French —is a straight-up lie," Quinn said. It was all he could do to stay calm. "He wasn't happy that I caught him screwing up. His client was in danger of getting hurt. His elbows were hyperextending when lifting weights."

Any reasonable gym owner would have been horrified. But Marv's lips just pinched. "He says you tried to pick up his boyfriend at work, too. That was how he found out you're stealing his clients."

"What?" Quinn yelped. Oh, that asshole was going down. "First of all, I don't have a single one of his former clients. They're probably all in PT and rehab from what he's doing to them."

Marv held his hands up. "I'm just saying, man. I need to keep an eye on how everyone fits into the place."

"Well, he doesn't fit in. Unless you want this place getting a reputation for injuries."

Why was Marv still looking skeptical? It was like he had it in for Quinn and he wasn't going to let Quinn change his mind.

"Be that as it may," Marv plowed on ahead like he hadn't said a word, "you gotta watch yourself." He smacked Quinn's belly with the back of his hand. "Okay? I'm not losing him. He impresses people. I need more examples like him to motivate people."

Quinn's brows crept up. Was Marv implying that he had to drop the couple pounds he'd put on from eating real foods this month? Even though Quinn could no doubt still bench-press him without a second thought?

Oh my God, what a dick. Quinn struggled to come up with words that weren't *Fuck off,* but Marv was walking off like it was the end of the conversation. At the same time, Quinn's first client of the morning had just come in.

"Quinn, hey," Janet greeted him, unaware of everything Quinn was burning to say to Marv.

And it ought to stay that way, Quinn reminded himself despite the tightness in his throat. Clients didn't care about his problems. He was there to fix theirs.

"Hi," Quinn said, only a little strained. "How's it going? I'd better run and get changed." He fell into step beside her to the changing rooms, making conversation and trying to ignore all thoughts of Marv's smug little face.

After seeing both of his morning clients, Quinn threw himself into his own morning routine. He pushed himself further than usual, going fast and hard without a break until he was out of breath and his muscles burned. Even then, he paused long enough to gulp down water and headed for the cable machines.

They were both taken—and by two familiar faces, of course. Quinn suppressed his groan.

Neither Troy nor his boyfriend were *doing* anything, but they were leaning on the machines and talking like they had all day. Anyone with manners would have moved aside to let someone else use the machines.

But it wasn't an accident. Troy started casting glances in Quinn's direction and smirking like he knew what was going on.

Quinn wasn't afraid of them. He strode up, alert for any trouble from the brick walls of Dumb and Dumber. "If you're resting, can I use these?" He jerked his thumb at the machines.

For a moment, he wondered if they were going to pretend not to hear him like it was third grade. But then Troy finally bothered to look at him. "Nah. We're busy." Troy wrapped a hand around the handle of the cable above his head, giving Quinn a whiff of terrible armpit smell. "Obviously."

Fine. If they were going to sit there and hog the machines like a pair of wrinkled old nuts, he'd find another way to work out his abs. He could do it without equipment, because unlike these douchebags, he actually knew what he was doing.

What he wanted to say was, *Maybe that attitude is why you're losing clients, not me.* But any mention that Marv had talked to him would only make Troy gloat more.

So instead, Quinn smiled at them like he didn't give a fuck. "Great. Thanks." He walked to the mat and dropped onto his front, then found a comfortable position and raised his arms and legs off the mat.

With them watching on, he went through half a dozen exercises, pushing himself to his very limits.

The moment he was done and staggering for the showers, they moved away from the machines toward the rowing machines. Assholes.

Luckily, Quinn couldn't bring himself to care about them anymore, with his body feeling like he'd just run it through a shredder.

If Marv wanted his trainers to have an eight-pack, Quinn could do it. And he'd still be stronger, pound for pound, than the guy who now had it out for him. Sure, it meant giving up cheat days over Christmas, but Quinn's job might well count on it.

Suddenly, worrying about Aaron was a lot more fun than thinking about his job, so Quinn let himself change tack.

Sorry, Aaron, Quinn thought as he leaned back into the hot, blissful spray of water. *I'll keep drinking your coffee, but you're on your own when it comes to Christmas dinner.*

Which reminded him of the unspoken elephant in the

room: what they were going to do next week. Would Aaron agree to spend time with Quinn and his family? Or was he going to hang out with his friends after the coffee shop closed? Could Quinn spirit him away to spend the evening all by themselves? That would be his dream outcome.

But no—Quinn couldn't launch into that conversation while things were still so fragile between them.

He sighed and turned off the water, drying himself off roughly. In the cold, hard light of day, it looked a lot like avoidance. But it wasn't, right? He just didn't want to lose Aaron. Keeping this fragile bond together had to come first.

Always first.

15

AARON

Aaron was officially not in the mood to handle this shit. It had already been a long day at the coffee shop, and who should walk in but Floyd Hart, renowned asshole of the town.

He'd tried to burn down the art gallery only a few months ago, and had given Rain hell for coming out. Even Cher had banned him from her bar, which was almost unheard of. As far as Aaron was concerned, that made him instantly bannable from the premises.

Whatever he was here for, it was bound to be trouble. Aaron drew a deep breath and straightened up, preparing to chew him out.

Then he stopped, because Floyd wasn't alone and he couldn't yell at him in front of a perfectly nice customer. Aaron's brows furrowed as he saw who Floyd was with—an old lady with snow-white hair and a cane. Floyd was holding the door for her. When he looked up at Aaron, his expression was as guilty as a fox in a henhouse. He even trailed a few paces behind, like he didn't want to be here. Like he knew he was about to get a telling-off from someone or another.

But the older woman was briskly approaching Aaron at the counter, already smiling. "Well, hello, son. How do you do?"

"I—um, I'm well, thanks." Aaron fumbled for his words. He was busy noticing the resemblance between the two. Floyd had to be in his sixties, and this woman in her... eighties? Perhaps even a spry ninety-something? "Welcome to my coffee shop."

"I suppose you know everyone around here now." Her voice was wry. "But not me." She stopped at the counter and leaned on her cane, catching her breath. She looked around the place, studying faces and nodding in recognition to a few people. The place was half-full, with maybe a dozen people around different tables. They all looked just as surprised to see her.

Aaron nodded. "Sorry. I don't think we've met, Ms...?"

"Hart. Elsie-Mae Hart." She looked at him. "And you are?"

"Aaron," he said. So she was a Hart, yet he'd never heard of her. He glared at Floyd, not bothering to say hello. Already, he liked her more than Floyd.

"I see you've met my son." Elsie-Mae glanced between the two of them. "What have you done now, Floyd?" She sounded impatient.

"Um..." A flush crept up Floyd's neck. He looked like he was panicking, his eyes flickering to the door. But he couldn't very well run away from his own mother.

A grin crept across Aaron's face. Was *she* the secret weapon Cher had threatened to unleash on him before? Everyone else in the place was quiet, turning to watch the unfolding drama.

While she stared her son down, Aaron jolted at the soft chime that rang and looked at the door. Cher was there, her arm slung casually around Jesse's shoulders like she was a protective mama hen. No need to warn them, then. Aaron managed a smile at them both.

"If you don't tell me true, I'll ask someone who will," Elsie-Mae told Floyd, her voice tarter than an unripe blackberry. There was no mistaking a mom who meant business.

Floyd grimaced and folded his arms, shifting from foot to foot. "I didn't exactly welcome the newcomers into town."

"Well, you were a damn fool, then." Elsie-Mae tutted. "What you need is someone strong enough to put you in your place. Ever since Nancy died, this place got rusty. That's why you sent me to retire in Cedar Lodge, wasn't it?"

Floyd gulped and started to shove his hands into his pockets, then caught himself and folded them behind his back. He was sweating now. "Yeah. I lost track of things."

"That's why you came to me, wasn't it?" Cher spoke up from the doorway, finally approaching the counter. "Hi, Mrs. Hart." She leaned in to gently kiss Elsie-Mae's cheek.

"Ah, there you are." Elsie-Mae patted Cher's arm. "I'm glad you're still here."

"As am I," Cher agreed. She leveled her gaze at Floyd as she straightened up. "I figured out you were struggling, but you kept pushing me away when I wanted to help."

Floyd stared at his feet, working his jaw around. He was breathing quickly, looking like he wanted to disappear into the floor. "My pride got the better of me," he finally said, not looking up at her. "I've never been good with numbers. Nancy did that for me."

For the first time, Aaron actually felt a little bit sorry for Floyd. He was overdue a big comeuppance, but even so, this had to sting.

Elsie-Mae shook her head. "I don't want to live in that

home knowing this place is falling down around its ears. I'm happier here, Floyd. That's why I wanted to come back and visit for Christmas. I missed you."

That made Floyd's gaze finally snap up, his eyes widening in shock. "You can't mean that?"

"I do." Elsie-Mae looked determined. "Someone has to keep an eye on you and this whole place."

Cher broke into a smile. "We'd love to have you back, Mrs. Hart. Not just because your son needs a clip around the ear now and then."

Even Floyd chuckled quietly, rubbing his face as he finally looked at Aaron, then Jesse. The apology in his expression was more than Aaron had seen before, but not quite enough.

"Go on." Cher pointed at Jesse. "I know you want to. It'll get it off your chest."

Floyd drew a deep breath and turned, facing Jesse. "I'm sorry. I found reasons to hate you and your friends, just 'cause I knew you'd do better than me."

"And?" Cher prompted. When Floyd looked at her, she folded her arms.

"And because... well, my grandpa hated people like you."

"Like us," Jesse echoed, his lips twitching into a smirk. He was so tormenting him.

"Gay," Floyd said quickly, like he didn't want the word on his tongue for too long. "And his father before him, and so on. Right back to the founding of Hart's Bay. My namesake—he got screwed out of a deal by a couple of gay guys and had to come down here to find his fortune."

"Only he wasn't your namesake," Elsie-Mae said impatiently. "He was called Albert. He only named himself Floyd to get away from the law, you know."

Cher choked with a stifled sound of amusement, and

Aaron bit his lip hard, too. From what he'd heard, Floyd had leaned on the leverage of being named after the town's founder for his whole life.

"But that was a long time ago, and there's no sense in keeping that grudge alive."

"Especially since it's barely true," Cher muttered under her breath, then held up her hands. "I overheard you meeting that historian you were going to get to write a book about you—I mean, about the Harts. Suddenly that went away."

"Anyway," Floyd said quickly, as if to cut off any more embarrassing anecdotes from Cher, "I'm sorry."

A moment of silence fell as Floyd waited for an answer. It took long moments before Jesse spoke, and Aaron found himself holding his breath.

"Will you tell my boyfriend that? And Rain?"

Floyd didn't even flinch, but he did drag a hand down his face. "Finn and Rain? Yeah. I'll have a word soon—if they'll let me. My son might be slower to come around, though."

"Because you've taught him to hate?" Jesse said quietly. "That's on you."

"I know." Floyd sounded sincere when he looked at Jesse. "And I'm sorry for that. I doubt people will let me forget it."

"I think you'd be surprised. People here will forgive you and move on. But you're right, they won't forget," Cher warned. "You've used up all your last chances, buddy."

Floyd nodded, and then he looked at Cher and Aaron, his gaze searching. Like he was waiting for an answer.

It took Aaron a moment to realize what they had in common: they both ran the gathering places of the town. Floyd was asking if he was welcome here. He opened his mouth, but Cher put a hand on his arm for a moment, stilling him. They made Floyd say it out loud.

"I owe you an apology, too, I guess," Floyd finally said, nodding slightly at Cher. His cheeks still burned like fire. "I'll keep my attitude out of your bar."

"Good." Cher's voice was clipped. "You know I don't give people second chances every day."

"Then... if my friends are okay with it... you're welcome here," Aaron said. He would never trust the man, but he'd serve him coffee and give him the chance to mend fences.

"I'd be glad to bring my business here. The town's looking better than it has in a long time," Floyd admitted. "I guess it's time to admit I was wrong."

Aaron caught his breath. He hadn't expected that much of an apology from the man, ever. He nodded slowly, biting his lip as the knot in his chest loosened.

It felt like a sigh of relief had just passed through the whole coffee shop. The old wounds mending, the rift closing... it could only be good for everyone.

"Well, I think I need to open tonight," Cher said briskly, clapping her hands together.

Shit. It was nearly closing time here. Aaron glanced at his watch, trying to keep it subtle. He'd stay as long as Mrs. Hart wanted to keep the place open. But she had a shrewd glance.

"Are you closing?"

"Er... I'm supposed to be, but it's okay," Aaron started to say. "Cher doesn't do tea or coffee."

"Nonsense. I'll have plenty of chances to enjoy your craft," Elsie-Mae said and winked. "Besides, I can get my red wine. I swear by a glass a day. It's medicinal, you know."

Cher laughed. "I still have your favorite," she said, offering her an arm. Then she waved at the rest of the shop. "Okay, everyone. I'm opening tonight. Clear out and let the poor boy go home."

Aaron gave her a grateful smile. He still hadn't figured out how to tell people to go home except by strongly hinting. He could take a leaf from Cher's brusque attitude.

Still woozy and dazed from having suddenly become the town's therapist couch, living room, and gossip central, Aaron just leaned on the counter to watch people file out.

Jesse came up to the counter and leaned on it. "Wow," he whispered. "I can't believe that happened."

"I know." Aaron was dizzy. It didn't feel quite real yet. "Do you believe him?"

"Weirdly, I do." Jesse looked thoughtful, and Aaron followed his gaze through the door of the coffee shop as the knot of people followed Elsie-Mae across the parking lot. She was gesturing at the harbor, clearly in the middle of telling a story. "I see a lot of her in Floyd, you know. But not quite Floyd-like."

"You mean she's the center of attention, but in a good way?" Aaron laughed. He'd instantly had a good feeling about her, which was the complete opposite of Floyd.

But tonight, seeing him humbled, Aaron had actually felt sorry for him for a few brief moments. Maybe he wasn't bad through and through.

"That's it. She brings people together instead of... well, being Floyd." Jesse grinned. "Anyway, you need help closing up?"

"Sure. If you could help me bus the tables, that would be awesome." Aaron winked. "I'll pay you in nudes."

"Oh, God." Jesse rolled his eyes and smacked Aaron's chest with the back of his hand as he grabbed a tray and made for the tables. "Glad you haven't changed a bit."

"What do you mean?" Aaron tried not to sound anxious as

he leaped on the comment. Did Jesse mean he'd been less himself lately? Was he going tame? Was that a bad thing?

Jesse shrugged and stacked cups at the nearest table while Aaron locked the door behind the last stragglers, wishing them good night. When they were alone, Jesse spoke up again. "Just that I worry about you."

"Bad idea. That sounds exhausting." Aaron tried to keep his voice perky and upbeat, but even as he said it, he realized what he was doing: deflecting. Just like Quinn had said.

"You've had a hell of a year, Aaron." Jesse shook his head. "And I thought you weren't interested in relationships. When you were suddenly dating Quinn, it seemed... weird for you. Not bad, just weird."

"Nah," Aaron said. He hoped he sounded more confident than he felt. "It's not like we're getting married, you know? I'm just giving him a date to talk about for the holidays."

"Cool, cool." Jesse stacked plates and carefully brought the tray back. "As long as you're happy."

"I am." Aaron didn't have to fake that one at all. A smile radiated across his face at the very thought of his next date with Quinn. "It's been really nice."

Jesse shared a smile, like he was in on the secret. "It is," he agreed. Then he leaned over the counter and kissed Aaron's cheek. "Now let me out—I gotta go tell Ezra what happened and lock up the gallery."

"Aye aye." Aaron swung around the counter to do just that, waving at Jesse and watching him walk across the parking lot toward the art gallery.

When he was alone, he shivered and locked up again, glancing around. The evening had set in quickly while he was busy serving coffee and defusing potential townwide arguments. Being alone in here was usually fine with him, but tonight, he wished he had a little bit more company.

After shutting the machines down, wiping every surface, and counting his cash, Aaron headed to the office to deposit everything valuable in the safe.

Only after he'd done that did he spot the manila envelope he'd forgotten about from the other day, lying on top of a pile of paperwork.

Might not be a bad idea to hire someone else soon—even part-time—to take the pressure off him. Opening six days a week was starting to tire him out.

So he flopped at the desk, tearing open the top of the envelope and reaching inside to pull the papers inside out. But instead of a neatly formatted cover letter and resume, he found a single page.

Four photos filled the page, each one fuzzy like a cheap home printer job. And every one featured Aaron.

Naked.

A chill ran down his spine, and his hands started to shake. It wasn't hard to identify them—three were the usual nudes he sent guys to keep their interest until they could arrange a time to meet up.

In one picture, he looked over his shoulder at the camera, grinning, his ass up in the air. In the second, he was being fucked by a guy doggy-style. And in the third, he lay on his back, hard cock against his stomach, hands above his head. He'd gotten hookups to take each of them for him.

But one was newer than the rest, a selfie of him showing off his ass in the bathroom mirror at this very coffee shop. He'd sent it to Bryon during that hellish opening week, trying to placate him for ditching the hookup.

That meant this could only be one person—or that Bryon had shared the photos.

"Fuck," Aaron whispered. He'd never seen his photos printed out like this. On Grindr or WhatsApp, it was easy to send and forget. But seeing them here, in an unmarked envelope...

The shake in Aaron's hands intensified as he grabbed for the envelope and swept his fingertips inside, then peered in. No note, no other paper at all. Flipping the page showed only a blank underside.

With no message, the threat was implied.

Aaron's heart sank. He'd never had anything to lose by sending these photos before. Nobody had ever stooped low enough to use them against him, anyway.

After a lifetime unlearning shame and embracing his own sexuality, the mere sight of these photos brought him crashing back to the reality he'd escaped years ago.

To the conversations where his own family had dismissed him and taunted him—for being so desperate for love that he'd looked anywhere and everywhere.

"Fuck you, Bryon," Aaron hissed. But even the angry words couldn't shift the emotion in his chest from fear to the fury he deserved to feel. He just felt small, scared, and vulnerable.

What was he going to do?

There was no question—he had to hide it. This was the kind of stuff that would scare Quinn off for good. His parents barely tolerated Aaron as it was. Imagine if this got back to them. Quinn could deal with Aaron having a past, but what about when that past tried to invade his present? Threatened his future? Could he understand?

Aaron was terrified that the answer might be *hell no.*

Quinn was the kind of straight-laced guy that didn't dare peek out of the box. He might be able to tolerate Aaron, but that was it. Quinn wasn't going to get turned on by the idea that some loser was jerking it to his temporary boyfriend.

He ought to hold on to them, he knew, but the idea of keeping this where anyone could see it and judge him just sat in his stomach like a lead weight. What good would it do?

Before Aaron's brain caught up with his body, he was stuffing the paper back in the envelope, reaching for the shredder. He fed it into the slot, his breathing shallow and fast as he pulled his hand back and watched it chew through the rest of the paper before going quiet.

That was it. It was gone. He didn't have to think about it anymore.

Aaron focused on his breath—in and out. In the silence of the office, his hands finally stopped shaking and his gut settled where it should be.

All he had to do was wait out Bryon. One day, he'd get bored. Everyone did. And Aaron had learned his lesson—no more assholes who pinged his gut instinct the wrong way. The sex wasn't worth it.

It would all blow over; Bryon would see that he was well and truly unavailable and go away. In the meantime, Quinn could never know about this. There was no way that could end well.

16

QUINN

"What romantic stuff are you subjecting me to tonight?" Aaron laid the back of his hand on his forehead and pretended to collapse against the porch railing. "Splitting dessert? Baths with floating candles? Gazing into each other's eyes in the moonlight?"

Quinn laughed, turning to follow Aaron down the stairs from his house to the sidewalk. He knew Aaron wasn't being serious, because just a minute ago, Beau had answered the door but Aaron had pushed him out of the way and leaped onto the porch like an excitable baby gazelle.

"Well, you seemed to like looking at the lights," Quinn said. "So I thought we could walk around and see them."

Aaron's face lit up. "So that's why you told me to eat dinner before you arrived."

A flash of guilt coursed through Quinn. He should tell Aaron that he was back on his usual diet. But he couldn't bear the idea of giving up those candlelit dinners that Aaron was making fun of.

He just gave Aaron a smile. "Bingo. And then when we

need to warm up..." Quinn winked. "My house won't be far away."

"I like the way you think, Mr. Powell." Aaron wrapped his hand around Quinn's bicep and beamed at him. "Lead on."

They strolled out the front gate and turned to walk down the street. This time, they weren't rushing to find a private moment. They could slow down and enjoy the glow of warm lights in the foggy evening.

It was the perfect evening to look at the decorations around the neighborhood—it wasn't raining, but a touch of fog had rolled in. An orb glowed around every light, from the streetlights to the strings of LEDs decking trees and porches.

"How was your day?" Aaron asked, still firmly clasping Quinn's arm as they stopped to admire a small pine tree now wrapped in multicolored lights.

"Exciting for one reason," Quinn said, grinning. "It was my last day of client work before Christmas."

"Oh!" Aaron beamed. "How long is your break?"

"Just until the twenty-seventh," Quinn said. *By which time, Marv expects me to look like an underwear model.* He stifled the sigh at the thought. A crash diet was never fun, but if it was his best option... "How about you? Mom called and said she heard from—" No, he could cut out the middle of her story and get to the good part. "Uh, long story short, that she heard Floyd came into your place a few days ago. Everything all right? Cher told me to warn you he might sniff around..."

Aaron gasped and clutched Quinn's arm. "That's right! Oh my God. Did you hear everything that happened?"

Quinn laughed. "No. Mom got distracted telling me about Elsie-Mae Hart moving back to town or something?"

That was all it took to set Aaron off. The story rushed out

in a burble of words, punctuated with flourishing gestures and "Can you believe it?"s.

Quinn just nodded and shook his head at appropriate moments. It *was* a surprise to hear that Floyd had admitted he was wrong, and even tried to make up with everyone at the art gallery. And most of all, Cher.

"Well, that explains the rumors." Quinn rolled his eyes as Aaron lit up with curiosity. "It's nothing exciting. Just that Floyd tried to take Cher on a date once."

"More than that!" Then Aaron clapped a hand over his mouth and looked guilty, like he wasn't supposed to tell.

"Oh, God. There's a thought I didn't need." Quinn didn't care if Floyd had been a playboy in his day, but he still didn't want to know about it.

Aaron snickered. "No, no. Cher has better taste than him, I'm sure. I mean, it was a marriage proposal."

"Oh," Quinn blinked. "Well, I'm glad she didn't get pulled into his orbit."

"Seriously. He would have just bankrupted her, too, I'm sure," Aaron muttered. "If the business went down and took out her retirement fund, too... I can see why he's so touchy about it. But if he was stressed out about it, he could have... asked for help or something. Or told his own family. Rain had no idea. I haven't talked to Finn yet, but I bet he would have helped."

"You mean now and then, we all have to ask for help?" Quinn shook his head, swinging their hands as they kept walking. "Sounds fake, but okay," he joked.

Aaron hummed under his breath. "I mean, it's hard when it's family." That edge crept into his voice, like he wasn't quite standing on solid ground as he talked about the topic.

It still felt sore between them, and Quinn's guilt had never faded about that dinner last week. "Yeah? I guess you're right," Quinn said. The knife twisting in his belly reminded him that he hadn't been able to stand up to his own family just days ago for Aaron's sake.

"You should know. We both should." Aaron gave him a crooked smile. "We have more in common than I thought, considering how opposite we are."

Quinn wanted to protest. His words came unbidden, before he could think about them. "My parents might be higher-pressure than a tire factory, but at least they care. If anything, too much."

Aaron tensed up—Quinn could feel it just in the way his fingers tightened. "So do mine," he said, a little too defensive. "They just care about the wrong stuff."

"Yeah?" Quinn wanted to be relieved to hear that, but he wasn't sure he believed it. He wasn't even sure Aaron believed it himself.

"They thought they were getting a real boy who liked baseball cards and red meat. They didn't know what to do with someone like... well..." Aaron waved a hand up and down himself. His laugh was light, yet there was a forced note. It wasn't the full, rich laugh Aaron gave at Quinn's bad jokes.

"No, no," Quinn interrupted, letting go of Aaron's hand and gripping his thin shoulders. "Don't do that."

Aaron's brows shot up, and those pretty, soft lips parted. He tipped his chin all the way back so he could make eye contact. "Do what?"

"Put yourself down like that." Quinn squeezed carefully, well aware that his grip was stronger than he thought. "Sweetie, *I* know what to do with someone like you." But would Aaron welcome his words, or push him away? Quinn's anxiety ratcheted up another notch.

They were alone on the street, and Quinn was grateful. He didn't want this to be everyone's business. Aaron looked like he was hardly breathing. He looped his arms around Quinn's lower back rather than pushing him away and laughing.

That had to be a good sign, right? Either way, Quinn was about to plunge forward into the fog. He only prayed it didn't lead him over a dangerous clifftop.

"What's that?" Aaron's voice was a bare whisper over the breeze ruffling through the nearby forest and the steady hum of waves in the distance.

"Cherish you. Enjoy every smile and dirty joke. Let you soar in your own way, not try to force you into a mold that never fit." Quinn's throat was tight. If only Aaron knew how much his chest ached with the desire to do just that—to pull Aaron off his feet and into Quinn's world, headlong. To stand between him and anyone who dared to judge him.

To keep him and love him for his very own.

Aaron gulped hard, his reaction hard to judge apart from the surprise that widened his eyes. Was it a good or bad kind? Quinn couldn't tell. Aaron's gaze flickered between Quinn's eyes like he couldn't make up his mind on that very question.

"Well, that's not the worst idea." Aaron's voice wobbled as he tried to joke. The corners of his lips curled up in a soft smile. He didn't push Quinn away or snort derisively or anything.

He was listening. Quinn's shoulders sank with relief. His grin came instantly. "Yeah? I have good ideas. I'm full of them. Or full of *something*, anyway."

Aaron laughed, but as a cool breeze swept in, the fog shifted around them. He shivered and tucked his hands in his pockets. "Shall we keep walking?"

Quinn let go of him and kissed his forehead, then slid his hand into Aaron's pocket to hold hands. "Yeah. Don't get a chill right before Christmas." He tried to look innocent. "Oh, yeah. Speaking of which... totally randomly... we should talk about that."

Aaron laughed. "That's the most subtle segue I've ever heard. Well done."

"Thanks. I've been saving it up for days." Quinn was only half-joking, but Aaron laughed anyway. "So, what are your plans?"

"God, everyone around me seems to have one. Is it *that* weird that I don't?" Aaron asked.

"Three days before the big day, I'd say... unusual." Quinn chose his words with tact. "You don't want to see your family?"

"Whether I want to or not, they're away. Going on a cruise."

Quinn furrowed his brow, turning those words over in his head. "Wait, they're going on a cruise... over Christmas... without inviting you?" He straightened up indignantly. "Well, that's just bullshit."

"They did invite me, but then I decided to open Howya Bean and I backed out." Aaron worked his jaw around, but at least he wasn't *really* defending them. "I didn't really wanna go anyway, so I'm glad. They're a bunch of politicians. Literally. And they act like it."

"Politicians?"

"My dad's the mayor of some shitty city," Aaron muttered, hunching his shoulders and casting a quick glance up at him.

Quinn nodded once. "Ahhh." Well, that explained a lot. That was about the most un-Aaron career he could imagine. No wonder they'd driven him away—or he'd run away himself. "If you want, you can join me." Quinn tried not to sound like he was begging, even though he really, *really* wanted him to do so. Still, his puppy-dog charm was turned up to eleven. "Just the two of us? No pressure?"

It worked. Aaron took one look at Quinn's face and melted. He laughed, stumbling into him as he walked. "Well, who could say no to that face? But I don't want to... get in the way of you and your family."

"Pffft." Quinn blew a raspberry, which made the tension melt away from Aaron's expression again. "No way. I'd rather spend the day with you. They won't mind"—he crossed his fingers behind his back—"as long as I'm not alone."

Aaron squeezed his hand. "You could help me out at Howya Bean? I want to open that day for a few hours so anyone who doesn't have a place to go can... hang out and have a little party. I can't really afford catering or anything, but I'm collecting board games and that kind of stuff."

Oh God, I wish he were the marrying kind. Quinn couldn't keep the adoration from his face. "That's amazing of you."

"Gotta pass the time somehow. It was that or an orgy, but apparently that would be a *health code violation*," Aaron said with a playful grin. He stopped to study a yard full of tacky inflatable Christmas decorations. "We can have Christmas dinner beforehand. Just the two of us."

Crap. While they were planning, Quinn really should tell the truth about his diet, but then he'd have to admit how damn insecure the whole thing made him. And Aaron would assure him he was hot the way it was, and Quinn would be right back to an awkward eighteen-year-old with a bit of a belly, and a round face, and utterly invisible to everyone around him.

Without really noticing, they'd made it almost to Quinn's house. The lights were pretty, but Quinn was used to seeing them every year. It was much more interesting to watch

Aaron's reactions. As always when Aaron was around, Quinn's focus zeroed in on him.

"Oh, look where we are," Aaron said, giggling. "How convenient."

Quinn tried for innocence. "You'd think I planned it."

Aaron didn't buy his attempt for a second. He just smirked and fluttered his lashes, putting an extra sway into his hips. "What you want is another one of those mind-and-dick-blowing Aaronjobs."

"Aaronjob?" Quinn loved seeing him so blatantly seductive. It was silly, but still somehow sexy.

"Patent pending."

Quinn grinned and held open the front gate for Aaron, then led him up the steps. "If you're offering, I'd never say no. Anytime, anywhere…" At the gleam in Aaron's eyes, he reconsidered quickly. "Anywhere I won't be arrested."

"Damn. What's life without a bit of risk?" Aaron pouted, and Quinn stopped by the front door to kiss the pout off his pretty little mouth. Aaron stretched onto tiptoes, but after a few moments, he couldn't hide his shiver.

"Okay, let's warm you up," Quinn said, laughing as he unlocked the door and let Aaron in.

Growing up, his parents had been one of the few households to actually lock the door. Even now he always did it, but he knew some people in town didn't. With more tourists here lately, he figured it couldn't hurt to be too careful.

It did force him to be patient before he could suck Aaron's face off, though.

"Phew," Quinn sighed and ditched his coat in the closet. His shoes got tucked neatly in the bottom, and he bent over to place Aaron's in there, too.

Aaron pinched his ass. "Helloooo there. What a fine piece of meat."

"I have a name." Quinn pretended to be offended, clutching his chest as he stood up. He was starting to channel a bit of Aaron from time to time.

"It's on the tip of my tongue... or it's about to be." Aaron pushed his tongue into his cheek and grabbed Quinn's hand. With surprising strength, he towed Quinn into the living room. Quinn managed to turn on a lamp on the way past, but that was it.

Aaron shoved him onto the couch, and for a lithe little guy, he had some push in him.

"Oh, hello," Quinn said with a laugh, bouncing against the seat. He stretched out and laced his fingers behind his head, waiting to see what Aaron would do.

Aaron straddled Quinn, one knee pressing into the couch seat beside Quinn's thigh. As he swung the other knee up, he winced and held up a finger, then scooped his phone out of his pocket with his fingertips. "Ow." He laid it on the coffee table and tried again, his weight settling onto Quinn's thighs. "That's better."

Quinn laughed. "That's the downside of skinny jeans."

"But on the upside is the backside." Aaron winked. He leaned in again, but as if by unspoken agreement, this wasn't a wild rush to strip. They took their time to explore, lips wandering across jawlines, teeth closing around earlobes.

By the time Quinn kissed down Aaron's neck, he was whimpering and squirming. "Hold on," Aaron breathed out, peeling himself off Quinn. He gave him a sheepish grin as he trotted for the bathroom. "I hydrated too well."

Quinn grinned and stretched as he watched Aaron walk

across the hardwood floor on his tiptoes like he was trying to avoid the cool surface.

"God, my hands are cold!" Aaron yelped, his voice carrying from the bathroom, which made Quinn laugh.

The smallest thing caught his eye. He wouldn't have intentionally *looked* at Aaron's phone, but it was lying right there and it lit up, the sudden glare bright in the dark living room.

And he couldn't help but notice what app had sent Aaron the notification. The orange and black icon was easy for any gay guy remotely in tune with today's hookup culture—even one who'd never been on it.

Grindr.

The phone went off a few more times in a row before it went quiet, and Quinn finally realized he wasn't breathing. His throat was tight and raw all of a sudden, and a tight knot in his stomach didn't want to unfurl.

"Sorry about that," Aaron said, sliding across the floor toward Quinn with every step.

Quinn stood up, his head whirling. He didn't want to suddenly get sucked right into what they'd been about to do. Not without a chance to think. "That's all right. Want anything to drink?"

"Sure, I'll take some water, thanks." Aaron crashed on the couch and picked up his phone.

Quinn lingered for a moment, pretending to stretch so he could watch Aaron's reaction.

A slight frown, tension in his shoulders, and then his gaze flickered up to Quinn.

Crap. Don't give it away. The last thing Quinn wanted was Aaron to think he was spying on him. And it *did* feel kind of weird that he'd seen that notification—intrusive, somehow.

"Back in a sec," Quinn just said and smiled. Aaron didn't seem to notice anything off.

He made it to the kitchen before another dizzying wave of uncertainty swept through him. The hot and cold that flushed his cheeks and crept down his spine made his hands shake as he filled up water glasses.

Did he have any right to ask what Aaron was up to? They might be kinda-sorta boyfriendish, but not for real. And their fling was expiring soon. Ten days lay between this moment of shattered bliss and the moment it would really hit the fan.

What if Aaron was just biding his time, keeping his options open? That was unthinkable to contemplate. Quinn couldn't imagine another *option* besides Aaron. Couldn't imagine even flirting with someone right now, when all his dreams and desires were so intensely focused on Aaron.

Quinn clutched his chest and rubbed gently, but it did nothing to soothe the ache, because it was inside.

Crap. Aaron was going to expect sex today, and now Quinn didn't know if he was in the mood.

They'd rushed into unprotected sex awfully fast, taking it on each other's word that everything was negative. But he did trust Aaron. He *had* to trust Aaron. Was that a mistake?

One thing at a time, Quinn told himself. He couldn't dawdle in the kitchen anymore without an excuse, so he rushed over to a cabinet and rustled around, searching for a bag of chips.

All he could do tonight was give Aaron what only Quinn could: real care and affection, the kind he seemed to have been starved of for so long.

"I thought we could watch a movie?" Quinn announced as he came back into the room and Aaron put down his phone.

He forced himself not to wonder what Aaron had been typing —and to whom—just moments ago.

"Instead of an Aaronjob?" Aaron gasped.

Quinn smiled as he settled down next to him and put his arm around his shoulders. He pulled him in, kissing his temple. "Rain check? And, while we're at it, check-in?"

If Aaron was keeping his options open in order to call this off, he wanted to know right now. Not after Christmas, when he'd spent all this time daydreaming and hoping and wishing for more.

Aaron's face fell. He glanced down for a few long moments before visibly shaking off the disappointment and offering a smile. "No problem. About what?" Aaron twisted and reached behind himself, grabbing the blanket Quinn kept there. He shook it out and wrapped it around both of their shoulders, then leaned into his side.

"We're good, right?" Quinn asked. "You're okay with the romantic Christmas light walk, and a romantic cuddle and a movie right now?"

Aaron relaxed, like he'd expected something very different. That didn't put Quinn's heart at ease, because all he could think of was the deadline crashing toward them. "Oh! Yeah, babe, that's fine." Almost carelessly, he grabbed the remote. "It's part of the deal. I put up with being wooed, you put up with getting off a lot. But it *is* kind of nice to spend time together with our clothes on."

"Perfect," Quinn said, covering up the twist in his gut with a smile. "Then pick a movie and let's do this."

Hopefully something with car chases and explosions, and he then he stood half a chance of forgetting that quietly vibrating phone and the flash of guilt in Aaron's eyes.

Please let me be right about the man I've chosen, Quinn

thought as the movie started. He tightened his grip around Aaron's shoulders and smiled as Aaron shifted until he lay on the couch, his head in Quinn's lap. Instinctively, softly, he stroked his hair.

Quinn couldn't be wrong. He just couldn't. If he *was*, he wouldn't be able to handle it.

Everything was going to be fine... as long as he kept his mouth shut and didn't let that insecure, whiny Quinn out to the see the light of day. Ever.

17

AARON

Aaron could see his breath in the air. That meant it was an unusually chilly morning, even for December. So far, winter in Hart's Bay had been much like central Oregon, where they rarely saw snow—just a bit foggier. But today, the breeze nipped at the tip of his nose and made his fingers tingle.

The fog had stuck around, too, a thick blanket that dampened even the ever-present mutter of the waves. Aaron was walking to work by himself today, as usual. Surprisingly, Ezra had been awake at this hour.

At first, Aaron had thought Ezra was stressing out about the fog after his traumatic experience being lost in it just days ago. But instead, Ezra seemed delighted at the excuse to keep Rusty on dry land. He'd taken off for Rusty's before Aaron was even done with his toast. Someone was definitely getting laid, Aaron thought as he smiled.

Aaron squinted through the fog and picked his steps down the nearby path between houses, a shortcut to the town square. The route sloped and twisted around trees before emerging behind Cher's, where it was just a couple minutes' stroll to Howya Bean.

Despite Aaron's chattering teeth, it was a still, peaceful morning like any other. All Aaron heard was his own harsh breath as he tried to avoid twisting an ankle on the wet grass.

Until a branch snapped nearby.

Aaron skidded to a halt—but not in time to avoid crashing into a warm, strong pair of arms as a man stepped out from the trees, straight into the middle of the path.

His smile quickly turned Aaron's surprise into disgust. "Bryon?"

Without warning, the man's slimy little hands were on Aaron's hips. Not in the way one of his friends would have grabbed him to keep him upright, either. Bryon's fingertips rubbed in the hollow next to Aaron's hipbone.

The unwanted intimacy made Aaron's stomach lurch. He wrenched himself backward and out of Bryon's grasp. He skidded on the grass again, arms windmilling, but kept his balance and Bryon didn't try to grab him again—yet.

Instead, Bryon folded his arms and smirked at Aaron. "Fancy meeting you here." His voice was smooth and even, and it sent fear trailing down Aaron's spine in a single, intense wave. Bryon's eyes slowly slid up and down Aaron, head to toe and back again. He even licked his lips slightly, his nostrils flaring like Aaron was prey and he was on his trail.

If Aaron hadn't been chilled to the bone before, he was now.

What the hell was Bryon up to, lingering around this path at five thirty in the morning? Shit, this meant he was watching Aaron! He knew Aaron's daily routine and where to meet him —alone, without the prying glare of a security camera or other customers.

The adrenaline swept away the sick feeling as danger pulsed through his veins instead. Aaron hated it—hating being vulnerable, even for a moment.

"If you're planning to try anything, I'll break your nose," Aaron told him flatly. Grandma had shocked his parents by teaching him how to break a nose when he came out in middle school. It had come in handy now and again. He was already shaking with anticipation, not sure if he could snap into action fast enough.

Bryon snorted derisively, like Aaron was crazy. The way he stared down his very breakable nose set Aaron's teeth on edge. "Of course I'm not *trying* anything, gorgeous," Bryon said in the most patronizing tone ever, like he was talking to an airhead. "I like you, remember? I wouldn't hurt you. But you didn't answer me." He pouted, childish for a moment. "That hurts my feelings, you know. The deadline's tonight."

The more he said he wouldn't hurt Aaron, the less safe Aaron felt. He swallowed back the sick feeling, his fingers curling into fists.

Worse, Bryon tried to close the gap between them as he spoke. With every step he took forward, Aaron took one back. He didn't want to let Bryon close enough to touch him. Once was more than enough.

Aaron squinted at Bryon. What the hell was he talking about? "What deadline, you fucking creep?"

Bryon just smirked, and Aaron's eyes were drawn to the hand hooking a thumb through his belt loop next to his crotch. For a single moment, he'd thought Bryon's hand was going somewhere else.

Aaron stumbled over a root and reached behind himself, steadying himself on the trunk of a tree.

No, wait. Why was he letting Bryon command all the

space here? If he kept backing down, Bryon would think he was winning.

Aaron's heart pounded as he shook his head to get some sense into it. It was time to stand up for himself. Aaron felt like a trembling leaf in a windstorm, but he stepped forward. He had to tip his chin up to stare defiantly into Bryon's eyes. "What deadline?"

"The one I messaged you about." Bryon didn't try to touch him, but he leaned down, his breath hot and sour. Ugh.

His next words, though, plunged Aaron into a sudden, icy shock like he'd slipped on the cliff edge.

"I found out who your dad is."

Shit. How the hell did he do that? He must have Googled me or something. But Aaron had trained himself not to react to mentions of his family.

Aaron was expressive by nature, to say the least, but he'd learned early how to develop a practiced blank face. He just hated having to use it. It felt fake, and it took a toll on him.

He stared coolly at Bryon while his heart thumped harder. His palms were sweaty, and he heard his blood pounding in his ears, making it hard to hear anything else past the noise.

What would they think? Say? Do? God, Aaron knew the answers to each of those questions. They would do anything to put themselves as far from that scandal as possible. And that included handing him over to the media, letting them have a field day. Or worse, using the chance to remind him what he'd given up—a nice, all-American family—in his "quest for hedonistic pleasure," as his dad had put it.

But Aaron wasn't going to give Bryon the satisfaction of showing his racing thoughts. Instead he shrugged, letting a bored sort of annoyance creep into his voice so as not to give anything away. "Good for you. Am I supposed to give a shit?"

"If you don't give me what I want, I'll go to the papers."

Aaron could see right through those words. Bryon was bluffing. He didn't care about outing Aaron—who was already as out as it was possible to be—or embarrassing his family.

All he wanted was leverage. And the moment Bryon released those photos, he'd lose the only leverage he had. Despite the sickening roll in Aaron's stomach at the threat, he reminded himself over and over that he had the upper hand.

Please let me be right about this. If he wasn't... Aaron's life might be about to blow up. Again.

"Still not seeing why I should care," Aaron bluffed right back. God, it was hard to hear over the throbbing in his ears. He clicked his tongue and yawned, trying to bring the pressure down. Normally he hated lying, but he'd happily stretch the truth to get this perv off his back. "They've kicked me out. I don't give a shit about them. Hell, I should have thought of leaking my own nudes. I'd pay to see their faces."

Bryon's face fell for a moment—Aaron spotted it. He stood there for a minute, chest heaving.

"Now if you're done giving me fabulous ideas for revenge on a bunch of pricks who deserve me only *slightly* more than you do... I have a coffee shop to open and probably customers waiting by now." Aaron drew himself up to his full height as he stepped around Bryon. He kept his gaze fixed on Bryon, ready to dodge a blow or grab.

Neither came. Bryon's arms were still folded, his jaw tight. "I guess you're still fucking that..." Thankfully, he trailed off. His lip curled and expression twitched like he was deciding what word to use.

"Happily, yes. The only fuck I'll give you is this: fuck out of my life forever," Aaron snapped.

He shouldered past Bryon, pulse faster than a butterfly's

wings, and strode down the wet, grassy path toward Cher's. He was almost within sight of the building now.

Thankfully for his ego, the path held underfoot—no unexpected slipups to undermine his dramatic exit.

Aaron kept his ears peeled for any sound that Bryon was following him. When he was around the corner and Cher's bar came into sight, he broke into a sprint.

But Bryon didn't follow him. He cast glances over his shoulder by the time he got to the bar and saw nothing. Even as he reached the glass front window and slowed down, out of breath and wheezing, there was no sign of him.

He must have given up and went back to bed like a normal human being. Thank God.

Aaron was still jumpy as his day started, nearly spilling hot water over himself twice before Yolanda came in to join him for the morning rush.

"What's got you twitching today?" Yolanda asked once the rush had gone. She leaned against the counter, head tipped to one curious side.

"Just... nothing," Aaron said, rubbing his forehead. Then he couldn't help himself. He'd told enough lies today. "Just this guy who keeps coming in. Look, let me show you a photo of him in case he tries to come in when I'm not here. He's banned."

His screenshots of Bryon's Grindr profile were easy to find in his Safety folder within his photo album.

Yolanda leaned in to take a look. She raised an eyebrow. "Damn, that boy's good-looking." The question wasn't very well hidden in her statement.

Aaron sighed deeply. "I'm sure he knows that more than any of us." With an ego that size, he was sure of it. Didn't the guy have other cute twinks in the area he could bug? He wasn't ugly. He could get laid if he just treated people half-decently.

Not tried to bully them into sex, then blackmail them. If only he'd taken the chance to puke on Bryon while he'd had it. But he wasn't worth the aftertaste.

Oh, God. Was it blackmail if he'd sent Bryon the photos himself? How many other men had photos or videos of him just lying around on their phones? Aaron's hands started to shake, and he grabbed the Windex and a cloth to wipe down the display cabinet.

Yolanda raised her eyebrows and wiped down the machines, not saying anything. Waiting for him to talk.

But Aaron didn't want to. It was one of the few times in his life he'd felt shame, and he didn't know how to handle the raw, wretched pinch in his stomach or the stiffness in his back.

It hurt, and he hated it.

Every time he did, he was right back in one of the worst moments of his life: when his dad had hired the PR firm the day after they discovered him sandwiched between two men on the living room couch.

The whole hour-long conversation where they'd tried to grill him about his sex life, reminding him that he was "a risk" to his dad's mayoral career. His sexuality, his whole coming out, had just been an inconvenience—a political weakness for the people around him.

Fuck Bryon, honestly. He was taking the rejection way too personally, and Aaron feared he'd been wrong to call his bluff. What if he *did* release the photos just to spite him? He was that kind of person.

If it hit the news, even as a minor interest piece, everyone in town would know within hours. Especially Quinn—and worse, his parents. No way would they accept for their son the kind of boyfriend who would even take nude photos.

And Quinn was so wrapped up in wanting to please his family that Aaron wasn't sure this wouldn't be the breaking point.

Would this be a step too far? What if their little cozy arrangement went up in flames not because Quinn thought less of Aaron for it, but because the rest of Quinn's world did?

Or, knowing Quinn, he'd let the arrangement quietly expire before extricating himself, so as not to hurt Aaron's feelings. He was that stupidly considerate, the jerk. Aaron tried not to laugh as tears sprang to his eyes. He turned his back to dab them with his thumb.

Aaron wished he could just wrap himself tightly around Quinn, bury his head against his chest, and never let go. Never let anything get between them, never leave the room. Just him and the beautiful, sweet, gentle giant he'd been so utterly surprised to fall for.

"Go take a break," Yolanda told him. She was frowning, clearly worried but not intruding yet. "I've got things here."

Aaron managed a quick smile. "Thanks." He made it to the office before he opened his phone—and Grindr.

Until this month, it would have been out of habit. Anytime someone hurt Aaron, he could just find someone else to wallpaper over the pain for a few hours. Easy peasy, and totally not catching up to him now.

This time, he was doing it deliberately, but his interest wasn't in the other profiles in the area. He was looking for Bryon.

There. Easy to find, with his blank profile and signature handle: *suck me* with a string of five emojis: an eggplant, milk carton, droplets, closed fist, and pair of lips. Read in order, it was an efficient hint.

Except now, it read *Aaron*, with a string of winking emojis. His profile, instead of being a bunch of crap about him being a good lay, was also different. It said *Ready for me yet?*

The nausea made Aaron's stomach twist sharply. None of that was what he was looking for, though. He swallowed back his disgust and swiped past the shirtless, faceless photo.

Distance: 2,438 feet.

Good.

Aaron let out a sigh of relief. As long as he was more than a thousand feet away, Aaron would be happy.

A thousand feet. It didn't sound like much. It was a fraction of the distance Aaron wished he could put between himself and that creeper.

The best part of a small town was also the worst, Aaron was finding; he was never more than a few thousand feet from his friends and enemies alike.

Aaron closed the app and leaned heavily on the counter. At least he'd given up for now—but the threat hung heavily over Aaron's head.

Aaron's parents would be livid if they found out about this from some nosy reporter. Of course, they had left for the cruise yesterday. And he doubted they'd be paying for cruise ship internet, since mayors didn't actually earn the salary of a demigod. They just had the ego of one.

His dad's PR firm would want to know, though. His family had made it clear that anything he did that was "a risk" to them should be relayed through the PR firm. They didn't want to know about anything else. Not until he'd married a nice, decent man and lived a discreet, quiet life keeping up with the Joneses.

And Aaron might have left them behind, might only talk to them occasionally now, but he still felt some thread of obligation to warn them what was coming. If he didn't, there went the chance of him ever making up with them.

And a teeny-tiny part of Aaron had wanted to do just that for years. To be the kind of guy they'd approve of. He was closer than ever, hovering on the edge of giving Quinn a chance. They'd like Quinn.

Damn it, they'd like Quinn a lot more than they liked Aaron.

Sighing, Aaron told Yolanda, "Back in a minute." Then he headed outside, milling about and scuffing gravel in the border between the outdoor seating area and the concrete harbor.

The number was still saved in his phone book under "Cockblockers." That, at least, made Aaron snicker. For a brief month after that first time being caught by his parents, he'd actually *listened* to what these guys had to say.

Then he'd realized he didn't have to do anything they said, least of all live a chaste life trying to fly under the radar. It wasn't like his family was under the scrutiny of a national political campaign, after all. His dad was just mayor of one small city in Oregon.

"Layton's," the phone voice answered, cold and efficient.

"This is Aaron Fisher. I have a message for Michael."

"Let me transfer you now."

Aaron waited for his dad's PR manager to pick up. When he finally did, he only had a brisk "Aaron? What can I do for you?"

Aaron couldn't fail to notice that his tone was crisp, with perhaps a sharp edge to it. There was no love lost still. "I'm giving you a heads-up about something."

Michael didn't actually *say* "uh oh," but Aaron felt it radiating through the phone nonetheless. Could a death stare travel by radio waves? "Go on."

"There's a guy in my life. An ass who wants something from me. He's threatening to leak some nudes and make a scandal for my parents. I doubt anyone actually gives a shit what one mayor's kid does, but I'm sure Dad will care."

Michael's intake of breath was carefully controlled. "I see. Well, the first rule—"

"Don't talk to the press. I know," Aaron drawled, rolling his eyes. "I'm not saying jack shit to anyone."

"Let me talk to the team and see if we can suppress this, for your sake—"

Oh, Aaron was not going to put up with that snarky tone. Like Michael was doing *him* a favor. "I don't care if they do get published. I'll consider it an ad. I'm not asking for help with the situation. Consider this a warning, that's all."

"Noted." Michael's tone was stiff. "Compromising photos —is that it? Anything else we should be aware of? We'll issue the usual statement, if need be."

Aaron knew the one he meant: *The mayor supports his relatives' right to make their own life choices in due privacy.*

Like Aaron was something distasteful they wanted to hide from the world. No longer was he even family—just related to them. Which was true, really.

Today, all he wanted to do was go home and wrap himself in a blanket burrito. Maybe wiggle his way downstairs for supper.

That image, at least, brought a smile that helped Aaron breathe easier. "Sure. That statement's fine. Catch you later." Then he hung up and shoved his phone into his pocket, wishing he could slam the receiver.

Whatever Aaron said, he felt like he was three years

younger, staring sullenly across the desk at Michael's barely suppressed judgmental stare while his mother and father flanked him. Talked about him, like he wasn't even there.

One thing was for sure: he couldn't see Quinn tonight. Not after all this shit. He wouldn't be able to keep in his angst, and then sweet Quinn would try to ask what was wrong, and...

Well, Aaron couldn't tell him what had happened. It wasn't worth the worry he'd cause Quinn when Quinn hadn't even shown a sign he wanted him for longer than their little experiment.

Yeah. A blanket burrito was definitely happening. And wine. This called for a stop by the grocery store on the walk home.

If ever Aaron needed proof that he wasn't boyfriend material, he had more than enough now. Quinn didn't deserve a guy like Aaron—who only cared about getting his rocks off, never mind what it did to anyone around him.

Not being boyfriend material was supposed to be fine with him... but it wasn't. Shit.

But it was only the beginning of his day, so he had hours before he could think about any of this stuff. Aaron snapped to attention as Roy Hart, Finn's uncle, approached with a friendly smile and wave.

Aaron pasted a grin on his own face. It was gonna be a long fucking day until his reunion with Victor's finest five-buck chuck.

1 8

QUINN

Normally on Christmas Eve, Quinn was getting ready for a day of watching TV, day-drinking while relatives he didn't know visited his parents, and gossiping about those relatives after they left.

But for the first time ever, Quinn was excited to roll out of bed, chug his slimy morning protein shake, and grab a shower.

Before they'd even made plans, Quinn had gone clothes shopping on the off chance that Aaron agreed to spend Christmas with him. He was armed with new jeans and a red-and-white softly striped knitted sweater—like a candy cane but less obnoxious. He could see Aaron snuggling into it—and him. Hopefully his plan was subtle and compelling enough to work.

The plan had originally been for Quinn to come over last night so they had all of Christmas Eve and Christmas Day together. But Aaron had called Quinn after work yesterday and told him to wait until today. He'd given Yolanda the week off between Christmas Day and New Year's to visit her parents. In exchange, Aaron was taking all of Christmas Eve off. That meant more time to spend with him.

As for *why* Aaron hadn't wanted him over last night, Quinn tried not to worry. He'd said he was tired out, and Quinn had heard it in his voice. He didn't blame him one bit. With all the foot traffic in Hart Square, Aaron must have been pulling crazy days.

But it did add to Quinn's lingering doubt that Aaron was planning on keeping him around much longer. From the start, he'd known that Aaron just wasn't the type to commit. Or maybe more to the point, that Quinn wasn't the right guy to win his heart.

He only had a week to show Aaron what it would be like with him. That didn't seem like nearly enough time to persuade him to overcome a lifetime of holding people at arm's length. And the moment he tried to ask Aaron to make this permanent, Quinn was convinced that Aaron would walk out on him—agreement or no.

Aaron kept saying stuff that Quinn couldn't make heads nor tails of. Only little things, but things he could interpret as *interest* in him. But then Aaron would laugh and move on to some other topic, and Quinn would be left aching.

Quinn could read Aaron so well—so why couldn't he work out what Aaron wanted here?

Maybe Aaron doesn't know what he wants. But Quinn wasn't sure if that was the truth, or just him hoping that he had a chance with him.

After his morning workout, weigh-in, and reviewing some client notes, Quinn could finally call it midmorning.

His throat tightened as he ran his fingers across the wrapped gifts on the dining room table. Quinn suddenly found himself rethinking everything.

Maybe he should pick up roses and chocolate instead— woo him with all he had. Quinn bit his lip and shook his head.

No, he'd do better winning Aaron over with his actions than stereotypical romantic gestures.

Or maybe he'd pushed it too far. He could try to go the total opposite direction: buy Aaron a copy of *Die Hard* and popcorn, play it casual. But that felt like it would disrespect what they'd built together in the last week. And it would send the wrong signal—that he just wanted to be friends.

God, where was his fairy godmother when he needed advice? Probably in bed, having closed her bar in Hart Square late last night.

Quinn smiled and shook his head. "No, I'm an adult," he said out loud, like that would make him believe it. "I can figure out my own problems. Right?" As if answering himself, he nodded briskly. "Right." Then he swung one palm across his body to high-five his other palm before grinning at his own dorky moment.

Now was his one big chance. They were going to spend two days straight together being—well, not very straight together.

Quinn wiped his palms on his jeans and then pressed them on the cool surface of the table, leaning over it to take a few deep breaths.

Everything was going to be fine. He'd go see Aaron and his housemates today, charm them all over again, sweep Aaron back home, keep him company at the coffee shop tomorrow, charm *him* all over again... and, uh, convince Aaron to make their label permanent.

The pressure to get this right was so unfamiliar to Quinn. He didn't usually do anything that came with this many potential consequences or rewards.

Quinn pushed himself away from the counter and headed for the fridge to wolf down an early lunch. He'd either skip supper or claim a poor appetite and eat only the protein—he'd play it by ear. Aaron knew he was supposed to eat carefully anyway. Hopefully he wouldn't offend anyone.

One bland plate of chicken breasts and steamed greens later, Quinn was ready to head out the door.

He lingered by the door, his jacket and shoes already on, and sent Aaron a quick text first. *You up yet?*

It only took a few moments to get a reply.

Yeah! We've exchanged gifts and most of us are even dressed. ;) Come on over whenever.

If they're shy, tell them I'm on my way. Unless they're exhibitionists, then maybe don't, Quinn sent back and grabbed his car keys.

As he got behind the wheel, he felt his phone go off and peeked at it once more. It was a gif of some naked guy holding a gift-wrapped box in front of his crotch while he sang.

Quinn burst into laughter and shook his head, dropping his phone in the cupholder for the quick drive down his street and over to Aaron's place.

Having never spent this day with anyone but his parents and more distantly related family, Quinn had no idea what to expect. But it turned out to be pretty much the usual chaos there—from the moment he knocked and the door opened.

Jesse was there in skinny jeans and a garish green Christmas tree sweater, grinning at him. "Well, hello, Aaron's-totally—" he started.

Aaron charged down the hallway, sliding in his socked feet, and tackled him from behind, cutting him off mid-word. Then, with surprising skills, Aaron put Jesse in a headlock.

Jesse gasped and stumbled with Aaron backward into the hallway, right next to the arched living room doorway. "Augh!

Censorship!" He wailed over the round of laughter from the living room.

"Well, hello," Quinn greeted, laughing as he stepped inside.

"Hi," Jesse gasped as Aaron let go of him. Jesse mimed zipping his lips, winked at Quinn, then fled for the living room.

"Hello, too," Aaron said, grinning. Now that Quinn got a look at him, he saw the fluffy white PJ pants and a white T-shirt with a blue penguin on it. Aaron's feet were in enormous puffy penguin slippers.

"Cute theme." Quinn winked.

"Why, thank you. You're cute today, too." They were in full view of the others now, but this didn't seem to faze Aaron, who stretched onto his tiptoes and flung his arms around Quinn's neck, pecking his lips.

Wolf whistles greeted the move, just as Quinn had expected.

"Yeah, yeah." Quinn waved off the attention, sliding his hand around Aaron's waist to steer him to the living room. He couldn't see a clear space to sit, so he chose the floor next to the tree and patted his lap.

"That's right. Sit on Santa Daddy's lap," Ezra snickered, his grin wickedly unapologetic.

"Oh, I will." Aaron pretended to rearrange his skirts and delicately perched on Quinn's knee, his back straight and chin lifted. He stretched his legs out ahead of him and crossed them at the ankle. Then, he squealed as Quinn knocked him off-balance by hauling him in around the waist until he was more firmly settled.

"Better," Quinn declared, grinning over Aaron's shoulder at everyone else. He left his arm around Aaron's waist. "So, what's everyone's plans?"

"Finn and his brothers are coming by to pick me up so I can have dinner with the family today," Jesse said, smiling. "I'll see Mom tomorrow since she's spending time with her new boyfriend today."

"Aha," Aaron whispered, sounding smug. "Knew it."

"Dad's driving out here to pick me up," Benji said. "I'll be back in a couple days. Definitely before New Year's."

Ross sighed, examining his black nail polish, like a living stereotype. Quinn tried not to smile. He really was a grumpy little old man, wasn't he? "I just want everyone to leave so Beau and I can play games for two days straight."

"Fuck, yeah," Beau concurred and held up a palm. His sunny optimism was totally the opposite of Ross's gloom, but apparently it worked. "Come on, bro. Don't leave me hanging," Beau said and coaxed a reluctant high five out of Ross.

Quinn laughed, his attention lingering on Ross and Beau for a moment. Did they not have family?

As if sensing the question, Beau looked over at him. "My parents alternate years visiting me and my big sister. It's her turn this year, so I get to be a slob. It's great."

"Rusty's out working, but then he'll pick me up for supper and a boat ride," Ezra said. It was impossible to miss the glow of new love he had around him as he spoke. He tucked his hair behind his ear.

"Aww," Quinn murmured, smiling at the redhead.

Jesse beamed. "I'm glad that we have all the housemates here, even if we're missing a few honorary housemates."

"We still need a name for this place," Aaron spoke up. "If you won't let me call it Sass Chez."

A laugh rumbled in Quinn's chest as he held him a little

tighter. He loved Aaron's sharp tongue and mind equally. "That's a great name."

"But not really representative of us all," Beau said, leaning forward. "How about something ocean-themed?"

"Pineapple?" Aaron kept his face straight and glanced around for a moment. Benji reeled backward and stared at him, and so did Ross. Aaron winked and made finger guns at them both, clicking his tongue. "Found the kinky fuckers."

"How did you..." Benji covered his face as he laughed.

"Huh?" Ezra leaned forward.

Aaron gasped. "It's the most common safeword. Don't tell me you *don't have one?* Fix that, my babe."

Ah, fuck. Of course he was bringing up sex while sitting *right there.* But the way Aaron shifted on Quinn's lap told him that he knew exactly what he was doing here.

Ross just stuck his lip out and folded his arms again. "His knowledge scares me sometimes."

Ezra laughed and threw up his hands. "He's your problem tonight," he told Quinn.

Quinn smirked and flattened his hand on Aaron's chest. "Oh, good." Another round of knowing laughter went through the room.

"Penguins?" Beau suddenly said, pointing at Aaron—or his shirt, Quinn realized. "Like that meme online, how gays are a bunch of penguins huddling together?"

"Otters?" Quinn idly suggested. "They all hold hands to make a raft, and tangle themselves in seaweed to put down roots."

Aaron gasped and sat up straight again. "The Raft." His tailbone did something uncomfortable to Quinn's groin that he had to shift to compensate for. At least it helped with the boner situation.

"Oh," Jesse breathed. "That's perfect. All in favor?"

Quinn didn't put his hand up, since he didn't think he had voting rights here, so he just slid both arms around Aaron's waist.

"That's a yes, then. Thank you!" Beau beamed at Quinn.

Still rather surprised at his accidental helping hand in naming the place that clearly meant so much to them all, Quinn shrugged. "You're welcome?"

In particular, it meant so much to Aaron, who had fled here with his friends to escape the long shadows of his family. Maybe not just a raft of otters, but a life raft for those who had moved here.

The sound of a car outside made Ezra leap to his feet. "Okay, that's Rusty! Bye, all you gorgeous people! Merry Christmas to all!" He blew kisses at them and trotted for the front door.

Benji headed upstairs to pack, and Ross and Beau started to argue about what they were going to play first. Quinn was quite happy to sit here and listen to the friendly banter, a far cry from the stuffy holiday greetings that were no doubt taking place back home.

Then the doorbell rang, and Quinn heard a quick burst of men's laughter. Jesse stood up, his eyes shining with a sweet, nervous look. "That must be Finn's brothers."

Aaron sprang to his feet, too. "They'll love you," he told Jesse, kissing his cheek. "Go on, go answer. Let them in."

Awww. Quinn had to try hard not to smile as he watched Aaron cheering Jesse on. God, he was so sweet and supportive of everyone in his life.

After answering the door and greeting them all with hugs, Jesse waved the small group of guys into the hallway. "Come in, keep the chill out while I get my shoes."

A friendly face appeared in the doorway and smiled. He looked like a Hart, but for a moment, Quinn couldn't place him.

Then it clicked. "Oh! Dash?" Quinn grinned. They'd been lab partners years ago, when the science teacher had assigned partners and separated Dash from his twin brother, Baz. The two were usually glued together otherwise.

The relief on Dash's face was evident. "Hey," he greeted. "Long time no see." He came into the living room but lingered just a few steps in, like he wasn't sure how Quinn would react.

As if reading Dash's mind, Baz came up behind him. He stood there like he wanted to make sure Quinn knew he was listening.

Quinn didn't blame Dash for being cautious, though he did hope that Hart's Bay had been good to him since his return. Dash had transitioned just before leaving town for college. He'd really grown into himself—despite the nervous way he eyed Quinn right now, the confidence was hard to mistake.

Quinn smiled as he approached the twins and reached out to hug Dash first. "Welcome back," he told Dash firmly, squeezing him before letting go and giving Baz the same treatment. "What about you? Are you back for Christmas?"

"Just Christmas," Baz said. "But I'm looking into swinging a permanent move here." Baz clapped his shoulder as he let go and scrutinized him. "You're looking great, man. Damn."

That made Quinn beam with pride. "Thanks. I'm working as a personal trainer."

"Oh, that's awesome," Dash said. He lit up. "Does that mean there's a gym nearby?"

"Not yet, sorry." Quinn folded his arms thoughtfully. "But... you could come to one of my gyms, or I can give you a ride. Or teach you some bodyweight stuff from your home."

"I'd love that," Dash answered and grinned. "I've been wanting to get into shape. I feel ready."

Quinn remembered that point in his own life. Just four years ago, he'd finally grown tired of life being invisible, forgotten about as soon as he walked out of the room. Back then, he'd blamed it on being a couple of pounds heavier than the hot guys who got all the looks.

But as he'd learned about fitness and transformed himself, the confidence Quinn had lacked finally arrived. People respected him now, and when they didn't, he demanded it.

Sharing that feeling with other people was the best thing ever.

Quinn held up a hand to high-five. "Free first session, just for you."

"Aww, jeez. Thanks." Dash high-fived him, his cheeks pink but his teeth flashing in a genuine grin.

Finn and Elliott, the fourth and youngest of the boys, were talking to Jesse as he tied up his shoes, so Quinn waved in their direction. "I'll let you guys go kidnap Jesse."

"Our mom will think we've been filling up on Christmas cookies otherwise," Finn said with a wise nod. "Thanks."

There was another round of "Merry Christmas, guys!" all around before they finally departed.

Aaron sidled up to Quinn, putting his arm around his waist and kissing his cheek. "What does it take to get a free one-on-one training session with you?" He batted his lashes and lowered his voice to a sultry purr. "You can tell me on the way over to your place."

"Oh, God. Go get a room," Ross called out, waving a controller in their direction. "Merry Christmas and shit."

"No, hugs first," Beau insisted, jumping up to hug them both before he let them go. "Have a wonderful Christmas Eve. I'll try to drag this wet blanket to Howya Bean tomorrow to say hello! See you there! No—Ross, don't start without me, that's cheati—oh, you son of a cock!"

As Beau rushed back to the TV, Quinn's laughter made it hard to stay upright as he tied his shoelaces and pretended not to notice Aaron grabbing a bag of presents.

He and Aaron were about to be alone together during one of the most romantic times of the year for a new couple—or sort-of couple, or would-be couple. Now was Quinn's moment to show Aaron what his life could be like with him in it. Maybe even... forever.

The blood rushed to his head and stayed there, even once he stood. All he could think was: *Whatever you do, Quinn Powell, don't screw this up.*

19

AARON

Okay, maybe Quinn *did* know Aaron by heart already. Because Aaron's ideal Christmas involved a silky rock-hard cock filling his mouth.

And right now on Christmas Eve, Santa had come early. But not prematurely, thankfully.

They'd missed most of this cutesy movie's ending and barely touched their bottle of wine, too lost in exploring each other's bodies in the cozy nest of blankets on Quinn's couch.

Now Aaron was kneeling in front of the couch while Quinn sat on the edge with the strands of Aaron's hair twirled around his fingers. Every thrust slid that magnificent erection smoothly between Aaron's lips.

Quinn growled when the credits ended and the previews came on. He leaned forward to hit the power button on the remote. With his other hand still on the back of Aaron's head, he pushed himself farther into Aaron's mouth.

Aaron choked for breath, tears involuntarily springing to his eyes. But when Quinn cursed and tried to pull his hand away, Aaron snatched it right back and placed it where it had been.

Come on, he thought as he stared up at Quinn, his other hand fisting around his own cock and pumping slowly. *Go wild. I like it.*

But instead, Quinn gripped him gently by the elbows and pulled him to his feet. "There's plenty of time for that tomorrow," he murmured. "I want to make love to you tonight."

Love.

It was the first time they'd used that word with any degree of... seriousness.

Aaron's heart skipped a beat as he collapsed onto Quinn's lap.

Instantly, Quinn's mouth was on his, hot and insistent. Quinn's hands wandered up Aaron's back, slipping under his shirt to trail along hot skin from the small of his back to his shoulder blades.

Aaron's brain was still spinning. Love? Did Quinn mean that? Surely not. He just meant it as a euphemism for slow, sensual sex.

Lightning arced down his back as Quinn's nails raked gently down his skin, pulling him out of his thoughts and into the moment in a heartbeat. Aaron gasped and arched with a soft cry, his hardness throbbing between them.

"You like that, don't you?" Quinn murmured, pressing a little harder with his nails. "The sting."

"Fuck, yes." Aaron nodded his head so hard that he almost head-butted Quinn's nose. Luckily, as usual, he was nimble. He leaned backward just in time and laughed.

"And choking on my dick when you give head?" Quinn grinned. "I'll remember that, too."

"Just want to see you lose control," Aaron whispered. He

swayed into Quinn, nuzzling into his neck and kissing his collarbone. "Remember what I said the first time? Show me who you are. I can take care of the freaky sex positions—perks of being a proud slut. I just want to see who you *are*."

Quinn's lips were on Aaron's earlobe. His teeth sent another little shower of sparks cascading through his chest, straight down to the tip of his erection. "And I want to show you." His nails pressed firmly into Aaron's skin as he dragged them back up to his shoulder blades. "Line up our cocks," Quinn ordered.

That tone was so quiet Aaron had almost missed it. He caught his breath, cheeks flushing as he looked up at Quinn.

Was he... giving orders now?

The raised eyebrow and cool confidence made him squirm with pleasure. *Yes!* This was the Quinn he wanted to see more of—though embarrassing him in public was fun, these were the moments that they really seemed to click perfectly into place.

Aaron tried to play it cool as he shifted until his knees were spread just right and his shaft rested against Quinn's. "Now what?"

Oh shit, that felt good.

Instinctively, Aaron ground against the firm warmth of Quinn's cock lying against his.

"Stop," Quinn said, just as whisper-soft but firm.

A whimper escaped the back of Aaron's throat. Quinn was going to torment him again, wasn't he? "But..."

Quinn smiled at him, a gentle and tolerant expression. Like he was way calmer than he had any right to be, after a patented Aaronjob. "Wait."

"Hmmnngh." Aaron vented all his frustration and petulance in that one noise, sticking his lower lip out.

All Quinn did was lean forward to suck Aaron's

protruding lip between his own. Another riot of sensation exploded through Aaron's kiss-swollen lips, shattering any calm Aaron tried to achieve.

He just clung to Quinn's shoulders, his hips twitching forward in the smallest rocking motions he could manage.

Quinn drew the T-shirt up Aaron's body, the backs of his fingers grazing Aaron's skin as he went. Trails of sensation made him prickle all over.

Fuck, all he had to do was *look* at Quinn and he was turned on. Being trapped here, pressed close against his hot, hard body, their cocks wet and twitching against each other while Quinn slowly undressed him? Really, royally fucking unfair.

Quinn pulled away from the kiss to tug his shirt off and then quickly dispatched his own sweater and the shirt underneath.

Being shirtless was good. Aaron would take that. Without waiting for permission, he pressed his narrow chest against Quinn's, sinuously rolling their bodies together and burying his face in his strong shoulder.

His nipple caught for a moment against Quinn's before sliding past, and even that tiny shift in sensation made Aaron's thighs clench again.

He would give anything to have Quinn inside him right now, but he also didn't want to move to grab lube or anything. He was just calculating the spit-to-cock ratio when Quinn grinned.

"Bet I can make you come right here," he whispered.

Aaron's eyes flew wide open. *Without fucking me?* If he was going to go all the way with frot, they'd better add more spit, or that friction burn would smart.

Quinn wasn't waiting to explain himself, though. He tugged Aaron's pants down in one rough movement, his strong arm wrapping around Aaron.

Together, they managed to kick the offending garment off with only a few creative swear words from Aaron. Not purely from frustration, either—he was on edge from the sensation of his cock sliding across those washboard abs.

Quinn had been leaning back to help Aaron, but he stayed in this position, slouched on the couch. This meant Aaron could drape himself along Quinn's body. Bare skin slid on skin as he shamelessly ground against Quinn again.

"I need you," Aaron breathed. The world was hazy around him, Quinn the only thing that mattered. "Can't you feel how much?"

"I do," Quinn whispered, pressing kisses against his lips that quickly trailed over his cheek to his jaw, then his ear and neck.

Aaron rolled his head back and whimpered at the bursts of heat that coursed through him at every touch of those warm, wet lips, and every little flick of Quinn's tongue. "Don't think you do," he mumbled in complaint, which only made Quinn laugh.

"Patience, baby." Then Quinn's hand was there, between their faces, making Aaron jerk back in surprise. He pressed the tips of two fingers against Aaron's lips and slid them inside, never breaking eye contact.

Oh, that was hot.

Aaron relaxed and smirked at Quinn while he wrapped his tongue around his fingertips, showing off his skills with all he had. And if he did say so himself, he had quite a lot that deserved showing off.

When Quinn pulled his hand away, Aaron leaned in to kiss him instead, his teeth catching Quinn's lip for a change. But before he could take over and demand what he needed, those same wet fingers brushed his balls, then slid up to touch his tight hole.

"Fuck!" Aaron's whole body shuddered as every nerve ending in the area approved of the idea at the same time. He broke away from the kiss and clung to Quinn instead, involuntarily clenching and relaxing against those fingertips.

Slowly, Quinn's fingertips danced around the smooth, sensitive skin as Aaron whimpered and tried to press himself backward into them.

It felt like forever before Quinn spat on his fingers. The moment Aaron was waiting for was almost here—

One fingertip slid into him, a gentle yet confident movement. Quinn's gaze was fixed on Aaron's face, intently reading his every reaction.

When Aaron gasped or winced, Quinn paused for a few moments before he pushed his finger inside a little deeper.

Fuck, Quinn had cuddled him for a few hours, and now here he was, fingering him like a pro. Aaron really had found the man of his dreams.

That's a later-Aaron thought, he told himself, leaving that thought on a shelf somewhere in the back of his brain.

Quinn found the spot inside that prickled at first, quickly igniting into something more. Aaron gasped to let him know he'd found it. Very soon, the arousal deep in his belly became a flame and then a roaring fire.

"Fuck," Aaron gasped, riding Quinn shamelessly as his second finger slid in to join the first. He was hard again. This time, his hard-on felt even firmer. More raw, somehow. "That's it. Exactly there."

"Love seeing you all needy," Quinn growled. His other arm was wrapped firmly around Aaron's back, keeping them pinned together. "Hearing you beg me for more. Making you hold out for longer than you think you can."

Even if Aaron could have found the strength in his arms to push himself upright, no way would Quinn let him. They were wrapped together too tightly to pull apart.

Aaron reveled in this moment, basking in the way Quinn watched him like a starving animal. Aaron adored being the object of all Quinn's fantasies. Making him shake off that nice-boy image and indulge in his deepest desires made Aaron the happiest he could remember.

Being finger-banged hard and fast on the couch was a pretty nice perk, too.

"Now do you believe I'm going to make you come right here?" Quinn asked mildly, like he was inquiring about the weather.

Aaron couldn't swallow his whimper. Words were escaping him now. All he had was heavy breathing and *need* that pulsated through him like a living, breathing being taking over his senses.

"Good," Quinn whispered. "Then you're half as close to ecstasy as I want to bring you."

Aaron pressed his nose into Quinn's neck and breathed his musky scent in with each quick gasp of breath. "Please," he moaned. If Quinn tried to pull back now, he was just going to get a ruined orgasm and a lot of tears. "Don't stop."

Quinn just growled and pulled Aaron close. "Never," he promised.

If only he meant that.

Aaron swallowed hard and let the thought go as quickly as it had come to him. *Also* a problem for later-Aaron to think about. Right-now-Aaron wanted to come so hard he saw stars, thanks very much.

The heat was building through Aaron's whole body, his muscles taut from head to toe. Even his toes were curled, and he could hardly breathe. His throat constricted as he screwed his eyes shut. Fire rushed to his shaft, his balls drew tight, and he squeezed around Quinn's fingers.

Oh, God, Aaron couldn't last any longer. It was so good he never wanted it to end, but it had to.

"Let yourself go," Quinn whispered, burying his face in Aaron's hair. His arm loosened around Aaron's back so he could rake his nails up and down Aaron's skin. "Please, baby." Then, he pressed his flat palm in the small of Aaron's back.

Steering him through this—or claiming him.

Aaron couldn't hold back a second longer. He came with a shuddering cry, his voice half-broken as blackness swept through him and every muscle trembled somewhere far away. Hot jets rushed through him. Thank God for the pressure and firm ridge of Quinn's cock against his, or he would have been almost *too* sensitive.

He was heart-to-heart with Quinn, his heart hammering on his rib cage as he gasped raggedly for breath.

"That's it," he was dimly aware of Quinn whispering. His touch was soothing now, his fingers slowing their pace in Aaron as the orgasm drew to an end and the world knitted itself together again.

Then they slid out, and Quinn smirked at him. "Not bad?"

The first attempt to speak left Aaron making a weird syllable that went nowhere. He cleared his throat, licked his lips, and tried again. "N-Not bad."

Quinn laughed, gently gripping Aaron's hips to shift him onto his side on the couch so he could grab tissues. "Good."

Aaron blushed, his eyes drawn to the mess he'd made. "Thanks," he whispered. His load coated Quinn's throbbing erection, which was flushed pink and veiny. It looked needier than he had been himself a few seconds ago.

"Oh, I'm not done with you yet." Quinn's voice was a low purr.

Aaron's gaze snapped up to him, his interest instantly with him again. "Oh?"

"When you're ready, you can clean me up," Quinn said, his gaze intent on Aaron's again. "With that pretty little tongue of yours."

Aaron slithered to the floor in a single motion, though he was still so boneless that it ended up more like a drunken grass snake than a confident, sexy twink. To his credit, Quinn choked back his laugh, but Aaron giggled.

"I knew you had a dirty side, you know."

"Suck first, talk later," Quinn ordered, playfully batting Aaron's head toward his crotch.

Aaron laughed. "And a bossy side." Quinn's fingers laced through his hair. "Okay, okay!" He'd see how far he could push Quinn later. Right now, he wanted to make the most of this mess.

He leaned in to lap at the tip of Quinn's cock. God, his own mess tasted incredible mixed with the raw, natural musk. Maybe their body chemistry was naturally compatible or something.

Focus. Aaron was swimming out of the haze now, better able to focus on Quinn again.

Aaron lapped up every thick drop and swallowed it all down before he sucked the throbbing length between his lips. He tightened his grip on the shaft and slid his head down, all the way to the base.

"Yes," Quinn hissed, his grip tightening until Aaron's scalp stung. "Fuck, yes. Watching you come had me on edge already."

Aaron was so turned on just listening to Quinn. If he wasn't careful, he was going to jerk off a second time right here and end up a vaguely Aaron-shaped puddle on the floor.

Quinn's words turned to grunts, which became growls and nearly voiceless moans. True to his word, it wasn't long before Quinn's grip tightened in Aaron's hair.

"Yes...! Oh, you beauty." Quinn gazed at him, transfixed, even as he trembled on the precipice of orgasm. His words were soft, strained by effort, like he could only just hold out. "You perfect, perfect beauty."

It was almost enough to make a man blush, but Aaron was a little busy sucking cock to pay attention.

Then Quinn's nails dug into the back of his neck, and he gave a gasping shudder. A thick rope of salty mess hit Aaron's tongue, followed by another as he swallowed quickly, his gaze fixed up on Quinn's in return.

Even when Aaron pulled his mouth off him, he kept licking and kissing until the hardness under his mouth started to soften and Quinn tugged on his arms.

Aaron was too exhausted to stand, though, and he'd left Quinn too weak to do more than collapse back against the couch. They broke into laughter at the same time, each trying to catch their breath.

Quinn grabbed his hand and squeezed tightly, his other hand covering the back of Aaron's. He rubbed in small circles as he exhaled softly.

"Wow."

Aaron beamed to himself, nuzzling Quinn's knee. "Wow," he echoed. "Can I add that to my testimonials?"

Quinn laughed, a deep, warm, rich note rolling through the room. This time, when he grabbed Aaron under the arm, he hoisted him easily up onto the couch and pressed their bodies together.

"Thank you."

Why was Quinn thanking *him*? Aaron just gave him a bemused look. "Of course."

Quinn chuckled softly and pressed a kiss against Aaron's forehead. "For being you, silly. Now, come on. Let's get washed up."

The fears and excitement that had flitted through Aaron's mind in the heat of the moment were so far gone that he could hardly remember them.

There was no doubt they were safe right now. He was safe with Quinn, now and always.

Quinn pulling back from sex at the last moment the other day must have been nothing out of the ordinary after all... not Quinn preparing to ditch him on New Year's Eve.

Whoa, Aaron thought. *Check your baggage, please, me.*

He was just overtired now and overwrought after a long week and a long day of movies on the couch with Quinn.

Food would fix anything that sex and wine hadn't. Either that or sleep—tucked up against Quinn in that nice, warm, cushy bed of his.

Aaron smiled at the thought, finally patting himself dry and leaning against the bathroom counter. "So, supper? If your freezer is filled with boring identi-chicken, I can improvise something."

But Quinn frowned slightly. He turned off the light and led Aaron by the hand out to the living room. "I dunno about that. Are you hungry?"

"Not very," Aaron admitted. "We were feasting on leftovers. The house—the Raft—had Christmas dinner last night." He sat next to Quinn and pulled on his underwear. "But I could make something if you want."

Suddenly there was a tension that hadn't appeared in Quinn's face before. "I'm going to have to bow out of that. Just boring meals for me."

Aaron cast him a quizzical look before it clicked. Of course. The identi-chicken *was* his usual meal repertoire, after all. "You're not allowed to cheat over Christmas like the rest of us?"

Quinn shrugged in apology, his expression guilty. "Gotta be ready for the New Year's resolutions crowd. Sorry I didn't give you warning."

"No problem. Get your boring meal out tomorrow and I'll eat it with you," Aaron said, smiling at Quinn. He laid his hand on Quinn's thigh. "I want to be part of your real life, not just... dinners out all the time."

Oh God, he'd dropped the hint almost without meaning to. *Is that enough of a hint?* Aaron worried. Surely Quinn would pick up on it. He was the romantic, after all.

Quinn just laughed. Shit. Maybe he really was barking up the wrong tree, after all their conversations. "I can't subject you to my plain chicken breasts and egg smoothies."

"Oh, I don't min—wait, *eggs* in your *smoothies?*" Aaron's look of horror was enough to make Quinn break out laughing. "You sick man. I've changed my mind. You better not kiss me with an eggy mouth."

"I won't," Quinn promised, but he beamed at Aaron, his eyes bright. Aaron's heart fluttered at how damn pretty he looked when he did that.

Shit. He'd just caught himself thinking of the future, but yet again, Quinn either wasn't interested or was oblivious.

Quinn's smile faded into a little frown. "I've been under a lot of pressure from the manager of one of my gyms. I should have told you before, but I didn't want to worry you. He wants me to get into shape and lose what I've put on in the last month or two."

Aaron blinked, looked pointedly at Quinn's fucking *ripped* physique, and looked back up at him.

"I know," Quinn said with a sheepish laugh, but his smile looked grateful. He slipped his arm around Aaron's shoulders. "But the stress of maybe losing my place at the gym and everything... it's easier to just give in, for the short term."

"No," Aaron scoffed. "It's easier to cut that asshole out. And talk to me about your problems." He tapped Quinn's chest with a frown. "Men. The world turns smoother when you share your problems."

And Aaron was very good at ignoring the voice of his conscience. If he wasn't exactly forthcoming about everything, well... Quinn didn't have to know.

"In fact..." Aaron said, half to distract himself from his own moment of guilt, "I have an idea. Ask Rain and Colt about opening a gym."

Quinn looked horrified. "I don't want to do all that management crap. I just wanna lift weights."

Aaron laughed. "Yeah, but maybe they can run it as a little training space. Just for you."

"Or..." Quinn said with a grin, "I can just ignore him and be a rebel for a few days."

"Good," Aaron started to approve.

"It's only a week. It won't kill me."

Ouch. It felt like he'd just been slapped. To hide the recoil, to take a moment to shelve this feeling where it belonged—in a *drink and remember it later* place—Aaron stood up and stretched.

There was only a week left between them. Quinn couldn't have been clearer about that. He didn't want Aaron eating his boring meals, and he didn't want to cheat on his diet for more than a week.

Fuck, he needed to not think about this. For eight hours or more, preferably. His appetite suddenly gone, Aaron nodded once. "Let's get to bed, then. Christmas will come sooner that way, don't you know?"

"Sure," Quinn said, laughing softly.

Aaron led the way to bed so that he had another few moments to put himself back together. By the time Quinn pulled him in to snuggle under the covers, Aaron's breathing was *almost* back to normal.

If only he could figure out what he wanted, all of this would be easier. But it looked like even Quinn didn't know.

What chance did they have of making it out of this unscathed? Pretty damn close to zero, Aaron was pretty sure now. Whatever happened next, someone was going to get hurt.

Which was the way relationships always went, and exactly why sex without strings was always the better choice.

Today was a bittersweet memory now, fading in Aaron's mind compared to the future. A future he'd hardly dared hope for, and Quinn had taken pains to avoid talking about. That definitely made him a fool.

After his ex, hadn't he learned? All the times he'd tried to talk about his future with Kasey, he'd just been rebuffed. And here was Aaron again, getting ready for another New Year's Eve of tears.

He pressed his face into Quinn's arm, smiling slightly

when Quinn chuckled and pulled Aaron's back tighter into his chest.

If it was going to hurt later, he'd deal with it then. For now, Aaron would wring out every damn second of joy he could get.

20

AARON

Waking up wrapped in Quinn's arms on Christmas Day, it was hard to imagine that anything in the world could be wrong.

All Aaron's stresses yesterday seemed miles away when he was stirring awake with one strong arm draped over his side. For once, he'd slept in. Usually even without an alarm, he woke up at the same time every day.

But now he could relax and enjoy a gloriously lazy morning in Quinn's arms. Nothing else mattered. Maybe this whole faux relationship was too good to be true, but it was *so good*.

He didn't have to turn to look at Quinn to know he was still sleeping. The deep, even breathing fluttering the hair at the back of his neck told him that much.

After such a deep sleep, Aaron couldn't help a teeny-tiny stretch. He tried to keep from disturbing Quinn, but Quinn shifted and mumbled, then echoed him in stretching.

"Good morning." Quinn's voice was rough but clear. He tightened his grip on Aaron and pulled him in like a teddy bear. "Merry Christmas."

Aaron smiled and went easily, chuckling as Quinn pressed kisses along the back and side of his neck. "Merry Christmas," he murmured back.

He fully expected to feel Quinn grinding against him any moment now, but despite the obvious morning wood, Quinn didn't make it sexual.

Trying not to be anxious that Quinn was passing up another easy chance for sex, Aaron lingered in bed while Quinn pulled away and crawled out from under the covers. Quinn was clearly full of energy now, or he really needed to pee. He was bouncing on his toes.

"I'll make toast and scrambled eggs?" Quinn said. "And coffee? Tea? Juice? Water? Um... I don't actually have juice or tea. And the coffee is instant."

Aaron groaned and playfully flung an arm over his face. "You're killing me. I'll send you home with some of my own roast."

Quinn gasped dramatically. "Can you do that? Is it a trade secret? Should I guard your beans with my life?"

"No, silly," Aaron snorted, smiling affectionately at him. "Just don't start up a shop of your own. Now go make breakfast," he ordered.

"Yes, sir." Quinn pretended to salute and marched out while Aaron laughed and flopped back into the bed.

Aaron tried to relax and lounge in bed, glancing around the bedroom. The room was plain but elegant. On the dresser sat what looked like a recent photo of Quinn with his family, but no older pictures at all. There wasn't anything else to see here without spying.

Without Quinn there, the silence in the bedroom quickly grew uncomfortable. Aaron didn't want to be alone here while Quinn scoured his cupboards for something to put on toast.

So he eased himself out of bed and pulled on his underwear before padding down the cold hallway floor to the kitchen.

He smiled as he emerged, taking a moment to appreciate the tiny tree Quinn had set up on the kitchen counter. It was a little plastic one with a few ornaments on it. "Aw, how festive."

"I couldn't have nothing for Christmas," Quinn explained with a laugh. "I'm always in and out of the kitchen, so... I put it here so I'd see it more often."

As Quinn turned his back to slide frozen slices of bread into the toaster, Aaron poked at a bauble. The tree tipped off-balance, and he scrambled to grab it. After setting it upright again, Aaron leaned against the counter and tried to look innocent.

"Watch out," Quinn told him, not even looking around. "It's not the stablest."

"Like me," Aaron quipped without missing a beat. Quinn turned a wide-eyed stare at him, and he cracked up. "Sorry."

Quinn relaxed and chuckled, too, coming over to slide an arm around his waist. He kissed the top of Aaron's head as Aaron nuzzled into his chest. "It's fine," he murmured, his voice rumbling through Aaron's cheek. "I like how sharp you are."

Aaron snickered. "Not all over." He pulled back for a grin up at Quinn, then stretched onto tiptoe and hauled him down for a proper good-morning kiss.

They stayed like that for a few seconds, just sharing an affectionate, lingering warmth before the toaster popped and made Aaron jump.

Quinn smiled and gently tried to extract himself from Aaron's hold.

But Aaron didn't let go, so Quinn valiantly waddled over

to the toaster. Aaron was so lightweight he could just dig his heels in and let Quinn drag him like a cart horse.

"Do we have to wait long to exchange gifts?" Aaron asked once he'd regained his balance. He wiggled his way between Quinn and the counter, popping up under his arm.

Quinn laughed. He turned off the stove under the eggs and steered Aaron out of the way to grab a butter knife. "We can do it right now, if you want. Over breakfast. Do you want water?"

Anything was better than instant coffee. Aaron nodded hard. "Please."

"You grab the glasses."

Aaron gasped as he went for the cupboard. "I suspect you're trying to keep my hands busy." But however much a pain in the ass he made himself, Quinn seemed charmed. Weird.

"Guilty," Quinn winked. "Nobody wants cold toast." He took one of the glasses of water Aaron poured and exchanged it for a plate with the scrambled eggs piled on top of two slices of toast. "All for you." Before Aaron could object, Quinn waved him on to the table. "You go sit down. I'm not starving. I'll whip up my shake."

Aaron wrinkled his nose. "The eggy shake?"

"That's the one."

"Helllll nope. Too freaky even for me," Aaron declared and strode out of there while Quinn laughed. He didn't need to *see* the raw eggs going into that Satanic broth.

"If I'd known it was that easy to get you out from underfoot," Quinn stage-whispered.

"What?" Aaron whirled about so dramatically he took an extra quarter-turn on the hardwood floor.

"What?" Quinn blinked innocently and slowly took two eggs out of the fridge.

"Ew!" Aaron fled again, but he had to stifle his giggles as he settled down at the table to devour his toast while the blender whirred. He couldn't avoid noticing the presents, and the tags on them.

There were a handful of gifts there, some of which read Mom or Dad. That meant he hadn't been over to see his parents yet, then? But both the ones closest to him—a long tube and a smaller cube—had little tags that read *Aaron*.

While Quinn chugged his shake and then went to brush his teeth, Aaron escaped to the front hall. He grabbed the present bag from where he'd very sneakily hidden it under his jacket.

He scurried back and set up the gifts on the table just in time—Quinn joined him a minute later. "Phew. Sorry about that."

"Don't apologize," Aaron insisted. "As long as you brushed your teeth."

"I did." Quinn stuck out his tongue. "My taste buds suffered a minty disaster, too."

"Aww." Aaron waited for Quinn to sit and then scooted onto his lap before he could pull his chair into the table. He pecked those minty-fresh lips. "Thank you for your sacrifice, my hero."

Quinn laughed and looped his arm around Aaron's back before nodding at the table. "What's this?"

"Gifts. For you." Aaron bounced slightly. "Now?"

"Now," Quinn agreed, chuckling. "Yours first. Those two. Go on."

He went for the tube, since it was intriguing him. Aaron couldn't think of any conversations they'd had about bands or movies he liked. And it was heavier than a poster should be.

As he tore off the red-and-silver-striped wrapping paper, though, it became obvious. "Oh...!" Aaron whispered, turning over the plastic-wrapped tube in his hands.

It was a nonslip ergonomic mat—thick, heavy, and durable. Just the kind of thing he could stand on at work. This would make life a little easier every single day for both him and Yolanda.

Tears sprang to Aaron's eyes. It was such a *thoughtful* gift. Not just practical, but sweet as hell.

"I hope it's not too weird or unsentimental—" Quinn started, his brow creased in worry. Aaron didn't let him finish. He dove in for a kiss, so hard he knocked teeth with Quinn.

"Ow. Sorry," Aaron breathed out, but Quinn's laugh spoke of his relief.

"You don't mind it, then."

"Not at all. Thank you," Aaron whispered, and he meant it. He turned to his other gift and tore the paper off, then grinned.

It was a massage oil candle.

"I'll use that on you tonight," Quinn promised. He was blushing, looking embarrassed yet hopeful. Like he was being a little bit naughty and bold.

How sweet.

"I can't wait," Aaron murmured and grinned. "Your turn."

Quinn went for his practical gift first, too. It was a nice wooden cutting board with a curved handle and a pattern burned into it—a series of waves along the bottom.

"By one of my artist co-op friends," Aaron explained, blushing. "I thought it would make you smile whenever you use it to cook your replicator chicken."

Quinn burst out laughing. "You're never going to let my chicken go, are you?"

Oh, that was too easy. Aaron smirked. "Your cock's just so juicy. It's a gift that keeps on giving."

Quinn turned bright red and reached for his next gift, clearly trying to maintain his dignity as he reached past a giggling Aaron.

"And this is... it rattles," Quinn announced, as if it would make Aaron not notice the blush. Aaron just waited with bated breath to see that blush continue.

Sure enough, when Quinn realized what it was, even the tips of his ears flushed. It was a kit with a blindfold and feather duster, lube, and a cock ring.

"Oh, I..." Quinn swiped at his cheeks. "This is good. I don't have... some of these things. Thank you. I didn't even know where to start looking."

"I have plenty of suggestions." Aaron beamed at him and pecked his lips. "They start with my pretty little ass and end with... also my pretty little ass."

"I look at your pretty little ass all the time," Quinn promised, grinning at him.

So instead, Aaron just said, "Merry Christmas, Quinn."

Quinn fondly smiled at him and pressed a kiss against his lips. When he finally pulled away, he murmured back, "Merry Christmas, cutie."

Aaron finally stood up. "This calls for coffee. Let's head for the shop." Hopefully Quinn was ready for a few hours of welcoming Hart's Bay into their Christmas celebrations.

Quinn's enthusiasm didn't diminish one bit at the suggestion. He nodded and beamed. "Let's go."

As it turned out, the first few hours at the shop were quiet. While Quinn set up the board games, Aaron redrew the menu board with Christmas trees and a *first drink free* message.

And he caught up on his WhatsApp messages, which were a disaster. Hundreds of notifications. As it turned out, there was good cause.

"Rusty proposed to Ezra!" he exclaimed, nearly dropping his phone in the sink as he whirled about to stare at Quinn.

A moment too late, he thought, *Shit. I hope that doesn't come off as... pointed.*

"Oh?" Quinn smiled and looked back down at the Scrabble rules. "That's great. They seemed nice."

Aaron swallowed hard, trying not to take the reaction personally. At least Quinn was speaking mildly. He hadn't been weirded out or anything. "They are."

Thankfully, a couple other customers, Darren and Dan, came in then. That provided a few minutes' distraction as they shot the shit with Aaron and Quinn.

Still, there was no escaping it: the clock was ticking, and at every opportunity to show his interest, Quinn was steering around the subject so gracefully that Aaron couldn't even ask about it.

Aaron was positive that Quinn was just sticking around until the deal ended. Like everyone did, he'd move along to bigger and better when he'd gotten what he wanted from Aaron.

Aaron *knew* it was his insecurities nibbling at him like an unscratchable itch. It didn't make them any quieter, though.

At least he had one weapon in his arsenal: great sex. And Quinn was intermittently taking him up on it. So he turned up the charm, trying to make sure Quinn wouldn't be able to resist a third time.

He took every opportunity when they were alone in the shop to tease Quinn, brush closely by him, and whisper about the uses for their Christmas gifts. And Quinn reacted well, swatting at Aaron's butt when nobody else could see.

By lunchtime, there were actually seven people playing board games or talking to each other, and people came and left. Aaron made sure everyone got their first cup free.

When Colt and Rain came by to say Merry Christmas, Aaron spotted Quinn flagging them down. Hopefully he was asking about a fitness space. He didn't want Quinn to feel like he was hovering, so he gave him space and tried not to listen in. Besides, loading the dishwasher and wiping down machines gave him plenty to do.

Christmas was supposed to be a time of joy and celebration, but he hadn't heard from his family at all.

Not that he'd really expected to, but his spirits had been high with hope at the start of the day, and now they were steadily flagging. Self-doubt gnawed on him, eating away at his confidence. Everyone was on the cruise. He wasn't worth an expensive international phone call. He should have known that.

Aaron's throat was tight, and occasionally he blinked away tears when nobody was looking. He and his family talked during holidays, and maybe every couple of months otherwise. That was all. This shouldn't bother him so much. But today, it did.

Because if even my parents, who should care the most about me, don't want me... and the romantic with his heart on his sleeve who's desperate for a relationship doesn't love me... what hope do I have of ever being loved?

His thoughts cut to the bone, so he tried to ignore them and lost himself in talking to customers as they came in.

"Oh my God, Aaron!" Ezra burst into the shop and made a beeline for him. "Look!" He wiggled his left hand, showing off the ring.

That instantly took Aaron away from all the other crap. He beamed and rushed around the counter to hug Ezra and squeal with him first. "Oh my God! Show me, show me!"

"I can once you stop hugging me," Ezra giggled, stumbling back and presenting his hand again. It was a plain silver band, but it shone to perfection. "He said he didn't want to choose something super artsy that didn't fit my aesthetic." Ezra grinned. "So if I want, when we get married he'll pick out a pretty one with me."

"That's so sweet," Aaron gasped, hugging Ezra again as they both sniffled. "Congratulations!"

Oh, the sunshine radiating from Ezra's smile was everything.

Only after he rushed out to find the rest of the guys and show off did Aaron's spirits flag again. He wasn't an asshole. He really was glad for his friend.

But it weighed heavy on his mind that here Aaron was, not able to even keep a man for more than two weeks. Afraid of what it meant to date Quinn, but just as afraid that Quinn wouldn't want him.

By the time he decided to close up, Aaron was all too aware that Quinn's presents for his parents still sat on his dining room table.

He'd spent the day here, with him, instead of with his family, who clearly mattered so much to him. It touched Aaron that Quinn had chosen him over his family, but it worried him, too.

Maybe he'd pushed Quinn too much. Maybe Quinn was following him down the wrong path. Just because Aaron had a fucked-up family life didn't mean Quinn had to follow suit.

"You going to see your parents later?" Aaron asked.

Quinn looked quickly at him. "Well, uh… they did ask if I'll come over this evening, at least." He sounded guilty.

I, not *us*. Aaron didn't miss it. But he wasn't going to begrudge Quinn that time.

"Go," he said with a simple smile. "I have lots to keep me busy tonight."

"I promised you I'd spend time with you, though." Quinn's brow furrowed.

Aaron's smile wobbled. He put down his cleaning cloth and headed over to Quinn, pecking his lips. "Thank you. You did. I've had a lot of fun today—I'm really glad you kept me company this whole day. But I'm okay."

Quinn's shoulders sank, and he looked a little less stressed. "Are you sure?"

"Positive," Aaron lied through his teeth. "It's just another evening, isn't it? We had last night together by ourselves. I'll go torment whoever's around at the Raft. When you're done, stop by tonight, or come see me here tomorrow morning."

Somehow, his perky tone worked. Quinn squeezed him tightly. "Thank you," he murmured. "You really are the best."

Quinn didn't mean it. That was a thing people said when you gave them permission to leave and they wanted to go.

"I am," Aaron agreed. "Go on, scram. Merry Christmas, gorgeous. Go spread that cheer."

"I'll save a whole load of it for you," Quinn promised with a smirk that didn't even lift Aaron's spirits, for all he played at swatting him with a towel and shooing him out the door.

Just in time, too. As Quinn strolled back to his car, Aaron

made a beeline for the office and locked the door only just in time.

The first flood of tears was silent, hot, and fast.

Still no call, and now no Quinn to keep him distracted. It was for the best—he wasn't going to ruin Quinn's life just for this week of fun. But it hurt so badly he didn't know what to do.

After another round of tears and sniffling into tissues, he found enough sense to haul himself out of the chair and lock up Howya Bean.

Every time he took the little path to his house now, Aaron had a moment of fear. But this was an hour earlier than usual, so there was no way Bryon could know where he was.

When he crested the hill, he instantly saw that the car was gone. Some or all of the guys were out, then. Typical timing. Aaron wiped his eyes and headed for the porch, letting himself into the house.

Yep. The Christmas tree was on, but when he called out, "Hello?" there was no answer.

Like a sunbeam cutting through the cloud of Aaron's misery, his phone went off.

Maybe it was Quinn, ready to pick him up, or Quinn's parents inviting him over again, or his friends telling him where they were...

No, it was his parents. Aaron could have fallen over with surprise. Maybe he'd underestimated them and been a total drama queen all day over nothing. His heart lifted as he answered. "Hello?"

"Aaron," his dad greeted briskly. "You're on speaker, and your mom's here. Michael called us to warn us about what's going on. Luckily we're in port today so we have signal. You still have terrible timing." That was a sharp reprimand disguised in the thin veneer of a joke. "You're lucky your *friend* hasn't published those photos yet, as far as we know. But we've thought up a solution. I've come up with an anti-bullying campaign—have you seen it online?"

"*No*," Aaron spat, all he could get out.

"Well, you can be a poster boy for it—"

"*No*," Aaron said again, nearly shouting the word. Even his dad couldn't bluster through it. "No, I won't be your... political football."

"You should be grateful," his father said. "Most parents would be ashamed of their son for such a juvenile indiscretion."

"Most parents would be horrified that their son was being blackmailed," Aaron corrected, not bothering to keep the harsh note out of his voice. "I deserve better than this. Merry Christmas."

Thank God. Footsteps on the porch.

Aaron was just about ready to fall into the arms of whichever of his friends came through the door first and spill the whole situation.

But the doorbell rang.

Fuck. He wiped his eyes and pocketed his phone, wondering if his parents had sent Michael to go tell him off in person.

But as he yanked open the door, his brain couldn't quite process the sight.

Certainly not in time to do anything about it when Bryon put a hand on the doorframe and shoved his way inside, stepping into the last safe place Aaron really had in the world.

"Found you."

21

QUINN

Quinn had been trying to plan the best way to tell his family that he was serious about Aaron for the last week.

Hi, Mom and Dad. I want to make Aaron a part of my life, if he'll have me. Is this going to make things weird? Because he's important to me, and so are you guys, and I want to make this work.

That would be the adult thing to say—but it would also kick off a world of trouble. Mom would call his aunts and uncles, someone would gossip at the bar, where the walls had ears, and before he knew it, Aaron would find out that Quinn planned to ask him out.

But he'd reached the point of no return. As certain as he was that Aaron would run away from anything more committed than being *his guy* for these few weeks, they were near the end of the line.

And another week without certainty would kill Quinn. Better to take the chance, even with the risk that—despite Quinn's sculpted body and sweet intentions—Aaron would look right past him.

The drive back home was achingly quiet without Aaron chattering beside him. Quinn headed straight to the table to grab his parents' gifts. As he reached the chair where he'd sat, still pulled out, it felt like Aaron was a ghost by his side. He remembered that warm weight on his lap and his teasing grins.

Despite himself, Quinn grinned. Yeah. It was worth taking any risk for Aaron—even the risk of Aaron himself rejecting him.

As he drove to his parents' house, his resolve grew. Sure, things would be tough, trying to find the right balance, but life wasn't supposed to be easy.

"Quinn!" Mom greeted, beaming and kissing his cheek. "Come on in. Here are your gifts." She'd neatly filled a bag with them, and Quinn set his bag down next to theirs. "I wasn't sure how long you'd be staying around. Can you join us for supper?"

Quinn hesitated. Part of him wanted to get back to Aaron as soon as possible. He'd never had the chance to spend this much time with him. But then, Aaron had practically shoved him out the door. Maybe he wanted some time to himself, or with his friends.

"Sure. I'd like that," Quinn said, smiling back as he went to hug his dad. "How was Christmas Eve?"

"Oh, you know," Mom said before promptly launching into stories of what Aunt Brenda and Uncle Gideon had said. Dad was dishing up plates of supper—which, on Christmas Day, was always leftovers from last night's big meal.

But just as they sat down, his pocket vibrated. Normally Quinn wouldn't check his phone at the dinner table, but this was Christmas.

It was just one word from Aaron, and it was a word that

sent him standing up so fast he knocked the chair over, making both his parents exclaim in surprise.

Help.

No other explanation. Not a word.

"Shit," Quinn breathed out, and then clapped a hand over his mouth. *Swearing* at home was certainly not allowed. "Sorry, Mom. I need—I have to go."

"What?" Dad looked crestfallen as he set the plate on Quinn's placemat.

Quinn's gut lurched with shame. Letting people down was one of his worst fears—especially his parents. He didn't want them to be disappointed in him.

He's in trouble. I don't know where or how, but he wouldn't have asked if he didn't have a damn good reason.

"I'm sorry, I—I think Aaron needs me."

"But he's—you told us he's just a short-term thing. Now you're choosing him over your own family?" Mom sounded hurt, too.

Quinn couldn't wait—couldn't explain himself yet. "No, but... it's urgent. Look, I'll call when I can!" He shoved his feet into his shoes and grabbed his jacket. "Sorry! Love you! Bye!" He didn't even remember the bag of gifts by the door until he was halfway to Aaron's.

Oh, well. He'd grab it when he went back home to apologize. His main fear right now was far more important: finding out what was wrong with Aaron.

"Fuck," Quinn whispered when he found himself at the end of the street. Which way to go—home or work? Or somewhere else?

Home, he decided. Aaron had been closing up when he'd left. That meant he'd probably gone home—and if he wasn't there, someone there might be able to tell him where Aaron was.

In a matter of seconds, he was pulling up outside the Raft. He nearly broke the key in his haste to grab it from the ignition before he sprinted up the sidewalk.

The front door was ajar.

Fuck.

Quinn shouldered his way through, and it took him a moment to figure out what was happening.

Drips of blood trailed to the living room. Aaron's phone lay on the floor in the hallway, maybe kicked aside.

"Quinn!" Aaron cried. He was pressed up against the Christmas tree, which had toppled over in the corner.

The guy who swung around to glare at Quinn was holding one hand over his nose, blood dripping down his face and shirt. His other hand was fisted in Aaron's shirt, but he let go at the sight of Quinn.

Whoever this asshole was, Quinn didn't know him, but he was ripped and had several inches of height on Aaron. And the fear in Aaron's eyes alone would have made him tear this guy limb from limb.

"What the fuck are you doing?" Quinn shouted, striding across the living room in a couple of steps. "Who are you? Get your fucking hands off Aaron this *second*."

"Whoa. Didn't he tell you?" The guy pulled out his phone. "I'm his boyfriend."

Quinn stumbled to a halt for just a heartbeat. With an ounce less trust in Aaron, Quinn could have interpreted the terror in Aaron's eyes differently as Aaron shook his head just slightly.

Even in a moment like this, Aaron wouldn't lie. Which meant this bastard was lying, and Quinn hated liars.

"See, I have his nudes." The guy turned his phone screen toward Quinn. His phone background was a shot of Aaron on all fours, a guy fucking him—presumably this guy.

"So?" Quinn snapped. He grabbed the guy's arm and hauled him away from Aaron, putting himself between the two of them. "I don't give a shit who you are to him. He obviously doesn't want you here, if he broke your fucking nose."

"Stupid little whore," the guy growled.

"Shut up, Bryon!" Aaron gasped.

"Brave now you have your fuck buddy here, aren't you?" Bryon responded, trying to sidestep Quinn and get at Aaron again.

Quinn growled. "No. That's it. *Out.*" He grabbed Bryon by the shoulders. Like a lot of guys, Bryon might look big and tough, but Quinn understood simple physics. If Bryon fought back, Quinn could take him down in moments.

Bryon didn't. He just kept streaming vitriol and abuse at Aaron the whole way out the door. "Don't you get it? He sent me those photos! He's mine!"

"Lots of guys probably have his photos. No offense, honey," Quinn added to Aaron, who shakily smiled. "I love the perks of having a slutty boyfriend." He turned back to Bryon. "But he's *mine*, you hear me? I have him, and if I hear you so much as think about him one more time, I'm sending your ass to the hospital instead of jail."

Bryon whined, "But he told me he wanted me! Why'd he choose you?"

"Dunno. Because I'm not a piece of shit? That's for you to think about while I throw you down the stairs," Quinn growled. Bryon struggled, but Quinn easily hefted the man onto the porch and down the steps.

Bryon stumbled and fell, rolling to the sidewalk. "Asshole! He never said he had a boyfriend!"

"Didn't he?" Quinn folded his arms. "Hi, that's me. Get lost."

He stood and waited while Bryon picked himself up and dusted himself off, spat in his direction, and stomped down the sidewalk, one hand going to his nose again.

Then Quinn followed, making sure he made his way all the way down the street and around the corner. Only when he was out of sight did Quinn turn to head back up the sidewalk.

Aaron was on the porch, clinging to one of the support posts. His shirt and hands were still smeared in Bryon's blood. "Quinn," he breathed out.

"Oh, sweetheart." Quinn swept Aaron up and hugged him as tightly as he could. Thank God he'd trusted his instincts and gotten over here right away. "Did you break his nose?"

"I-I think so," Aaron breathed out. He managed a tiny giggle. "I didn't think I could, and then I... did. I'm sorry I interrupted things with your parents. Are they mad?"

Quinn didn't want to make Aaron feel worse, but he also didn't want to lie. He froze, but the guilt on his face must have said it all.

"Ah, shit," Aaron moaned. "Really mad? At you?"

"Yes. But that doesn't matter." Quinn took Aaron's hands and squeezed hard. "Ultimately, *this* matters. You matter."

But instead of beaming at him, Aaron's expression crumpled. "You can't just ditch them, though. They care about you. That matters, too." He wiped his eyes.

A car was approaching, and Quinn let go of Aaron and turned around. He half expected it to be Bryon coming back with a group of friends for vengeance, but instead...

It was Aaron's friends.

"Babe, what?" Jesse gasped as he scrambled out of the driver's seat. Ross and Beau piled out, too. All three of them rushed up the sidewalk to the porch and gathered around Aaron.

"What's wrong?" Beau breathed out, casting a worried glance between the two of them. "Did we interrupt?"

"This guy from Grindr who's been stalking me for weeks found me at home and burst in and tried to attack me, but I texted Quinn for help and broke his nose and Quinn abandoned his parents to come save me—" He gasped for air. "—and he threw Bryon out, and there's blood on the hallway floor now and the tree is a mess, and I'm so sorry!"

"Oh my God," Jesse breathed out and swept Aaron into a hug. "Thank God you're okay."

"I'm on cleanup duty," Ross volunteered and hurried into the house. From inside, he called, "This isn't too bad! Give me a minute. Oh. The carpet. Okay, I'll Google it. Don't worry."

Beau turned to Quinn and hugged him, too. "Thank you for helping out."

"Of course," Quinn murmured, but he took a step back when Beau let go. Aaron's friends were swinging into action like a well-oiled machine, cleaning up and comforting Aaron and everything.

He felt like he was being pushed out of the way, his job done. The voice of worry at the back of his head spoke up: was Aaron just using him... to ditch Bryon? No, he was sure that couldn't be true. Besides, Quinn would have kicked his ass to the curb no matter who he was trying to hurt or why.

Aaron finally pried himself away from Jesse and sent both his housemates inside, telling them that he'd be inside in a minute.

"You okay?" Quinn asked. Even he was rattled, not aided by the feeling that Aaron was about to send him away.

"I'll be fine." Aaron breathed in deeply and wiped his eyes, then hugged Quinn again. "Thank you, Quinn. You go make up with your parents, okay? I'll call you in a couple of days."

Oh, no.

Aaron had told him to pick him up tonight or tomorrow. "A couple of days" was a lot longer to wait, all of a sudden. Was Aaron that freaked-out? Had Quinn pissed him off? Or had this guy really gotten into his head so badly?

"I could come in," Quinn offered. More than anything, he wanted to talk this through now. Before he spent long days and nights trying to figure out what he'd done wrong.

But Aaron shook his head hard. "No. I'm not letting you sacrifice things with your parents just because I've made a mess of my life."

"You haven't," Quinn started, but he could tell from Aaron's face that it wouldn't get through. Aaron's laugh was a slight, sharp exhalation—like he didn't believe him.

Or maybe he was pissed at him. Shit.

"Did I say anything wrong?" Quinn added. "I hope I didn't make things worse, saying we were dating. I know you don't like the word." Word would get around town if this guy was a gossip, and Aaron might not like that.

Especially if he was planning to ditch Quinn and go back to his singleton life.

Aaron shook his head slightly. He sounded tired—like he just wanted it all to go away. "No, I think saying that was the only thing that stopped him."

Quinn swallowed hard. *Can't exactly ask him now if he wants to make this official. No way would he be thinking straight.* So he just cupped Aaron's cheeks and waited for him to meet his eyes, then kissed him softly. "You didn't do anything wrong," he said firmly. "The guy's an asshole, and I hope you report him to the cops. I'll back you up every step of the way."

Aaron relaxed and wrapped his arms around Quinn's neck, swaying into him for a few long moments before he pulled away. "Thanks," he whispered. "Go enjoy the rest of your Christmas."

That was a clear dismissal. Quinn straightened up and tried to ignore the lump in his throat. "You too," he murmured, kissing Aaron's forehead and nose again before he pressed one more lingering kiss against his lips.

The moment of warmth and tenderness seeped through the chill that had formed in his guts the moment he'd gotten that text, finally thawing him out.

But nothing else was better. In fact, Quinn was even less sure now of where he stood with Aaron.

He turned and waved slightly, strode down the sidewalk for his car, and tried to ignore the pieces of his hope shattering inside his chest.

Fuck, he thought as he started up the car and rested his head on the wheel for a minute that felt like an hour. *I don't know how, but I've screwed this up now.*

22

AARON

Howya Bean stayed closed for two days. It was a sensible precaution, everyone agreed. Nobody knew what Bryon might do next, now that Aaron had reported the assault with his housemates' support and help.

Besides, word had gotten around within hours of what had happened. Aaron's housemates had already fended off several neighbors who were "just checking in on" him. If he opened the shop, he'd never hear the end of people asking him for all the details.

And he wanted to forget it, and he couldn't.

He still remembered every moment, and it had played out in his dreams over and over. At first, Aaron had stood firm and shouted at Bryon to get out. Then he'd faked running to the living room before doubling back to the hallway. That had given him just enough time to text Quinn.

Bryon had swatted his phone out of his hand. His heart pounding, he'd done exactly as Grandma had once shown him and broken Bryon's nose. The split second afterward, rooted to the spot in horror of what he'd done, replayed in his dreams the most. After screaming and grabbing his nose, cursing him to the high heavens, Bryon had tried to grab Aaron. He'd run to the living room before finding himself cornered, Bryon looming over him. Stumbling into the tree, grabbing for anything he could use to defend himself, Aaron woke up every time before Quinn arrived.

If Quinn hadn't shown up when he did, Aaron would have looked out for himself, right? He wouldn't have been helpless. He didn't want to think so, anyway. Aaron never wanted to rely on someone else for anything. His friends and housemates had to make him accept their help and meals and company.

In a moment of weakness, he'd given in and asked Quinn for help. And now he'd screwed things up between Quinn and his parents. Maybe for good—who knew?

Aaron stayed in his pajamas for these whole few days. His friends let him sleep the rest of Christmas Day away, but by the following evening they were bugging him to come downstairs and watch movies.

He started to come around and feel more like himself the next day, but by then, he was all too aware it had been two whole days without seeing Quinn.

And Aaron missed him like hell. Even this short span of time had felt like forever. More than once, he'd woken up in the middle of the night wishing he could cuddle into Quinn's side, let those strong arms wrap him up and make him feel safe.

But another, tinier, more scared part of him wanted to let this time drag on until after New Year's. That way, Aaron would never have to confront reality about their relationship.

He could just write off this whole month and forget about it and try to move on with his life. Except that even thinking that made his whole world lurch like a meteor had hit his stomach.

Fuck, it was all such a mess.

At least he'd spilled his guts to his friends over the last few days. All but one thing—he couldn't quite bring himself to admit to how damn much he wanted Quinn in his life.

Which meant he found himself defending Quinn yet again as they ate breakfast three days after the attack. With Beau, Ross, Jesse, Finn, Rusty, and Ezra around in turns, and Benji getting back today, Aaron was hardly ever alone except when he was in bed.

"I just don't know if I should go see him today, or call him, or what," Aaron admitted. "I know I'm going to open the shop."

Ezra shifted and folded his arms. "You are?"

"I am," Aaron said firmly. "I'm tired of lying around. I need to earn money and keep this place open. It'll give me something to do. And I'm right downtown by the police station."

"*Police station*," Jesse echoed with air quotes and laughed. "You mean city hall?" The two shared a building, the town was so small.

Aaron laughed. "Yeah, but you know what I mean. Everyone in town will be watching out for him now."

"Honestly, his parents made you feel like shit, didn't they?" Ross said and brushed toast crumbs off his shirt. "Fuck that. There's only room for the two of you in your relationship. Plus whoever else you invite in. I'm not asking for details." Aaron managed a smile and rolled his eyes, but he didn't interrupt. "I mean, it was nice of him to rescue you, but it was only temporary, wasn't it?"

Aaron froze. He swallowed hard, his eyes falling to the cup of coffee he clutched for dear life.

"It was."

Beau caught that word. "Was?"

"Yeah." Aaron took a deep breath. "I... don't know where we're going," he admitted. "Which is why I want to see him."

Ross was right—Quinn did value his parents' opinion of him. He clearly tried not to disappoint them. How much stock did he put in their opinion of Aaron, too?

That was another risk for Aaron: another set of people to disapprove of him, judge him, fuck him over later. More charitably, Aaron knew they were only trying to look out for Quinn. But he would end up being collateral damage as always.

Aaron didn't want Quinn to lose what he had; at least Quinn's parents loved him. Aaron couldn't live with himself if he inflicted the same heartache on him.

It wasn't just the attack. Hearing from his family only to be scolded and used as a political pawn had hurt—badly. Thank God Bryon hadn't actually released those photos, though. He must have realized that he'd just give Aaron's case more weight if he did.

"Go open the shop, and one of us will keep you company," Jesse assured him. "We can manage short-staffed at the art gallery now that the Christmas rush is over."

"Thanks," Aaron said and smiled at them. "For looking after me these last few days. I don't know what I'd do without you."

"I accept payment in wine only," Ezra piped up and winked. "Come on, babe. Let's go. Who else is working today?"

Once they'd figured out who was driving there now and who would walk down to join them later, Aaron piled in the car with his friends. But despite their protests, he insisted on heading to open up his shop alone.

They'd bubble-wrapped him these last few days, and that

was no way to get his confidence back. He had to prove to himself that he was still the fierce, independent Aaron he'd worked so hard to become.

He wanted Quinn there, but every time Quinn had messaged, he'd come up with a flimsy excuse to hide the way his whole heart wanted him there.

They'd joked about it, but he had never expected Quinn to steal his heart for real. Meanwhile, all Aaron would bring Quinn was drama and trouble.

He couldn't deal with everything at once: the deal with Quinn slipping away like sand through an hourglass, his family using him for political points, and Bryon trying to break him.

Nobody could break through this bubble of fear until Aaron himself did, and he had to do that alone.

As he opened the shop, Aaron was in a fog. His chest felt like it might burst open, and his throat was so tight he kept thinking he had a collar on.

But the first customer was Gregory, and he didn't breathe a word about the attack, even though all of Hart's Bay knew. He just chatted about the gossip—some builders he knew were confirming the new school was underway—and left Aaron to it.

Aaron had never been more grateful for that kind of quiet understanding. He stood a little straighter and felt a little more normal without people fussing and coddling him.

But then the next customer came in, striding quickly and bright-eyed, chest heaving with exertion like he'd just sprinted all the way from home.

It was Quinn.

Aaron had to grab the counter to stand upright. Even with the last few days of absence—maybe because of it—his whole world tilted toward Quinn like a pinball table on edge.

Instantly, he needed to be in Quinn's arms again. He needed to hold him and cuddle and talk about nothing at all. Needed to share every story, whether it made him laugh or cry. Needed to spend every second of every day with him that he possibly could.

Fuck. There was no getting around this—he was in love.

Aaron didn't have to say a word. Quinn strode toward him until he reached the counter, then leaned in halfway and down to Aaron's level before he stopped.

Just offering Aaron a kiss—not taking what he wanted, like Kasey and Bryon and so many others.

Like that, all the tension in Aaron's chest evaporated. He pressed his palms backward on the counter and hopped up, straightening his arms to hold himself up off the floor as he kissed Quinn.

And God, what a kiss it was. Quinn's hands rose to his cheeks and then stroked his hair, shoulders, back—just touching, soothing gently.

Aaron lost himself in the slide of lips on lips, heat prickling through his chest and warming up the spots he hadn't even realized had gone cold with fear.

But Quinn didn't let it linger, even though Aaron whimpered quietly when he pulled back.

"Mom called to tell me you were open today. I just wanted to ask you if you'll give me a chance to talk about things."

"I don't think I'm ready to talk about anything serious today," Aaron admitted in a choked little laugh. It made his heart warm that Quinn's parents had, at least, encouraged him to come over—in their own way. "I'm doing better, but my mind's still miles away."

"Okay," Quinn agreed easily, resting a hand over Aaron's on the countertop. "I can give you a few more days."

By then, Aaron might feel normal again—not jumping at shadows or crawling into bed in the middle of a conversation. Already, just being open for a few hours had exhausted him.

"Yes, please." But Aaron was hardly breathing. Was that before or after New Year's?

Quinn smiled, as if knowing what was on his mind. "New Year's is coming up, and we've been avoiding it for... well, forever. Would you come over for supper that day after you close the coffee shop? And then we can go to the party at Cher's together? I really want to spend that day with you. More than anything."

Goddamn it, Quinn spoke in a soft voice, earnest and gentle and plain. No hiding his feelings or playing games.

Aaron believed him, too, despite the doubts that had churned through his mind. Most of them were just distractions so he didn't have to face his ultimate fear.

Aaron was afraid that Quinn was just pulling a Kasey, pretending to love him, putting on a show for other people, and biding his time until he found a real future.

But Aaron couldn't hold on to those doubts when Quinn watched him like this. Unlike Kasey, Quinn always gave him the chance to say no. He asked and didn't take; he suggested and didn't sneer.

"Yes," Aaron whispered. "I've missed you. More than I realized."

Quinn broke out in a smile and cupped his cheeks again to kiss him. "Me too. Are you okay?"

"I'm fine," Aaron assured him, hoping he didn't have to rehash things yet again.

But Quinn didn't make him. He just nodded once, pulling back to look Aaron over like he was checking for injuries. Then he relaxed and breathed easier. "Okay. Good. I'd better go—I've got a meeting about some gym equipment, and I'm already kinda late. But I'll text you?"

"Okay," Aaron breathed out. "Thank you for coming here." He smiled after Quinn, waving to him as he left.

His spirits soared like they hadn't for days. Like a sunbeam through the mist, a foglight through the night, Quinn swept away the confusion and gave him a homing signal to lock onto.

A way home, if Aaron could only swallow his fear and step onto that path at long last. With Quinn's hand in his, maybe he finally could.

23

QUINN

It was the third or fourth time Aaron had run straight into Quinn while they cooked. This time, Aaron was reaching for cutlery and nearly stabbed Quinn with the forks. He squeaked and jumped backward. "Shit, sorry!"

Quinn nearly knocked over the pot on the stove while he tried to grab Aaron and steady him. "Whoa. Sorry. You okay?"

"Yeah." Aaron gave a breathless laugh but turned on his heel to stride to the kitchen and set the table.

Quinn paused as he stirred the pot of stewed vegetables and chicken. The rice was already sitting on the stove and done, just waiting for the rest of their meal.

All afternoon, they hadn't quite gelled together like before. Quinn was trying to hide how much this upset him.

Aaron was jumpy and not himself, while Quinn wasn't quite confident in how and when he could touch Aaron. No longer did he want to grab him and haul him in for a cheeky kiss or flick his ass with a towel in passing.

But things were good between them. Quinn had reassured him that his parents weren't mad at either of them. That was half-true; they'd been shocked that someone would try to hurt Aaron, although he hadn't explained the details, obviously.

Since then, Quinn had been subjected to the local side of his family telling him several different versions of the story during the nonstop visits and family parties that fell between Christmas Day and New Year's.

In some people's thirdhand retellings, Bryon was a jealous ex, and in others he was a customer Aaron had spilled hot coffee on and who had come to get revenge. Quinn never gave them any details, except that Aaron was fine. Thankfully, nobody seemed to know about the nude photos.

But he also had to find a way to show Aaron that he loved him—in a way he'd never be able to ignore. Quinn wanted him to know that he didn't care about disappointing anyone else in the world as much as he cared about Aaron.

So tonight, in front of everyone at Cher's, on the closing evening of their agreement, he was going to ask Aaron out. For real, like he should have done from the very start.

That way, Aaron couldn't worry that Quinn would choose other people over him. No explaining things to their friends or families, and no room for gossip. The word would spread to anyone who wasn't there, but it would be firsthand—or at least secondhand. Everyone would know it like it was.

Quinn was thankful to spare Aaron from the gossip he'd endured these last three long days, but otherwise, he'd missed him like hell. At least they were texting almost constantly again and calling each other every night—nearly back to normal.

"So what did Marv say?" Aaron asked, his tone forcibly cheery. "About your diet and stuff? Do I have to go break his nose, too? I might develop a taste for it."

Quinn chuckled and shook his head. "He agreed to keep

me on *just for January*," he air-quoted. "So I'm calling in contacts and working with Rain and Colt to get some kind of space set up here. It'll be super basic. I don't want to open my own gym, thanks."

"Why not? You'd be great at it."

Quinn smiled as he turned off the stove and ladled rice into dishes. "Then I'd spend more time pushing paper than pumping steel."

"What you need is a co-owner." Aaron grinned. "Don't be an idiot like me and do it all yourself."

"That's... not a bad idea," Quinn admitted. "Maybe I'll keep an eye out around town. Some of my clients aren't happy with their jobs, too."

Instantly, he thought of Andrew, who had come so far in his training sessions. He was looking for any kind of work that wasn't his boring office job. Would he really be up for the risk? Who knew, unless Quinn asked?

"I'm brimming with ideas," Aaron said with a smug grin and sat at the table. "And a couple of them are even safe for work."

Quinn laughed, dipping the ladle into his stew to pour it on top of each bowl of rice. "And all of them are good, in my experience."

Aaron pretended to preen while Quinn chuckled again. "Oh, stop."

"Here you go." Quinn sat opposite Aaron, smoothing down the tablecloth. He'd gotten the good plates out, too, and he'd lit a pillar candle.

Hopefully it wasn't too much. Either way, Quinn would find out tonight.

"This is nice," Aaron said suddenly. "I missed this. I've

been kind of hiding out in bed the last few days when I'm not at work."

Quinn nodded slightly and held up his glass of wine. "Well, here's to a good New Year's Eve."

Aaron clinked glasses, and their gazes caught and held for a few moments. It was nothing short of magnetic, the way they were drawn to each other and had been from the start.

"To a good night," Aaron said simply. That was all.

They dug into their supper without saying much, both of them clearly hungry. It was already late, and the party at Cher's would be starting soon. Quinn, for one, was ravenous for something more interesting than his last week of meals.

Slowly over the course of supper, Quinn relaxed. He'd only seen Aaron in the mornings when he picked up his coffee, so Aaron told him about movies he'd watched while Quinn talked about the highlights of his parties.

The whole time, Quinn could hardly focus from jittery nerves. He was going to put himself out there like never before, and he might never have done it if it weren't for that attack from Bryon.

Aaron had called *him*. Of all the friends he could have texted or called—it wasn't the cops, it wasn't his best friends. It was Quinn that Aaron had reached out to and trusted to come with a single word. That said more than any of Aaron's joking complaints about romance.

After supper, as they got ready, Aaron went over to his coat pocket and yanked a thin strip of fabric out. For half a second, Quinn thought he might be about to learn about bondage, but Aaron just grinned at him.

"Can I have help tying this?" Aaron asked, looking up at Quinn. "I want to match you. My knot will be all over the place if I try." Then he snickered and muttered under his breath, "So to speak." As usual, Quinn had no idea what he was talking about but probably didn't want to know, given that tone.

Oh, my God. I'm doing the right thing. Quinn's whole heart melted at how nervous and hopeful Aaron looked with those round eyes and fidgety feet.

He wanted to kiss Aaron and sweep him off his feet, but now wasn't the right moment. Quinn had a plan to show Aaron that he was worth showing off.

So he stepped close to Aaron and looped the fabric around his neck, sliding the cloth across itself and twisting. It took focus to figure out which way to go, so he mentally reversed it as he went.

Aaron held still and Quinn kept his touch gentle, sliding the knot up the tie when he had it figured out at last. He let his thumb caress Aaron's skin and slid his hand up the side of Aaron's neck. Aaron shivered and closed his eyes, a quiet sigh escaping. Quinn cupped his cheek and pulled him in for a soft kiss.

Aaron was vulnerable and needy, and Quinn was captivated—heart and soul. He needed this man. He'd risk anything: humiliation, his parents being pissed off at his choice of life partner, anything. He didn't care.

He'd move mountains for Aaron. No more letting Aaron push him away. From tonight on, he wasn't going to let Aaron deflect his own needs.

"There. Ready to go," Quinn whispered against Aaron's soft lips.

"Mmm." Aaron stirred, sliding his arms around Quinn's back. "We could show up late."

Quinn chuckled. "Later," he promised. "I have too much I want to do. If we start, I won't want to stop."

Aaron swallowed hard, his eyes flying open as he stared up at Quinn. His cheeks were flushed. Good—a blush. That was rare. Quinn felt kind of proud of himself.

"Oh," Aaron whispered. "Well, when you put it like *that*. Let's go before I peel your clothes off and ride you like a flying carpet."

Quinn took Aaron's hand and laced their fingers. "Do you mind walking?"

"Not at all." Aaron smiled up at him, bright and cheery despite all he'd been through lately. The man was made of something else, stronger than Quinn could ever imagine—steel didn't cut it. Stardust, maybe.

God, Quinn loved him.

His voice was strained as he declared, "Then let's go."

The time flew by as soon as they reached Cher's. Everyone in town seemed to be there, crammed into every corner of the little place. Since it was a gorgeous, relatively warm winter evening, they were even spilling out of the bar from the tables outside into the square. Even the Harts were around—from both branches of the fractured family. Some of them, Quinn hadn't seen in years.

Rain's parents kept their distance from Finn's parents. Elsie-Mae was the only one who drifted back and forth between Harts like they were all her very favorite child. She left at ten, declaring midnight an unsociable hour, and the glares resumed.

Half an hour before the new year, Finn made like he was heading for drinks. But he instead walked over to Floyd, bold as day.

"What's he doing?" Quinn whispered to Aaron from their spot at the bar, but he shrugged.

"No idea. Shh."

The hush that fell over much of the bar made Cher turn around from counting glasses. She nearly fell over at the sight: Finn facing his grandfather as they scrutinized each other.

"Thank you for your apology. Jesse told me what happened, but I wanted to talk to you myself. It's not going to fix everything, but I hear you. I want this to be over. This whole stupid damn rift."

Quinn inhaled sharply. He'd never paid attention to the blow-by-blows—*so-and-so ignored so-and-so at the grocery store, did you hear?*—but he knew what this meant.

Floyd nodded slightly. "Me, too. It's done enough damage. *I've* done enough damage. It ends now."

Like that, he reached out to offer his hand. Finn took it and shook, and a ripple of gasps and a smattering of applause went through the audience.

"Thanks, Grandpa," Finn said, a little quieter. "I hope we can get past this one day."

"Me too, Finn. Me too."

After that dramatic highlight, the only thing to do was drink wine, chat with all of Aaron's friends, and wait for the new year to count down.

And risk everything to ask Aaron out for real.

No big deal, right?

"Be right back. Gotta make space for the midnight champagne!" Aaron winked and slid past Quinn to make for the bathroom. Quinn nodded, watching Cher move around the bar and pass out plastic glasses of champagne.

Shit. It really was now or never. Quinn was sweating buckets, enough that he rolled up his sleeves.

"Doing all right, honey?" Cher asked.

Quinn gave her a quick, nervous smile. "I'm about to ask Aaron out, to be my for-real boyfriend."

"Oooh. Putting a name on it? That's big." Cher winked and slid him an extra glass of champagne. "For the nerves."

Quinn nodded in thanks and downed it in a gulp, then burped and coughed as the bubbles engaged in hand-to-hand combat with his lungs. "Sorry." Once he caught his breath and Cher stopped snickering, the anxiety crept back in. "It is big. But I don't know. It feels right. You can find love in the place you least expect."

Cher nodded and leaned in. "Are you asking him out at the stroke of midnight?" When Quinn nodded, she raised an eyebrow.

"What?" Quinn asked, biting his lip. "Wrong choice?"

"Are you doing that for you or for him?"

Ouch. Blunt, but effective as always. Quinn opened his mouth for a moment before he closed it and shook his head. Aaron had always been fine with their relationship being their own business.

Quinn had told himself he didn't care about disappointing anyone anymore. He couldn't live his life for other people. Kind of like he'd started off working out to get others' attention before realizing it was about himself, he'd really thrown himself into this relationship for his and Aaron's sakes, nobody else.

But by asking him out in front of the whole town, was Quinn just seeking approval in a subtler way? To replace the validation his parents would never give him about the relationship?

Ouch. It felt true, deep in Quinn's bones. He couldn't see how he hadn't spotted it until now.

Seeing that she'd hit a sore point, Cher reached out to pat his hand. "Sorry. But you know, you've got a few minutes left. Make 'em count," she advised. "Here he comes."

Aaron joined Quinn, sliding onto the stool again and giving him another adorable little smile. "Ooh. Champagne's been delivered. Must be really close."

Quinn licked his lips and turned to Aaron, taking both his hands. "Yeah. But first, I wanted to ask you something."

Aaron tilted his head, his eyes bright. "Yeah?"

"Five minutes left!" someone hollered, and Quinn felt the whole room lurch.

Shit. He was running out of time. No grand speech, then.

"Aaron, I... I love you." He gulped hard, squeezing Aaron's hands a little tighter than he meant to. "And I don't want this to end. Will you be my boyfriend?"

Seconds turned into hours—no, years—as he waited for Aaron's answer, scrutinizing his every expression for some clue to his answer.

But instead of lighting up like he'd hoped, or even gently letting him down, Aaron looked... disappointed. No, that wasn't it. *Crushed*.

"Quinn, I... you..." He pulled his hands out of Quinn's and grabbed his champagne glass, lurching to his feet. "You just broke the one promise we had."

"I—what?" Quinn's mind whirled as he tried to figure this out. Not to tell other people? Not to give it a label? But that was the point—he needed more than to call Aaron *my guy*.

Aaron's eyes shone, tears streaking his cheeks as he shook his head slightly. "Just let me down easy, right here. I'd prefer that."

Quinn shook his head hard. "I'm not going to let you down. I mean it. I want you."

"I can't believe you're not faking it," Aaron whispered, a quiet desperation in his eyes. "I'm not the guy you want to love. I want to be, but I can't."

Then he turned and fled, champagne glass still in his hand. He wove through the crowd easily, turning sideways to slide between people toward the door.

Quinn's whole world had stopped. It was plunging down, falling further and faster than he could have imagined.

And all he could think was: *What promise did I break?*

24

AARON

Aaron had only caught a snippet of it through the crowd.

Love in the place you least expect.

He knew he was the last resort for plenty of men in town, but this was a harsh reminder of the way everyone saw him— the slutty trophy guy. Not a keeper, and certainly no one you should *expect* to love. Just keep around until the novelty wore off.

Aaron had only ever asked Quinn to promise one thing: not to fake love at the end of this deal.

They hadn't even talked about that word before. And now, all of a sudden, minutes before the deal came up, Quinn wanted to tell him this? No. That was the kind of shit Kasey had done—blindside him with declarations of love, ask him to move in, tell him when it was over.

Was Quinn just doing this for show? Because, like everyone else, he wanted something from Aaron—not Aaron himself?

Scarier by far was the fact that *Aaron* loved *Quinn*. He couldn't even keep his own heart in check. However hard he'd tried to keep it just sex and friendship, from the moment Quinn had smiled those pearly whites at him, Aaron had been screwed.

It was happening all over again.

He was falling for a man who saw him as a convenient solution to his problems. Maybe for Quinn, that problem was needing a relationship instead of needing a political pawn or a quick fuck. Either way, Aaron was still the voiceless object, the trophy. He'd be stripped of everything he'd worked to be and tamed for one man's desires.

Aaron's feet carried him, and without any conscious decision, he found himself fumbling for his keys to unlock the door of his shop.

"Fuck," Aaron breathed out, wiping his eyes as he slipped inside and sat on the counter. If only he could have talked about it with Quinn. But he'd panicked, his worst fears suddenly rearing their heads.

Not there, in public, in front of everyone he knew, with the clock counting down to midnight and expectant eyes on him and ears listening to everything he said.

Not under the microscope like that. Expected to nod and smile and say yes because what else did someone say in that situation? With Cher looking on, and people nearby turning to listen in?

The thought of losing his free will, being the nice, submissive, compliant little guy that so many men wanted him to be... it scared the shit out of Aaron.

For a few precious days, it had looked like Aaron could have it all. Everything he wanted, and everything he hadn't even allowed himself to dream of having. Maybe even forever.

And then it had come crashing down.

Happy New Year to me. It's like the old year, but more of

the same, Aaron thought and allowed himself a bitter smile. He stared at the number counting down on his phone, tightly clutching the plastic stem of his champagne flute as the silence gnawed at him.

Thirty seconds to go. If this month hadn't saved him, nothing could now. Instead, it had damn near broken him.

And all because of one man who had stolen his heart along the way.

The door opened, a tinkle in the utter stillness of the dark shop.

Aaron turned his gaze up, feeling frozen. If this was Bryon, he had no fight left in him. Nothing to give anymore.

But it wasn't. It was Quinn, and he held his hands up before carefully approaching. "I'm sorry, sweetheart. I'm so sorry I upset you."

Damn it, Aaron's tears fell again. He slid down from the counter to his feet and opened his arms, letting Quinn wrap him up in a hug that pulled all the little broken pieces of Aaron's heart back together.

"I had to hold back your friends from coming to aggressively love you, so please hear me out before they trample me," Quinn murmured in his ear.

Aaron laughed breathlessly and let go, leaning on the counter. "Well, you've got about twenty seconds."

Quinn didn't even hesitate. He was stricken yet serious, nothing but honesty radiating from his face as he cupped Aaron's cheeks. He spoke quickly but with passion. "I'm serious. I want you. Only you. I fell for you from the moment I saw you, and I've been too afraid to scare you off to tell you until now. But please—*please*—believe me. I'm not faking this."

Aaron caught his breath. "You... aren't? But look at who I am. I'm all wrong for you."

"No, you're not." Quinn didn't speak over him brusquely. It was soft and gentle. "Sweetheart, you're *perfect* to me. You've thrown up every obstacle: your sex drive, your past, your friends, my family. I don't care about any of those. I want you, Aaron."

It was midnight. Fireworks went off outside, crackling from the end of the pier and backyards around the city.

And Aaron grabbed Quinn and kissed him, hard, tears streaming down his face as he answered Quinn in the best way he knew how.

Honestly, with no words to hide behind anymore. Forceful and bold, he showed Quinn who he was.

And Quinn swept him off his feet, crushed their bodies together in the strong loop of his arms as Aaron wrapped himself around Quinn.

The missing pieces Aaron hadn't even wanted to admit seemed to slide into place when Quinn held him like this.

Maybe he didn't have to be complete.

Maybe he had to be okay with letting Quinn complete him.

Maybe, in that vulnerability, Aaron would find the greatest strength of his life.

But if he kept these walls up for the rest of his life, he'd never get to find out. And he'd lose the man who made him feel things he'd once thought he could never feel again.

"I love you, too," Aaron breathed against Quinn's lips. "And I'm so sorry I hid it. *I* was the one breaking our rules. I was so afraid to tell you. Afraid you'd... I don't know, use me. Like every other man does." He cleared his throat and wiped his face before pressing more kisses along Quinn's jaw and throat. "But you don't, and you never have. Fuck, I fell for you from the moment we met, and that scares the hell out of me. I'd marry you tomorrow, and that *definitely* scares the hell out of me. I've never felt more complete than when we're together, but I never thought you wanted me like I want you."

He could feel Quinn shaking slightly, but holding on to him like he might slip away at any moment.

"Oh, baby," Quinn whispered, nuzzling his neck and cheek. "I'm so sorry I made you think that. The number of times I just wanted to tell you. But I thought even talking about commitment would scare you off, and I couldn't risk that."

Aaron chuckled, his voice hoarse with emotion. He was tired already with the exhaustion of relief, like all the emotion in the world was spent. Like he could sleep for a year. "It doesn't. But I... I've only ever been a chess piece for other people. I came out and my parents hired a PR firm to deal with it. Now they want me to be the poster boy to score some political points. My ex told me when we were dating and when it was over. Guys come along, fuck me, and leave me when they're done. And then I... I thought you wanted me to be the thing you need me to be, too. The perfect boyfriend. But your parents hate me. It wouldn't work."

Quinn set Aaron down gently, taking his hands again. "Fuck all of them. I'm serious. Anyone who's hurt you, I wish I could take that pain away. I'm proud to have you. In every way, in public and private. Our life is our business. I want you to be yourself in front of them. I want both of us to be ourselves. Not scared like I was, cutting away pieces of myself to try to get their approval. That's not my job, and it's sure as hell not yours. If you scar them for life, well, they'll get used to it. Or not. That's their choice. But I love you for *you*."

Aaron's knees wobbled as he leaned backward on the

counter for support, then tugged Quinn closer, pressing his nose into his chest again. "I love you, too," he whispered.

He believed Quinn. He wanted him. No more hiding things and hoping for the best.

It was going to be different—so very different—from Aaron's last year, let alone any relationship Aaron had had before that.

But, he thought, it was going to be perfectly worth it.

"When I see my future, you're there," Aaron admitted, his chest fluttering. "No, not just there. You're it. The one." He gulped hard and then managed a tiny, shaky laugh through the tears now spilling over again. "How romantic is that, huh? Guess you won."

Quinn wrapped his arms around Aaron to hug him for a long time. "Yeah," he murmured at last. "*We* won."

With that, they walked back to Cher's hand in hand.

They didn't need to say a word when they entered the bar; a round of applause started, and toasts were raised to them. Their smiles—teary, yet overjoyed—said it all.

QUINN

The walk back to Quinn's house felt warmer than the trip down. It could have been the triumphant, even joyful glow in Quinn's chest, or their extra glasses of Cher's "champagne"— which was really sparkling wine, but nobody was sober enough to care.

Quinn tugged Aaron onto the porch and sandwiched him between himself and the door. "No getting away now."

Aaron giggled. "I never want to." He beamed up at Quinn and then slid his arms around his waist.

"Okay... here goes." Quinn unlocked the door and pocketed his keys, then slid his hands down to Aaron's ass and squeezed.

"Ooh!" Aaron giggled. "Cheeky."

Quinn hoisted him up, ignoring Aaron's gasp of surprise, and steadied him with one forearm under his ass, the other hand groping for the door to push it open.

With Aaron wrapped around him, Quinn stepped carefully through the doorway. "Happy New Year, baby. Welcome home." He set him carefully in the entryway and closed the door.

Aaron beamed at Quinn as he fumbled to toss his jacket aside and kick off his shoes. "Thank you. You know, the Raft is yours, too. You're definitely an honorary member. Have I told you that before?"

No, he had not. Quinn's chest was tight with emotion for a moment. He knew what that place meant to Aaron—the sanctuary he'd found in his new family there. Opening it to Quinn meant everything.

"Thank you," he said, trying not to let his voice wobble.

Aaron just grinned. "You can thank me with your dick. I've been waiting for hours, you know. *Hours.* Days, in fact. Maybe a lifetime."

Quinn laughed. "Oh, have you?" He took Aaron's hand to lead him straight to the bedroom. "Thank you for your bravery. This superhuman feat of endurance will be rewarded."

"By making me perform another superhuman feat of endurance?" Aaron eyed him suspiciously, their shoulders bumping as he steered into Quinn playfully.

Quinn bumped him back. "Maybe I'll be nice to you."

"Phew."

"By making you wait," Quinn continued, smirking. When Aaron groaned at him, he just winked. "You can't deny how good it feels afterward."

He so badly wanted to get Aaron naked, explore his body from head to toe, until Aaron squirmed and whimpered and begged for release.

"I hate that you're right," Aaron lamented. But the moment they stepped through the bedroom doorway, he pressed against Quinn with every inch of his hot little body. "Take me, Quinn. Show me what this year has to hold."

Quinn swept his hands from Aaron's hips to his back, reaching under his shirt to run his nails ever so lightly across his skin.

"Oh!" Aaron gasped, a ripple coursing through him as his eyes fluttered half-closed.

Quinn growled playfully, then loosened Aaron's tie. He tugged Aaron's shirt off under it, and tossed it aside. "Better. You don't need that. Or these." He unfastened Aaron's trousers.

But when Aaron tried to reach for his tie, Quinn batted his hand away. "I need a grab handle."

Aaron burst out giggling.

When Aaron stood there naked but for the tie, an adorable blush spreading over his cheeks, Quinn just stood there and looked him up and down. He was so damn sexy, and he knew it, but Quinn never wanted him to forget, so he said it anyway. "God, I'm lucky you're mine."

"And only yours," Aaron said instantly, pressing against him. His smooth, bare skin was hot to the touch as Quinn ran his hands from Aaron's shoulder blades down to his ass. Much better without all that pesky fabric.

That reminded him. "*Do* you want to be exclusive? I realized we never really talked about it, and since you enjoy sex so much..." Quinn trailed off, anxiety thrumming through his chest. "I want to make you the happiest you can be."

Aaron just smiled at him. "I've hidden behind my label for a while. Let people see me as a joke, or as a slut without any depth. So to speak." He winked. "But it wasn't until you that I realized I can be a slut with you, and be happy. So, no. I want you and only you, baby."

Well, someone had lit a whole campfire in Quinn's chest.

He swallowed hard and nodded, his beam lighting up the room.

Then Aaron deadpanned, "And if we decide to take in an innocent young man and corrupt him with my sex toy library in twenty years' time, we'll deal with it then."

Quinn threw back his head and laughed. "Oh, Aaron. I love you so much."

But his chest might just burst with happiness. Aaron wanted to be with him in *twenty years' time?*

"Besides, this way I can pass along my condom collection."

"Your...?" Quinn blinked at Aaron several times.

Aaron smirked. "They were on sale. Forty bucks for five hundred. How could I pass them up? Surprisingly, I even have some left over."

"Oh, my God," Quinn snorted with laughter. "Now you can be the condom fairy."

Aaron squealed and clapped his hands. "Yes! That's my Halloween costume, too. You genius."

Quinn started laughing and he could hardly stop, even as Aaron tumbled onto the bed and tugged him on top of him.

"You—I don't know what to do with you," Quinn finally managed. Then, before Aaron could get out any dirty suggestions, he smiled. "No, scratch that, I do: love you. And fuck you, some nights. And make love, other nights."

Aaron sighed happily. "I could deal with that," he teased. "I suppose. Now kiss me, love."

So Quinn did—a deep, lingering kiss that spoke of the pull between them, irresistible as the earth's tides themselves. In Aaron's eyes, he saw everything he could ever need.

He ground against Aaron, careful to hold himself above his adorable little boyfriend so he didn't squish him. As their hard shafts lined up and slid together, all he could do was moan throatily.

"Perfect," Aaron gasped. It was his turn to dig his nails into Quinn's back, on either side of his spine. "Oh, you feel perfect above me."

Quinn knew just what he meant. He shifted until he straddled Aaron's thighs and then pulled his legs together, closing Aaron's legs. Then he slid down a few inches, the tip of his cock sliding between Aaron's smooth thighs and brushing past his balls. The tip of his cock nearly reached Aaron's smooth little hole with each thrust, but the angle wasn't quite right.

Still, it was a tease along the sensitive skin all around, and Aaron gasped. "Oh." He squeezed his thighs harder, wrapping his forearms firmly around Quinn's back. "Hello there, big boy."

Quinn ran his hand through Aaron's hair, gently closing his hand into a fist.

Aaron's hiss was sharp-edged pleasure, his eyes lighting up as he went still under Quinn. Wordlessly, he rolled his head back when Quinn tugged on his hair, exposing the pale line of his throat.

"Gorgeous," Quinn whispered. He kissed his Adam's apple, then the soft spot just under his chin, and his rapidly flickering pulse point. "I want to eat you all up."

"Yes, please." Aaron whimpered, and the note vibrated through Quinn's kiss-swollen lips.

Quinn licked from the hollow of his collarbone all the way up to his cheek, then nibbled his jaw. "What shall I do with you?" He gave a hard thrust, his cock nestled snugly in the warm crook of Aaron's groin. "Slide inside you? Fill you up? Leave you dripping wet with my cum and your sweat?"

Aaron's strangled sound of response didn't have any clear syllables.

"I'll take that as a *fuck, yes*," Quinn chuckled gently. He bit Aaron's earlobe and then kissed behind his ear before he swooped back to his lips and kissed him hard, sucking on his lower lip until Aaron yielded.

When Aaron's lips parted, he slid his tongue between his lips, gently yet demanding. He wasn't going to turn away until they were both satisfied beyond belief.

But before he fulfilled the dirty fantasies he was outlining to Aaron, true to his word, he was going to make him wait.

Aaron gasped when Quinn scooted down far enough that his cock slid free, so that he could reach his nipples. "Quinn—" he started and then bit back a cry when Quinn's lips closed around a nipple.

"Mmhmm?" Quinn pinched the sensitive nub between his lips and pulled gently. He gazed up at Aaron, and then his tongue darted out to circle around the nipple a few slow times.

By the time he made it to Aaron's other nipple, Aaron was kneading his back and crying out softly with every brush of Quinn's lips on his skin.

Quinn could feel Aaron's shaft pulsating against his stomach, achingly hard. He didn't grant him an ounce of relief, though. Not yet. There was time yet.

When Aaron tried to reach down, Quinn playfully smacked his hand away. "No."

Aaron squirmed and pouted at him, raising his hands above his head. "Oh, no. I knew it."

Quinn smirked, confident in everything he did and said right now. It was incredible, being able to read Aaron so well that he knew this protest was part of the fun for him. "Sorry. It's for your own good, you know."

Sure enough, Aaron gulped hard, his cock twitching against his belly. "But I need you."

Quinn smiled gently, pressing a finger against Aaron's lips. "Shhh. You don't want to miss this."

He gently unlooped the tie and took it off. And then he slid down the bed, kissing a trail down Aaron's stomach. He stopped at all the little spots he'd noticed drove Aaron crazy, tonguing at them until Aaron's cries were sharp and insistent.

Then he carried on, straight down through the sparse curls of his treasure trail to the tip of Aaron's cock.

Aaron's cry was wordless. He arched off the bed and trembled before he managed to settle.

"Mmm," Quinn moaned at the salty taste he found there. Aaron's belly was already slick, his tip wet and needy. He licked every drop off, keeping each stroke of his tongue light and teasing, then worked his way down the shaft.

"Fucking *suck* me," Aaron groaned. "Jesus, what does a guy have to—"

Quinn interrupted him by sweeping his tongue up, then sucking the head of Aaron's cock into his mouth with a dirty, wet sound.

Aaron cried out again, his toes curling into the bed as his nails scrabbled against Quinn's back.

The heat of the heavy shaft against Quinn's tongue was addictive. He sucked hard, wrapping his lips tightly around the shaft and sucking his cheeks in. Then he slid his mouth down, taking Aaron in to the hilt before he pulled back up.

It took moments to find a rhythm that worked for him. His other hand was free to pinch Aaron's nipples firmly, rolling them between his fingers and sliding his nails gently across them when he wanted to turn Aaron's volume up.

"Yes, yes, yes," Aaron panted. He bucked and squirmed,

but Quinn's other hand easily pressed him to the bed when he rose too high. Then, Quinn reached down to his own hard cock, giving himself a squeeze and gentle rub to take the edge off. It almost hurt, how much he needed attention. Needed to be inside Aaron's tight body, claiming and filling him almost beyond belief.

Don't worry, Quinn told himself. *Soon.*

First, he wanted Aaron desperate and squirming with need. Not just need—that didn't feel like a strong enough word. He wanted him going out of his goddamn mind, unable to wait another second.

And Aaron was rapidly approaching that point. "Please," he gasped. "I want you in me, please."

Finally, Quinn pulled his mouth off Aaron, giving him one more gentle lick before he smiled up at him. "And I want to be inside you."

Aaron spread his legs so fast that one knee almost made contact with Quinn's face. One hand wandered south toward his cock, like he thought Quinn wouldn't notice.

Quinn let him get away with it for a few moments while he grabbed lube, but when he turned back, he gave him a mock stern look. "Now, what did I say about that?"

He didn't waver even under Aaron's pleading look, until Aaron guiltily drew his hand back and laid it above his head again. "Fiiiiine."

Quinn smiled, slicking his fingers. "I'll make sure you get your chance. Tonight and tomorrow morning. No way are you opening the shop on time, just FYI."

"That's fine." Aaron laughed breathlessly. "Nobody else will be out of bed that early anyway. I can take the morning off."

"Good." Quinn rested one hand on Aaron's thigh to keep

his legs apart, then grinned as Aaron raised his knees and clutched onto them for dear life to make himself even more accessible.

"Perks of a slutty boyfriend," Aaron said, but he sounded proud now. There was no edge of self-deprecation there.

Quinn beamed at him. "I'll remember that and bend you in two more often," he promised. With that, he ran two fingers around the tightness and inside, taking it slow and gentle at first.

One knuckle at a time, he worked his fingers inside to spread and slick Aaron open, getting him ready. He let Aaron have another few minutes of pleasure as he fingered him, rubbing the firm prostate until Aaron quivered.

But before he could run the risk of letting Aaron finish too quickly, Quinn drew his fingers out and chuckled at the inevitable pout. "I've got something even bigger and better for you."

"Is it... a cucumber?" Aaron pretended to guess, a hand over his mouth in shock. "Or an eggplant? Oh, my."

"See if you can guess." Quinn grinned at him, adding more lube to his palm. He stroked himself until he was wet and burning with need, then pressed the tip against Aaron's sexy little hole.

Quinn slid into Aaron slowly, grunting at the tight ring that enveloped him. Meanwhile, Aaron rolled his head back and squeezed his eyes shut, his breathing quick.

"Definitely eggplant," Aaron managed a minute later, his eyes fluttering open again. He beamed up at Quinn, spreading his legs and hooking them around Quinn's back. "More, please."

So Quinn pushed into Aaron in slow, shallow thrusts.

Deeper and deeper he went, until their bodies were locked together.

"Yes," Aaron whimpered. "Quinn, you feel... *so* good."

Pleasure thrummed pleasantly through Quinn's whole body, an electric crackle. Every nerve was on fire, but most of all, his skin burned where he touched Aaron. Their chests brushed against one another's when Quinn leaned down to kiss him, and their thighs rubbed as he found just the right angle.

And then he was so deep inside Aaron that he bottomed out, their eyes locked together just like their bodies.

Aaron just nodded once at him, a small and eager movement. So Quinn smiled, leaned down for a kiss, and started to thrust into him. These were fluid thrusts, ripples of his whole body. His muscles worked in ways they never did at the gym. But every ounce of strength that Quinn had trained came in handy now.

It wasn't just Quinn, though. Aaron was flexible and graceful, enveloping him and squeezing around him in short, sharp ripples of pleasure.

His moans and whimpers drove Quinn onward, and his hands roamed across Quinn's back, sometimes caressing him tenderly and sometimes digging into his skin.

They kissed hard and fast now. Neither of them held back. Nobody else mattered—nothing at all mattered but the slick thrusts of Quinn deep inside Aaron, and their hands on each other's bodies, and the wordless moans of pleasure that soaked the air.

"I can't last much longer," Aaron gasped, fast and low and desperate. "I love you too much. I love *this* too much. Did I mention I love you?"

Aaron was squeezing tight around him now, his whole body tense as his breathing came in fast, harsh pants.

"I know," Quinn soothed him, kissing him gently. They'd have plenty of chances to make love—every day, if they wanted. "You can come for me, baby. Let go. I've got you."

"Yes...!" Aaron choked off his cry, tossing his head back and clutching Quinn.

Quinn held Aaron close and gasped for breath. It was his turn, now that Aaron clenched around him so tightly he couldn't hold back. Bliss crashed into him, utterly and completely carrying him away from the world.

He was just here, in the throes of ecstasy, with the person who mattered more than anything.

"I love you," Quinn gasped, pressing kisses into the crook of Aaron's neck and cradling him close. "I love you so much, too. I want to hold you like this forever."

"Yes," Aaron breathed out, his hands going still against Quinn's back. "Forever."

When Aaron finally went limp in his arms and Quinn collapsed on top of him, they just pressed kisses against sweat-soaked skin, rubbing and touching like it was their last chance ever. Or maybe the first chance in forever.

All Quinn had to do was roll onto his side and Aaron went with him, nuzzling into his chest and tucking himself in.

They needed no words. Touch alone spoke volumes. At the end of all their uncertainty and hopeful yearning was the start of a bone-deep certainty.

This was it—Quinn's forever. And he couldn't wait a moment longer. It began now.

EPILOGUE

AARON

There was never a question that they'd go out to dinner at Millie's for Valentine's Day. Quinn called a month ahead to book a table, and they even picked coordinating ties.

It had been more than a month since they'd gotten together, and Aaron knew at every moment that he'd made the right decision. It wasn't even a choice, really—it was a decision to let his heart lead.

Living with Quinn for the last month, they'd gotten to know each other even better. Aaron had already started to influence the place; his condom bucket had stayed behind in Benji's capable hands, though Aaron had dibs on it for Halloween. But his sex toy library had found room in Quinn's closet.

Slowly but surely, he was broadening Quinn's horizons. None of Aaron's wildness had been tamed, that was for sure. Aaron's fears were a thing of the past, because Quinn only loved him more for it. And sure, Aaron had shocked Quinn's parents a few times already, but they seemed to like him more now that they saw Quinn so much happier. One day, they might even see eye to eye.

"Are we splitting dessert?" Aaron beamed when Quinn gestured to the waiter and winked.

They'd been lucky to get a table by the window; on this day of the year, more of the booths and regular tables had suddenly turned romantic, decked out in tablecloths and candles. But the lucky few got these tables, with a view over the moonlit wilderness and ocean beyond.

"You bet your pretty little head." Quinn grinned at him. "And I hear they're making their chocolate eclair-cake with a certain coffee..."

Aaron beamed. His new flavor—the Roast of the Town—was on sale at Victor's store so customers could get their fix on their way to Howya Bean. It was even used as a mixer for one of Cher's drinks, and even as an ingredient in a few desserts here at Millie's.

"Oooh." Aaron snickered at the long, narrow cream-filled cake in the shape of an eclair when it arrived. He glanced up at Quinn. "You had to know I was going to comment on this."

Quinn gave him his best long-suffering sigh. "Of course." But he still laughed as Aaron enthusiastically pressed his spoon into the cake to make cream burst out of the end.

"This is the best Valentine's ever." Aaron beamed at him. "Thank you for taking a cheat day."

"I wouldn't dream of subjecting you to my... what was it you said this morning?"

"Breasticles," Aaron said with a cheery grin.

"That's it. How could I forget?" Quinn deadpanned.

Aaron ate Quinn's food—even those chicken breasts— some days. But Quinn was a lot more relaxed on his diet now that he was working mostly from his little gym here in Hart's Bay.

He only opened the place at specific hours, mostly when he was working with clients. Already, there was such a demand that Quinn was looking at hiring a former gym client to manage it full-time.

Once the cake was gone, Quinn stretched in satisfaction and then smiled at Aaron. "I bet I can make your Valentine's even better, though." He reached across the table to pass Aaron a box.

When Aaron squinted down at it, he laughed in sheer surprise.

It was a cock ring box. One of the fancy, stainless steel ones with a nice little wooden box and velvet-lined interior.

"Oh my God!" Aaron breathed out, trying not to giggle. He knew Quinn was getting bolder, but this newfound sense of mischief was absolutely breathtaking.

He tried not to attract *too* much attention as he flipped it open.

And then he stopped, staring at the contents.

Wait. No way.

Quinn smiled softly at him and got up, only to sink to his knee.

Aaron had told him cheerily several times that he'd get engaged in a heartbeat, but... he hadn't known if Quinn was listening.

In the box—rather than the velvet interior he'd expected with its bright silver ring—was a much smaller ring. One sized for a finger. And the simple design was unmistakable.

It was Aaron's grandma's wedding ring—one of his most prized possessions. Sure, they'd talked about Aaron wearing it one day, but Aaron had thought Quinn was talking about someday. Not... right now.

Hot tears pricked in the corners of Aaron's eyes. Quinn had been truly listening during those long, late-night conversations about their pasts.

Only Quinn would think to do this. Aaron's heart only swelled that much more. And the fact he was doing this in public, after the last time Aaron had turned him down?

They were miles away from that night now; Aaron knew how much Quinn cared for him, in a way nobody had before, and Quinn knew that Aaron was serious about wanting him.

This wasn't a show for anyone else. It was for Aaron alone.

"Aaron Fisher," Quinn said, his voice that low, sincere tone that struck at Aaron's heart. "I've wanted you since the moment we met. I've been blessed to spend these last few months by your side."

Oh, damn it. Aaron was tearing up. He fanned himself slightly and managed a wobbly smile.

"It makes me proud to be your boyfriend. But it would mean everything to me if I could have the honor of calling you my husband."

"Yes," Aaron whispered. It was the only word he managed before the tears choked him. "Yes, I... *yes.*"

The ring was beautiful—white gold, inlaid with a single square diamond in the middle. Subtle yet beautiful. He'd always loved it, but he'd never thought he'd actually get a chance to wear it.

As Quinn gently took his hand to slide it onto his finger, Aaron grew aware of the applause around them.

It was almost strange, how little the attention mattered to him. Sure, it was nice, but unlike six weeks ago, he wasn't acutely aware of it. There was no weighing up others' opinions, and how they might be feeling about the two of them. With Quinn here in front of him, smiling only for him, Aaron knew what it was truly like to only care about what Quinn thought.

To care more deeply for Quinn than he'd ever thought possible, in fact.

Aaron sprang to his feet, nearly knocking Quinn off-balance as he threw himself at him, hugging so fiercely that Aaron saw stars.

Quinn caught him and spun him around once before gently setting him down.

"I love you," Aaron breathed out. "More than anything."

"And I love you, too," Quinn whispered.

At last, when Aaron could think straight again, he let Quinn guide him to the seat again as he dabbed his eyes.

All he could think to say was, "But you didn't throw away the cock ring, right? Those things are expensive."

Quinn tipped back his head and laughed. "No, hon. I saved that for later."

"Perfect." Aaron beamed. "Then I think I know how to celebrate this occasion—before we tell our friends and they mob our front door with congratulations."

Quinn snorted with laughter. "You think we can beat the news spreading to them?"

Aaron rose to his feet again and grabbed his coat. "I don't know, but I'd sure like to try."

As Quinn swept him away, hand in hand, Aaron's soul felt light like it never had before. In giving up the walls that had kept his little world safe but gray, he'd found the most vibrant rainbow of all. And the pot of gold at the end? That was Quinn.

Life was just better now. There was no arguing with that.

And with Quinn's ring on his finger, Aaron could see clearer than ever the road that lay ahead.

All roads led to Quinn, and he couldn't be happier about it.

AFTERWORD

Dear reader,

Thank you for reading *Stolen Hart*, the fourth book in the cozy, heartwarming world of Hart's Bay!

I'm delighted that Aaron, everyone's favorite inappropriate sassy friend, has finally gotten his chance at a happily-ever-after. And from him, Quinn has learned the courage to be himself! I cracked up constantly while writing this book thanks to Aaron in particular. I miss these guys already.

There will be more stories coming from Hart's Bay in 2020—next up is a bonus short story about Uncle Roy. I can't wait to share it with you! The town has come a long way, but there's lots of love yet to be found...

Thank you to my dream team—Amy, Sandra, Meg, and Kitti—for bringing my guys to life and slaying overexcited sentence structures. As always, I would be remiss if I didn't thank all the Petals in my wonderful Facebook reader group for your patience and support while this book germinated. And, of course, my Cheesebags who keep me believing in found family every day.

Stolen Hart will be brought to life as an audiobook narrated by Greg Boudreaux in May 2020!

If you haven't already, make sure you sign up to my newsletter so you hear when Uncle Roy's short story is available, as well as the next Hart's Bay novel! You can sign up here: edaviesbooks.com/subscribe

You'll also hear about: exclusive Hart's Bay Bites; freebies and deals; new releases in ebook, audio, and print; preorder alerts; sneak peeks at upcoming books; event appearances; and other exciting news as it happens!

I also have a reader group on Facebook if you want to chat about your favorite parts of *Stolen Hart*, see cute bee photos and good news stories, and keep on top of my upcoming releases with a whole bunch of lovely readers: facebook.com/groups/edavies

Last but not least: always be you!

~Ed

ABOUT THE AUTHOR

E. Davies grew up moving constantly, which taught him what people have in common, the ways relationships are formed, and the dangers of "miscellaneous" boxes. As a young gay author, Ed prefers to tell feel-good stories that are brimming with hope.

He writes full-time, goes on long nature walks, tries to fill his passport, drinks piña coladas on the beach, flees from cute guys, coos over fuzzy animals (especially bees), and is liable to tilt his head and click his tongue if you don't use your turn signal.

facebook.com/edaviesbooks

twitter.com/edaviesauthor

instagram.com/thisboyisstrange

bookbub.com/authors/e-davies

Brooklyn Boys

Electric Sunshine

Live Wire

Boiling Point

F-Word

Flaunt

Freak

Faux

Forever

After

Afterburn

Afterglow

Aftermath

Men of Hidden Creek

Shelter

Adore

Miracle

Redemption

Audiobooks

You can see all my books available in audio here: www.edaviesbooks.com/audiobooks